To Fran,
thanks for
inviting me

Wanda

Karl Shoemaker Mysteries

Justice Comes After Death

The Enforcer

The Enforcer
A Karl Shoemaker Mystery

By Werner Hoppe

All rights reserved. No part of this book shall be reproduced or transmitted in any form or by any means, electronic, mechanical, magnetic, photographic including photocopying, recording or by any information storage and retrieval system, without prior written permission of the publisher. No patent liability is assumed with respect to the use of the information contained herein. Although every precaution has been taken in the preparation of this book, the publisher and author assume no responsibility for errors or omissions. Neither is any liability assumed for damages resulting from the use of the information contained herein.

Copyright © 2011 by Werner Hoppe

ISBN 978-0-7414-6608-2

Printed in the United States of America

This is a work of fiction. Names, characters, places, and incidents either are the product of the author's imagination or are used fictitiously. Any resemblance to actual events or locales or persons, living or dead, is entirely coincidental.

Published January 2013

INFINITY PUBLISHING
1094 New DeHaven Street, Suite 100
West Conshohocken, PA 19428-2713
Toll-free (877) BUY BOOK
Local Phone (610) 941-9999
Fax (610) 941-9959
Info@buybooksontheweb.com
www.buybooksontheweb.com

Acknowledgment

Again I want to thank my son Andreas Hoppe, PhD for accepting the tedious task of editing another novel of mine.

And Bo for, well, you will see.

Author's Note

It is important for the reader to understand that the atrocities committed in Nigeria, some of which are described in this novel, were a direct result of the Biafra conflict and should not be interpreted as being a part of everyday life in this West African country.

Prologue

The alabaster-white flap was opened and a hand slowly pushed the ivory tray holding a cup of freshly brewed Earl Grey tea, a glass bowl with hot porridge oats, and one slice of dry toast across the platform through a one-foot square opening that linked the living area with the bedroom.

In his sitting position the man on the bed only needed to reach over to retrieve the tray.

"Close the hatch, Ahmadu," he demanded from his cook when this wasn't done right away; growling a few choice words – none of them likely to be listed in the Queen's Royal Vocabulary Manual for British Diplomats – more so because of the inconvenience of having to get up than the servant's disobedience. And when he reached his hand over to the other side of the wall in an attempt to pull the hatch, the razor-sharp machete flashed down in a wail of high-pitched shrieks from one side and a hellish roar from the other side of the wall.

The muffled thump of the severed limb, when it hit the floor, was the last sound the man who referred to himself as the Enforcer discerned before he woke up, bathed in cold sweat.

The dream was over, but the memory of what came afterwards lingered in the man's head. He was seven years old when the screams coming from his dad's bedroom propelled him out of his bed so high, that he got entangled in the overhead mosquito net. It took him a few horrifying seconds before he reached his father, who was lying in a pool of blood, alternately screaming and wailing in excruciating pain. Helpless, panic-stricken, he ran from room to room, yelling for help: Ahmadu, the Fulani cook, didn't answer, was nowhere in sight, Benjamin, the Igbo steward, Sarah, his wife and house cleaner – where were they?

But there was no time to be squandered with retracing the past; the new day asked for action.

The manner in which he reacted to that horrific dream was very different from the way other people would have. What would have been a nightmare of the worst kind to anybody else was an invigorating event for him, giving him the confidence and reassurance that today would be special.

So it went without saying that this morning he takes extraordinary care in selecting the proper attire. Standing in front of the mirror one more time to reassure himself that he was portraying a flawless image for today, the Enforcer feels good, no, he feels real good.

The thick, shoe polish-black moustache almost stretched across the width of his angular face and equaled the full set of hair in color and texture. With demonic-like pride he strikes the moustache, at the same time making sure it is firmly attached to the skin. The sandpiper-grey three-piece suit, complemented by the matching white shirt and burgundy tie and kerchief sticking out of the chest pocket, give the wearer an impression of debonair worldliness. And he prefers to overdress, even when the job doesn't demand it.

After all, there was always work to be done. In fact, most of his days, and nights for that matter, he spent laying the groundwork for future transactions.

However today could be the day where it would all come to a head, the culmination of a three-week long streak of tedious planning and daily surveillance; anything out of the ordinary, responses to weather changes, weekend habits, clothing preferences – all supported by entries in his tiny leather-covered notebook of his favorite color – black.

He lets his eyes fly over the last few recordings. Analyzing them in his proverbial methodical way, he deduces that there are two possible meeting points, three different time slots, one of which could make it extremely challenging to accomplish his task. But he's not worried – he's a pro. And he would prove them all wrong again.

They called him a madman, a psycho. He didn't like that. His precision and craftsmanship could not have been the work of a madman. But then again, they didn't know. The only name he approved of was the one the second of his two inner voices had given to him: the Enforcer.

And when Michelle Brown at precisely 7:15 p.m. turned the key to open the front door of her Garden City condo, she had no idea that this was the last time she would do this.

Chapter One

Highway 17 hadn't changed all that much. Traffic southbound seemed a little heavier since the last time Karl Shoemaker had traveled this road about four years ago.

Ten months after he had left Georgetown with Brenda and Bo for Cody, Wyoming, Miss Davenport had changed her last name to Shoemaker.

Without hesitation had Karl agreed for the wedding to take place in Georgetown, this homey town on the South Carolina coast. Not only full of history, which is rivaled by very few, Georgetown was also Brenda's hometown. Some of his closest friends had spared neither trouble nor expense to join them here in the Low Country.

And for just a second, while he was passing the diner in McClellanville, his mind flashed back to that fateful day more than six years ago when a guy by the name of Salomon Sandhurst III spent his last day of freedom in this cozy little roadhouse.

But the here and now returned as soon as the South Santee Bridge came into view. Karl's respiratory system had elevated his heartbeat substantially in anticipation of his reunion with the people who he had embraced and added to the inner circle of his closest friends.

Although Brenda and he had stayed in regular contact with Marge and Amos Grimm, Bobby Moore, and a few others by phone and e-mail, these were only measly substitutes for actually being in their presence again. Last time they came down, it was to celebrate Amos's seventieth birthday. Although he had unofficially passed the sheriff's torch on to someone a couple of decades younger, he still was called to help out when matters had gotten out of hand or diplomacy rather than quarreling was the wiser action to take. Amos retiring? *"I'll believe it when I see it,"* Karl mused. *"Most likely he did this to please Marge."*

The visit this time was unplanned and unannounced. To make sure, however, that their innkeeper friends weren't on a cruise somewhere in the West Indies or hiking one of the knobby trails in the Appalachian Mountains of North Carolina, Brenda had called Molly Cordell.

"As a matter of fact, they just got back from a visit to Marge's oldest son in Alabama. He has three, how did she call them, 'rambunctious' pre-teenaged boys. She says the sheriff is so depleted that he had already embarked on a 'leave of hibernation'. I have a surprise for you too when you get here."

Brenda, in training to become a clinical nurse, had taken advantage of a two-week long seminar conducted by the Medical University in Charleston. The school in Wyoming had no objection as long as she paid for the trip.

And as for himself, his friend and colleague at Scofield University, Stewart Bramble, had agreed to take over his classes in exchange for him to do the same for Stewart during February of the following year. Bramble was an avid skier.

After crossing the entire state to take her to the airport in Cheyenne, he and Bo launched their seven-day journey to South Carolina in the brand new Jeep Liberty, which had dispatched the two-hundred-fifty-nine-thousand miles old Cherokee into a well deserved retirement.

Turning into Main Street past the welcome sign, he thought of making a quick stop at the Bay Restaurant and say hi to Bobby Moore, but decided against it. So he drove on until he came to the place on Princess Anne Court, where half a decade earlier a planned one night stay had turned into a heart-stirring adventure that lasted for over a week.

Although his friend Bo was no longer the champion sprinter he used to be and more often needed some help now to get in and out of the SUV, the instinct related to his perception was undiminished and his discernment as sharp as ever. He wore the undeniable white dusting under his chin with an air of inborn pride only a thoroughbred Rottweiler could display.

"Holy Lord Almighty!" was all that came out of Marge Baker's, or rather Marge Grimm's, mouth. The two were married shortly before Karl, Brenda, and Bo had left for Wyoming. She literally pulled him inside the lobby of the Carolina Bed and Breakfast Inn, the '*Inn*' for the informed. Her mouth remained open, as if in preparation for the instructions to fire off a barrage of onrushing questions, but decided that they could wait and enveloped the stumbling visitor with her legendary embrace instead.

Bo, not consenting to being left out of the reunion, kept pawing at Marge's apron.

But then the questions poured out of her mouth non-stop until a disgruntled voice from inside one of the rooms behind the kitchen twirled their heads in that direction.

"What's all that ruckus out there? Can a man not get a lousy fifteen minutes of undisturbed sleep around here?" The sheriff, as he was still referred to, was teed off, to say it mildly.

"Oh Amos, fifteen minutes my foot. Now get decent, and hurl your butt over here. We have visitors."

Karl Shoemaker displayed an approving smile at their rugged way to communicate, since their love for each other was unquestionable and the most genuine he had ever witnessed.

"Well, I have to say in his defense, he's still recuperating from having been taken hostage by my grandkids in Montgomery, Alabama, from where we returned yesterday. But enough is enough. Other than going to the bathroom a couple of times he hasn't shown his face – uh, finally."

A rather disheveled, but an undeniably trimmer Amos Grimm appeared. As soon as he recognized who the visitors were, the size of his eyes doubled as he rushed over and gave his younger friend a long bear hug and a number of alternating pats and strokes on the back.

After Bo had received his share of the welcome, water and another bowl with half a dozen pork chops, the Q and A session could begin in earnest. Patiently Karl explained his spur-of-the moment decision to come down to Georgetown. "After Brenda was accepted at MUSC, I thought it would be great to pay you guys a visit."

Two of Marge's giant mugs of coffee later most of the gap between their last visit four years ago and the present had been closed when the sheriff started shaking his head.

"What's with you?" the innkeeper turned to him, puzzled.

Amos ignored the question, grabbed Karl's arm and said, still shaking his head, "You sure haven't lost the knack for showing up at prime time."

And when the other two's faces were still covered with question marks he added, "Only this time I think the crime is even more sinister." While he said this he went back into the bedroom. He returned with a newspaper in one hand and tossed it in front of the visitor.

"Not again," was all that came out of Karl's mouth, remembering the newspaper head line from six plus years back. And it was almost identical. Only that instead of a teenaged girl this time it was a twenty-eight year old woman and she was not found in Winyah Bay but in her apartment.

After he read the first few sentences, Karl Shoemaker's eyes widened in reflection of what they just read. Then he continued to read out loud,

The Georgetown County Sheriff's Department found the body of a young woman in a condo inside the Palmetto Plantation and Golf Course Reserve north of Murrells Inlet. The body was identified as that of Michelle Brown, twenty-eight. The cause of her death was described by Deputy Antonio Caparelli as 'one of the most grisly I had the misfortune to witness in all my twenty-three years in law enforcement.' He added that the victim's torso was covered with gaping zigzagged slash- wounds too horrific for his eyes to bear for any length of time.

The murder weapon was not found at the crime scene and neither were any other kind of objects, finger- or footprints, to give the investigators even the hint of a clue.

The coroner placed the time of death shortly after seven-thirty pm on Wednesday.

Karl Shoemaker couldn't stop shaking his head, but finally uttered, "But this time I can't get involved. And—"

"And neither will he," Marge didn't wait for Karl to finish his thought, leaving no doubt how *she* felt about this.

Amos looked at her, then at Karl, shrugged his shoulders and said, "There you have it. And I haven't even been asked to do anything. Linus, you remember Linus Thompson, one of my deputies, knows what he's doing – most of the time, anyway."

"The guy who kicked in the door in the South Santee woods with a Karate move."

"That's the one. I was able to convince County Council to make him interim sheriff. That gives him about three years to prove himself to the public and it leaves him another year to get prepared for the election."

"I don't want to hear another thing about this murder. We just came back from an exhausting trip and I don't want to know how long you have been without sleep.

"Let me see what I can whip up for us. Since you aren't going anywhere tonight, why don't you go into your room, have a short nap, freshen up and then the three of us have an early supper and Amos and I bring you up to date with the latest gossip from Georgetown, uh, minus any murder investigations."

"You have it all figured out, haven't you? Well, it's not that this comes as a surprise to me." Shoemaker pulled himself out of the chair and walked over to this amazing woman, giving her a heartfelt hug. Still the same, Karl thought with great compassion for this lady; she didn't query him why he hadn't called, instead she offered him *his* room, as if this was the most natural thing to do. After so many years. *Yes, she truly is an amazing woman.*

They had finished a huge bowl of shrimp salad, a much lighter fare than Karl remembered Amos to have been indulging in before Marge began to keep a tighter rein on his food consumption. Now they were having their second glass of Pinot Noir, which most likely had found its way to the *Inn* from the Bay Restaurant inside a box full of shrimp from McClellanville. Bobby Moore and Marge had been close friends ever since Bobby and his wife Amy came down from Winston-Salem, North Carolina and started the restaurant from scratch.

That thought was still on his mind when he asked her with sincere curiosity, "How is Bobby doing?"

"Oh my Lord," Marge shook her head, as if still not comprehending what she was about to say. "Well, as they say, it would be funny if it weren't so serious."

"Now you got my full attention and don't keep me on tenterhooks any longer."

Turning towards her husband Marge said, "Do you want to tell the story, honey?"

"No, you go right ahead; makes me sick to my stomach even thinking about it. Never thought this could happen here in Georgetown."

"Alright then. When Bobby is looking for help in the kitchen, a dishwasher, fry cook, or whatever, he first picks a kid he knows. Or he just mentions it to patrons who have teenaged boys.

This time he needed a bus boy and this couple, he a plastic surgeon from, uh, Boston, was anxious to give their seventeen-year old youngster a glimpse into the life of 'the less fortunate'. Thought this would be 'enlightening' for him; keep him from lying on the beach all day or lounging in front of the TV.

"They owned one of these Holiday Inn-sized mansions right on the beach in that super-rich development north of De Bordieu – not to say that one isn't plush in its own right.

"So the boy, what's his name again, Amos?"
"Bradley?"
"No, Bradford. Bobby said he insisted on being called by his full name, no abbreviation. So last Thursday two weeks ago Curtis came in a little early – you remember him, I'm sure, he's the one who took over the bar from Brenda – to meet a liquor salesman, when he saw Bradford tinkering with the cash register. Bobby had just bought a brand new one, completely digital, like a computer. As a matter of fact they call it the computer. I don't know too much about that modern stuff—"

"Well, sweetheart, why won't you let me help you out here," the former sheriff suggested with a wink in Karl's direction, knowing that their visitor was eagerly waiting for the essence of what actually happened, but would never have stopped her from weaving tidbits of local chatter into her report.

"Yeah, yeah, go ahead. I need to do some work in the kitchen – where I belong." And with a mock impression of indignation on her round face, the sweet innkeeper left the two men to themselves.

"Both of us know that she can't be fooled that easily," Karl said to Amos, unable to hide a faint touch of 'Schadenfreude'.

"She's way too smart for me. I knew that already before I married her. But let's get back to the story, or to the case, as it has developed into.

"When Curtis Wilson approached the boy and asked him if he had a personal number and how he knew the password, both necessary to open the computer, the boy took off.

"And as it just so happened, the cleaning lady, a woman by the name of Vanessa Simmons – she's been working for Bobby from the day he first opened the doors to the restaurant, I know, because I recommended her to him – was mopping the floor in the entrance hall. There was no reason for her to know that anybody else was in the building. The staff, kitchen workers and waitresses normally don't show up before four o'clock."

"Seems to me you're not exactly hightailing it yourself, if I may say so. Karl is about to doze off," Marge's remark, sprinkled with a mixture of sarcasm and a victorious smile, caused her husband to concede, again.

"I heard you loud and clear, honey. I'm gonna step on it. So Karl, the boy stampedes out of the barroom, around the corner toward the door and promptly slips on the wet floor, lands flat on his face with the mop Vanessa was holding under his belly and the panic-stricken Mrs. Simmons scrambling to heave her backside off the floor...

"Curtis said that the boy was screaming like a 'cow in the slaughterhouse'. He called Bobby and the three bandaged up a two-inch long but shallow flesh wound in his left calf about four inches below the knee joint as well as they could. Then the two men carried him to Bobby's pick-up and took him to the hospital on Black River Road.

"From the hospital Bobby came straight to me with Curtis in tow. After he told me what happened I strongly suggested for him to go to the Chief of Police and press charges.

"But, you know Bobby Moore, he wanted to talk to the boy's parents first and see if the matter could be settled among them without involving the law. 'Could mess up the boy's life for good', that's all he said.

"Well, so far so good. Bradford was back home that same evening. They had brushed some, what do you call that antiseptic stuff— "

"Peroxide?"

"Yeah, that's it. Anyway, they closed the cut with a Band-Aid and called his parents to pick him up. And here's the killer. Two days after that Bobby received a letter from the Law Firm *Ballister, Wastewater and Collins* in which he is sued by Mr. and Mrs. Jacques Sutton – Marge tutored me how to pronounce that first name – bet you a dollar his real name is Jack."

"What possible reason could they have to sue Bobby?" Karl got his question in while the former sheriff had to catch his breath.

At this point Marge couldn't hold back any longer. She stomped in, drying her hands on the apron. "That's what we wanted to know. But obviously the nose-job doctor and the lawyers stuck their heads together and came up with this cockamamie charge. Would you believe they claimed the boy just wanted to get into the internet? Mistook the cash register for a real computer. Beats all, don't it?

"And if that weren't enough, they charged that there should have been some sort of sign to warn people, the public was the word they used, of the wet floor. Oh, and then there is the *rough* handling of the two men in the restaurant – 'he's still in a state of shock.'"

"What is Bobby going to do about it?" Karl, perplexed, wanted to know.

Amos answered, "Well, Bobby, reluctantly, said, 'If these people are stupid enough to carry this all the way to the courthouse I have no problems to sue them for punitive damages. I know, Sam' – that's Sam Marquette, his attorney – 'has already a handful of arguments should that action become necessary.'"

"You said it right, Marge, it would have been funny if it weren't so serious. Amazing what people are capable of nowadays. But guys, right now I think I'm trying to soak in a few of the last South Carolina sun rays before their owner moves on to the other side. I also want to see if Bo remembers our outings to Winyah Bay."

"Would you object to one more or does 'three's a crowd' apply here too?" Amos asked which resulted in a voiceless open-mouth expression on his wife's face, until her speech came back – two full seconds later.

"I declare, I never thought I would hear you volunteering for a walk further than to the mailbox. But I'm pleased as a lark. You three get out of here."

Amos gave her a peck on the cheek; Karl retrieved the leash from one of the key hooks, called Bo, who wasn't as enthusiastic as the two humans, to leave his comfortable place by the French window.

Furthermore he remembered the good times in this house, especially when he and the innkeeper were all by themselves. Mouthwatering memories. Reluctantly he got up after the third, more insistent command.

"Actually, I wanted to talk to you a bit more about the killing north of Murrells Inlet," the former peace officer of Georgetown County clarified his uncharacteristic course of action.

"I knew there had to be more to it than getting a bit of fresh air; not that that wouldn't have been a good reason all by itself." Karl threw his right arm over his friend's shoulder and said, "So, how are you getting involved in this case without making Marge aware of it, which, by the way, is just simply not possible."

"You know me too well, and, yes, there is no way I could pull this off without her finding out."

They had just reached the corner of Princess Anne Court and Saint Philip, one street further from where Bo had always taken the lead, not stopping until they had reached the Bay and the playground.

Today the canine turned his head up, looked at his master, who knew right away what was on the mind of his four legged companion of more than a decade. "No, we are not trying to deceive you, Bo. You are right on. Go ahead and be our leader."

"What are you talking about?" The sheriff looked a bit confused, but quickly his face lit up and with an 'I got it' grin added, "Forgot that you two converse on a higher plane."

"Alright, that being settled, now Amos, what's really on your mind? Do you know more about the case than what I read in the paper?"

"Not a hell of a lot more. Just that the perpetrator must have gone through extraordinary trouble to elevate the expression 'brutal' to a brand-new level."

"Because of the weird slash wounds." Karl agreed.

"The way Caparelli described the scene in that apartment made me feel my blood pressure shoot up like fireworks on New Year's Eve. Whoever did this crime went about it in an eerily methodical way."

"Would that be so unusual?" Karl asked, puzzled.

"Well, I accept his precautions regarding the fingerprints, murder weapon, or any other 'legacies', so to speak. But cleaning up afterwards? I had talked to Linus and the deputy a couple of times before you got here – contrary to my wife's offhanded remark ... I wasn't just recuperating from the trip; her grandkids were great, by the way – and he felt that such a brutal piercing of a human torso back and f..., I can't even say it..., would leave wall to wall splashes of blood and, of course, huge pools of it on the floor under and around the body, unless ....

"I feel that pervert actually liked what he was doing. And Linus Thompson claims he's already talking to a suspect, or a 'person of interest', as they call them nowadays. A man by the name of Clarence Woodburn. And that kind o' worries me."

"Was she still wearing her clothes?" Karl asked, not oblivious of the sheriff's uneasy trepidation.

"No, not a stitch. But there was no sign of forceful sexual penetration."

"So, what do you intend to do? Whether you plan to have me in on this or not, you have to convince Marge first. She takes your retirement and your health very serious.

"Brenda and I consider both of you our best friends and it would break our hearts if anything unhealthy, physically or mentally, would come between the two of you."

A slight irritation appeared on the lawman's face. "She's the best woman the Good Lord could have given me, but when it comes to my line of work she'll have to back down. Retired or not, there is something eerie about this murder I don't want to let Linus handle by himself."

Chapter Two

The ritual hadn't changed. Immediately after the successful transaction, he followed the plan, which had served him so well the last time. First he had to undress his victim, before he began with the clean-up. Since he had no feelings towards his prey he was always sufficiently composed to take great precaution when stabbing his victims with the precision of a brain surgeon, minimizing the spread of blood. But this time his prey fought valiantly to resist his attack. Though he was sure that she was dead after the first time his reshaped machete punctured her heart, he stabbed her two more times. He had carried everything the woman was wearing in a plastic bag to his place. And it wasn't until then that he removed the surgical gloves.

Over the years his conscience had adopted a do-not-care attitude with respect to his lifestyle, and there were certainly no sensations of guilt about the annihilation of human life.

And whenever his reflections took him back to that fateful day his father bled to death he could follow his subsequent path with emotionless ease. His brain cells had retained the memory of the indescribable pain, the fear, and afterwards that sense of absolute abandonment with stoic complacency.

When he ran out of the house as fast as his short legs could carry him, yelling in his high-pitched voice for help, only to see Benjamin and Sarah on the steps with streams of blood flowing freely out of the front of their necks. He survived the following weeks by snatching anything from the market stands in the city, an apple here, a banana there.

When he was lucky he landed half a loaf of bread or even a few slices of sausage from one of the open-market stands.

Gradually the life he had lived with his dad and the servants faded away from his memory. His current circumstance demanded his full attention.

More and more kids shared his predicament and before too long the older boys used the smaller ones to do the dirty work for them. It was hard and unfair, but it did give him a new sense of belonging. It also marked the beginning of an increasingly blurred understanding of right and wrong and the ever so slow destruction of his soul.

The unrest in this war-torn country made it possible for gangs of any kind or age to flourish. The conflict about the Biafra region, which resulted in an ill-fated three-year secession of that province from the motherland, had left the largest nation on the coast of West Africa in a state of virtual anarchy. Fulani and Hausa from the north and Yoruba from the oil-rich south fought the Christians who belonged to the Igbo, a.k.a. Ibo, tribes without any regard or respect for human life. In one single riot thirty thousand Ibo were slaughtered.

Brought up in an environment of lethargic agnosticism, the boy was unable to share the beliefs of any of these combating factions.

So after a few years he gave up life with the gangs and continued his path alone. By that time – he was now a lad of almost ten years – he had become what could be labeled a juvenile delinquent.

He had learned not to shy away from even the most callous methods of achieving his goal, which so far comprised mainly food, pocket money and clothing. But that was about to change too.

The turning point, which elevated his street-smart pillaging and vandalizing to an even higher, more sinister plane, came years later during the half time of a rugby match between the Capital City teams of his country and Togo. The stadium was filled way beyond capacity.

Expectations on both sides were high, surpassed only by the tension in the heads of the predominantly younger male spectators. The winner would carry the title of West African Champion and as such was qualified to take part in the final round to determine the overall rugby champion of Africa.

Next to soccer or football, as it is called outside the US, the sport of rugby is extremely popular on that continent.

There was no better place than a cramped stadium to make some extra money by separating a few wallets from the pockets of their rightful owners – a skill the teen had developed to an art close to perfection.

He had already filled his own pockets with just about ten billfolds, loose bills, even a handful of coins to last him for at least a week. Snaking his lean body through the maze of sweat-dripping bodies, he and thirty-thousand fans were cheering on their respective teams with ear-piercing force.

Ten minutes before halftime the cheers by both factions, home-team fans and Togolese, who were outnumbered three to one, were gradually replaced by equally fanatic jeers and whistles the sound of a screeching freight train. What they wanted had eluded them so far, a five-pointer for their team. Not one of the players on either team had been able to ground the ball past the goal line. So far the match had been riddled with fouls. And the formation of the tunnel followed by a regulation-specified scrumming to put the oval ball back into play constantly interrupted the flow of the contest.

The fans are almost relieved when finally the referee vigorously blows his whistle announcing the half-time break. A wave of boos accompanies the thirty players into their underground dressing rooms.

The crowd, disgruntled about the lackluster game, isn't paying a lot of attention to what is taking place on the field. But the one who can hardly conceal the content of his bulging pockets is watching every single operation on the far side of the field with intense curiosity – the approach of one Unimog flanked by two Jeeps, and a truck, probably French-made, since the French had joined one side in the Biafra war, which one, he didn't know.

What happened now was like a movie reeling off before his eyes, set on fast forward. Five wooden poles with a circumference of telephone poles, just half the length of one, flew out of the truck.

Right behind them several bundles of rope as thick as hawser hit the ground. Within seconds about a dozen soldiers, no, thirteen exactly, jumped off the Unimog, lifted two wooden boxes from the vehicle and dropped them beside the rope and the poles.

Gradually the fans were beginning to pay more attention to the strange occurrences on the field and the initial murmur grew louder. And what they were about to witness left an icy chill in the spines of even the most hardened guys.

Four twenty-foot pieces of the rope were tied close to the top of each of the five poles, which were then brought to an upright position and secured by the stretched-out rope in a tent-like manner and fastened with the help of oversized pegs from the boxes.

Five shirtless males were literally forced out of the open rear of the lorry by guns in the hands of another group of military men who jumped off the truck and kept pushing the guys toward the erected posts.

The five men, who appeared to be in their early to mid-twenties, had difficulties getting on their feet. It was at that moment that the crowd noticed that their hands were tied behind their backs.

Suddenly a surreal silence fell over the stadium. The fans had all but forgotten about the rugby match. The expressions on most faces foreshadowed a sense of eerie anticipation.

When at last the men had reached the five poles, they were blindfolded and tied to them from neck to toe.

The firing squad included the soldiers who had guarded the five men in the truck. After the command was bellowed out from what looked like a highly decorated officer, the automated rifles discharged a hail of bullets in the direction of the victims.

After their chins had dropped to their chest, another officer with a stethoscope checked their heartbeat, or lack of it. The poles were dislodged, carried and thrown back into the truck, still united with the bodies, and within seconds the vehicles were gone and the spectacle was over.

Shortly thereafter the yellow-shirted home-team players and their Togolese opponents in green with black shorts double-filed back into the arena, ready to raise the level of their performance as well as the mood of the fans with renewed energy.

The troubled teenager, however, never remembered the final score, but the halftime exhibition remained unabridged in his memory like the brand mark on the upper arm of a holocaust survivor.

This kind of exhibition, open-air executions, released further fateful messages to a mind already in an endangered mental state. The slashing of his father's arm which left him bleeding to death, the early demise of his mother, an almost casual disrespect for human life during the post-war era, and now the government-endorsed shooting of five young men, most likely for the same crimes that had been part of his routine for nearly his entire life, had prepared him for what was about to enter his mind. Reluctantly he listened to the battle of the two voices inside his head.

This way of life will destroy you. Remember the good times with your father when he took you to the hills in Jos, or to the beaches of Lagos.

In Kano you learned the language of the Hausa. Everybody laughed when you yelled from the confines of your playpen, feeling neglected: Ga ni - Here I am! Your father was an honest man. He didn't deserve to die the way he did. And Carlotta, your beautiful mother, before she was fatally stricken by malaria, was the proudest young woman the world has ever known. Return, run away from this road of destruction, before it ruins your soul! Ka yi gudu da iyakar saurinka – as fast as you can!

*Don't listen to that garbage. Stay with me! The other side wants you to recall the times you had with your father and mother. How could you? You were just a little boy. The only incident you **can** remember is the day you found your father lying in a pool of his own blood, killed by his own cook Ahmadu from the tribe of the Fulani. Did you know that he also massacred Benjamin and Sarah?*

What about the years after that? The Biafra uprising and subsequent secession – thousands of people lost their lives during these three years before the region was returned to the country.

*With nobody taking care of you, you had to fend for yourself. And in the murky niches of the streets you found a way to survive. But today you saw for the first time that the rulers of the re-united country are sparing neither efforts nor methods to eliminate abandoned survivors like yourself. You have the right to go on, and with it the prerogative to apply any means necessary to accomplish this. You will be the Enforcer, don't ever forget this. I'll eventually lead you to a life of **true** prosperity.*

The latter voice made more sense to him.

Chapter Three

"I think I'm going to check in on Bobby, just to say hi," Karl Shoemaker said to his companion when they approached a new building housing the Chamber of Commerce and the Maritime Museum that had replaced the old Gulf gas station.

The sheriff concurred, "Good idea. Maybe he has heard more from *Ballister, Wastewater and Collins,*" trying to pronounce the names with the sophistication of an Oxford-raised British chap, but failing miserably.

Karl chuckled at his friend's stab at comedy, wanted to say something, but decided against it.

Amos Grimm glanced at the taller man and smiled at his own ineptitude and quickly changed the subject. "If you think Bo will let me take him back to the *Inn*, you might as well go straight to the restaurant from here."

"I don't think there will be a problem. He's getting a bit thirsty by now, anyway."

Bo knew they were talking about him, pulled the leash in the right direction and the transfer worked just fine.

Karl said, "I am glad he remembers. And right now he thinks, 'Ready to go home. Don't care who takes me there.'"

"How do you know that?" The sheriff had always been amazed at the degree of understanding between the two.

"I just do."

"Well, well, just take a look who the cat dragged in. The unparalleled *shyness* in the voice of Lois Catbury thundered through the barroom hitting Karl's eardrums like the duck on those Aflac commercials.

"Hi guys," Karl Shoemaker, who wasn't expecting this many people in the bar at five o'clock and not quite ready to face the never-restrainable Lois Catbury on his first day back in Georgetown, greeted her rather timidly.

"I should've known you were coming."

"What makes you say that, Lois?"

"Well, someone got killed again. Isn't that when you usually show up?"

Karl chose one of two empty chairs at the far end of the bar, ordered a beer, and instead of having to endure a barrage of long-winded questions, he gave her the reason of his visit voluntarily.

Undisturbed by the fact that she had to talk over two heads to reach Shoemaker, the predominantly one-sided dialog continued for some time.

Karl patiently listened to her rendition of local gossip while keeping an eye on the aperture for Bobby. Lois was the only person at the bar he recognized and wondered how the other patrons he had met during his previous visits to this lively southern town were doing. He didn't have to wonder for long.

"…and this coming October three years ago – is that right, Curtis? – Yeah, can't believe it's been this long. Anyway, Boots Cornthresher had a heart attack smack in the middle of a shave and haircut he was giving to no one other than his old nemesis, the mayor. By the way, Jim is still in charge of the town, or so he thinks. Boots always said, 'Before I retire I want to give the mayor one last cut. And I'll mess that one up that even his hat won't hide it.' You must know the mayor never forgave him for what he did to him years before. You remember that one, don't you?"

"Sure do," Karl replied. He remembered the morning when Mayor Jim Livingston made his entrance to Betty's Luncheonette, where several locals were gathered for their weekly breakfast Stammtisch, lifted his broad-rimmed straw hat, which revealed his brand new skinhead. Boots had shaved a biker's head before his and forgot to install a comb into the electric machine.

"But wait," Lois was determined to finish her story. "This time he was about to trim the side of Jimmy's head – he always wears the sides razor-short – when the barber's body fell into his shoulder with his hand pushing the cutting machine from one ear to the other, leaving a one inch wide road across the mayor's top, right above his pituitary gland."

Karl lifted his glass and took a deep swallow of his favorite German beer which Curtis had placed in front of him. "Bobby around?"

The bartender who had replaced his wife Brenda was just about to answer when Lois beat him to it. "I just heard Amy tell the air conditioner repair guy that he just called her. Was leaving the Surfside Package Store and would be here in about twenty minutes. How does that rate on your scale for customer satisfaction?"

"Lois, you are off the chart." As much as Karl liked the ever-perky woman, he just needed a break from her verbal bombardment. "I think I'm going to step out for a minute and say hi to Amy." And while he walked by the two men sitting between him and her it seemed they were both breathing a deep sigh of relief.

Amy was Bobby's wife and partner in the business; no more than five-four and barely topping the hundred pound mark on the scale, blond, wavy, shoulder-length hair, indigo-blue eyes, always cheerful. She was both liked and respected by the staff. Brenda once told him that a lady from Virginia approached Amy after she and her husband had finished their meal that she reminded her of Meg Ryan.

Karl thought that was a valid observation, slightly flattering the actress, when he walked up to her at the hostess stand. An instant of surprise in her face gave way to genuine delight to see him.

"Where have you been this long?" giving him a friendly hug and a few pats on his shoulder.

"It's only been four years," Karl answered jovially. "I just got here a few hours ago and thought to say hi. Bobby okay?"

"Oh yea, he's fine. Particularly tonight. His night out with the guys. He called me from Surfside. Did say he was on the way home, but there are quite a few more challenges to overcome between there and here, if you know what I mean."

"Well, the last leg of our trip was pretty rough. I also ought to get back to the *Inn* shortly, before Marge sends the sheriff." And with a wink, "can't even make a decent joke anymore. Have been listening to Lois since I came in."

Amy rolled her eyes and said, sympathetically, "That does it all the time. Let's give her fifteen more minutes. After that I'll come to your rescue."

Two of the patrons had left the bar, and a third one was beginning to show signs of inebriation – he was trying to repeat what Lois and Curtis were saying, only no sound escaped his freelancing mouth.

"There's no way Clarence could have anything to do with this. He's got to be the dumbest outlaw I've ever known."

Karl recalled the name from his earlier conversation with Amos Grimm and knew what and whom they were talking about. He stayed back and listened when Lois slammed her hand on the bar and released a thunderous guffaw that caused the dishwasher to drop a stack of plates behind the wall in the kitchen.

"Curtis, calling this guy dumb is like saying Einstein was bright. Let me only mention three of his numerous brilliant break-ins."

Lois downed the bottom half inch of her vodka Collins in her theatrical fashion – banging the empty glass on the bar with the force of a sledge hammer. Lifting her left index finger as in one more and proceeded with the criminal biography of some Clarence Woodburn.

"Okay, there was the one in the Lassiter house on 701 in Ringle Heights. A stakeout that took him two months, during which time he observed that Mr. and Mrs. Lassiter attended the fellowship meeting at the Community Church every Wednesday. And when he finally crouched as low as possible with his surgical instruments, notably the universally applicable crowbar, in front of his intended target of entry, the main door, the porch lights came on, the door opened, and Mrs. Lassiter greeted the would-be burglar with a look of disbelief. Unfortunately for him that day it was Thursday."

When Lois uttered the last words the muted man, who had developed a severe top-heaviness, jerked his torso up as if bitten by a swarm of irate honey bees, and blurted out with an uncooperative faculty of speech and blurry saucer-size eyes, "Today's Thursday? I promised to be home by five, on Tuesday." Then he slid down the barstool, almost lost his footing in the process and stumbled out of the barroom.

Karl decided to enjoy the free variety show a little longer and stayed back, kind of behind the scenes.

Deeming the polluted patron to be unworthy of interrupting her demonstration of local news, she continued with her proverbial crooked grin and a discarding wave of her bracelet-studded arm. "About time he left. Anyway, another one of his botched unlawful ventures happened during a robbery attempt in Choppee—"

"I don't know about that one," Curtis broke in, but abstained from further comments when he saw the impatient lines between her eyebrows.

"I was about to tell you. The house was actually empty. The owners, an assistant principal at Carversville High and his wife, had pinned a note on the door, making their daughter, Libby, I believe that was the girl's name, uh well, it's not important - anyhow, the note said that they had gone to have dinner at the Barbeque Grill in Conway. The note even let her know that her mother had left a pizza in the fridge for her to put in the microwave."

By now the bartender, known for his patience when confronted with long-winded gibberish, looked around, spotted Karl in the aperture.

His face lit up in hopes the man from Wyoming would put an end to Lois' monologue. But Shoemaker had no such intention. He enjoyed listening to this plainspoken, albeit indefatigable woman; in a peculiar kind of way he liked her. So he shook his head to let Curtis know that he intended to stay back.

And after Lois had assured herself of the bartender's attention she continued. "Ok, he walked around the one-story brick house and found the back door leading to the kitchen open.

"As you know, that's nothing out of the ordinary in the South. Walks through the house, picks up a few things here and there, jewelry in particular, but also some cash, when the phone rings. What does our genius do? Of course, he picks up. The conversation goes like this; I heard this from Sammy Robert's, who was a detective in the sheriff's department at the time. He interviewed Libby afterwards.

'Hello!'
'Who's this? Uh, sorry, must have the wrong number.'
'Well, who you want to talk to?'
'My mom, Rosaline McClary.'
'Well, this is the, eh....'

Libby called 911 and the rest is history. Now give me another drink. The last one for today. Where is Karl?" She turned around and saw the visitor leaning against the entrance frame, grinning.

"Right here, hanging on to every word you said. The guy you were describing doesn't seem to be made for the career he chose."

"You can say that again. He's a bona fide loony. How Linus Thompson could possibly think he's had something to do with that murder. He must be desperate to show he can handle the job. Not this way, Buster."

And shifting her plump anatomy in Karl's direction, said, "Are you sure that's not the reason you're here?"

"Heard about it less than an hour ago for the first time."

"Then you must have this extrasensory …, what is the word? Anyway, ESP. Just in case the sheriff, and I mean the old one, enlists you in the investigation, you might want to know, that there have been more comedy acts performed by the accused. Once he broke into a trailer home of a young couple, which evidently had left the place in a hurry, with no time to clean up.

"While pocketing the usual items earmarked for the pawnshops in the region, our super robber washed and put away the dishes, made the beds, and picked up some stuff lying on the floor.

"The zillion finger prints played a great part in the inability for the stolen items ever reaching their intended destinations."

Karl shook his head in disbelief. "You had to research the comings and goings of this man in earnest to come up with all that detail."

"I looked them up in the courthouse after I read about his arrest in the Gazette. I seemed to remember a few things about the guy.

"Yeah, I almost forgot. One day he took away the shopping cart of an elderly lady full with groceries. The problem was the cart had not yet gone through the check-out counter. Now, don't that beat all?"

Chapter Four

Back at the *Inn*, Karl felt as if he had stepped into the middle of a performance by the Georgetown Swamp Fox Theater Group: Intercepted by the squeaky sound of the door that connected the lobby with the private area, the landlady's mouth was still half open, but her fierce scowl in the direction of the sheriff, who himself had little more than a puny apology written all over his face, didn't require an absorbent amount of perception for him to suspect something was the matter.

He threw a look over to Bo, who by his demeanor could often help him to better assess the severity of an occurring or even a brewing unpleasant situation.

And the canine didn't let his master down this time either. Upon Karl's entrance he lifted his head and released an unequivocal growl that could put the fear of God into a stranger.

"Something wrong?" Shoemaker cautiously inquired, knowing very well there was.

"See, even the dog is on my side. I can't even let you go around the block without cooking up another one of your dubious schemes.

"I have a good mind to call MUSC in Charleston and let Brenda know what you two are up to again." And with her hazel eyes boring into her husband's, who stood there amazed at her unreserved emotions, she snapped, "What about that holy promise, *'Honey, now comes our time. You've taken care of other people all your life and I've chased crooks for longer than I care to remember. From now on we'll enjoy the rest of our lives – together.'* Great speech! But you never meant it, did you?"

As if she realized that her last remark was just a tad too petty, her voice changed more into a plea now, "I waited long enough for you to finally make a move, and don't want to lose you before I really get to fully enjoy this new life."

Karl felt a considerable uneasiness invading his well-being. He knew the two loved each other unshakably and their occasional rough lines were always emitted in jest. But this time Marge left no doubt – she was angry, and Karl knew the reason.

But he didn't have to wait any longer for witnessing the conclusion of their differences.

"Honey, I know you're upset. But before I say any more you have to lay off our friend here. He told me to make sure I ran it by you – whether with or without him being involved. Now, just listen how I feel about this. And if, after I give you my reasons, you still insist that I should stay out of this I'll scrap the idea."

"I fail to be able to think of anything you can come up with that would change my mind." Marge's counter-move was a bit more restrained, but indignation was still written all over her face, making it visibly difficult for her to keep an open mind.

"Alright, I understand. However, honey, I am after all a law enforcement officer, retired or not. You remember when you told me that you wanted to keep running the *Inn* after we had tied the knot?"

"Getting shot at by a sizzling spark from the frying pan is not exactly the same as takin' a slug from one of these automatic contraptions in the hands of them savages out there."

Karl didn't like the direction this discourse was headed and injected gingerly, "Nothing, Marge, nothing has been decided on this yet. I can only imagine how Brenda will react when she finds out about this. That reminds me, her classes will be over in about half an hour. I need to call her then."

The innkeeper, true to her reputation for swiftly recognizing an opportunity, jumped on this one. "Oh good, then you can tell her that I have to talk to her," looking grim-faced alternately at her husband and Karl, both dumbfounded.

The visitor waved his hand in surrender and said, "I guess you have to work this out among yourselves and I'm sure I'll get an earful from Brenda." With this he walked over to Bo, who was still in alert mode, indicated by the partially upright position of his inbred floppy ears.

In an effort to divert Bo's attention he engaged his friend in the dog's favorite game, a rough mock-wrestling match.

Marge and Amos followed his advice and were still locked in a heated debate with no winner in sight. The sheriff kept on pleading his cause. "Sweetheart, there is another reason why I want to, no, need to nose around a bit. And I mean just nose around, not chase the killer or anything that requires a gun. That would be a wild goose chase, now wouldn't it? No, I only asked Karl if he would like to come with me to find out more about the victim. What kind of work she did, or if she has any relatives close by. That stuff, detective work.

"Need a glass of water." He walked over to the refrigerator, pulled out a liter bottle of still water and gulped half of its contents down.

Marge was still standing in the same spot, silent, uncompromising.

"What I was saying, the other reason is Linus, Linus Thompson. As you know I put a plug in for him to take over from me. He's a good guy and a hard worker, but I know that his reasoning at times defies common sense.

"Would you believe he arrested that Clarence Woodburn, who deserves a place in the, what do you call that book again…?"

"Guinness Book of World Records," Karl's muffled announcement came from underneath the Rottweiler's massive belly, evoking a temporary truce between the two combatants.

Amos, trying to take advantage of the lighter moment, went on driving his point home. "Okay, whatever, as the dumbest burglar on the planet."

"And what," Marge asked, shaking her head, "in Heaven's name has the arrest of this sorry, deranged vagrant got to do with you having to *nose* around? How'd you know he didn't do it?"

"I just do. I stuck my neck out when I talked County Council into letting Linus stay on as interim sheriff. You don't need to do a lot of guessing who they'll come after if he messes this up."

"I just don't want you to get hurt. You know that. It's not like you were after a shoplifter."

"You're right there. Whoever did this had his mind set on something else altogether."

At precisely a quarter before seven Karl called 247-9980, Brenda's cell phone number. They had been married now for four years, but still behaved like newlyweds.

"I missed you," were the first words that vacated his mouth after Brenda's 'hello?'

A girlish giggle escorted her response. "Me too, sweetheart."

The questions on both sides came out faster than the answers, but at the end they were able to sort them out to each's satisfaction. And after they decided to meet the coming weekend for lunch at the Cracker Barrel in Mount Pleasant – Brenda's schedule ran pretty much around the clock with lectures, hands-on sessions, and preparations for the final exam – she said, "Make sure you give Bo a rigorous stroking behind his left … you know the spot. Oh, I almost forgot, how are Marge and Amos? And what was their reaction when you showed up right out of the blue?"

"Well, you know, nothing has changed much here. A little while ago I was witness to one of their pseudo-quarrels, which, I'm sure, will end up similar to the ones we used to watch, a hearty whip from Marge's dish towel or an innocuous slap on the butt, hers.

"Give them my love and I'll see you soon."

Karl knew right away that he was going to be in trouble for not letting her know what the quarrel was all about. No doubt she would be able to connect the dots between that one and the planned sleuthing.

He had placed the call in the lobby to give the two a bit more privacy. He waited for a moment before opening the frosted glass door to ensure himself that things were calm inside.

Marge and Amos were sitting at the tile-top table in the kitchen, each of them munching on a fried chicken leg with a dish of a dozen or so more between them.

Without looking at Karl Marge Grimm said, trying to sound grumpy again, "You aren't off the hook either, and don't for a minute think otherwise. But now sit down and help us annihilate some of this chow, straight out of the health food store."

Vintage Marge Grimm, Karl thought to himself. "Let me just check with Bo. Maybe he's in the mood for another walk."

Marge mumbled while ripping a slice of juicy dark meat off the soon-to-be bare chicken limb, "Don't think so."

And when Karl moved around the corner toward the bay window, he didn't have to guess about the meaning of Marge's remark.

Bo was stretched out like a cat in front of the fire place, with one eye half open as a generous gesture to his master, a sheet-metal bowl, empty, or rather licked spotlessly clean, next to his head with one ear dangling over the rim.

Karl shook his head, returned to the table and said, "Now why'd I even entertain the thought, that it would be different this time." He was referring to the innkeeper's feeding habits, better over-feeding habits of his dog.

"Well, he had to eat too."

"Yeah, but I can pretty much tell how much he had to eat when he covers his eyes with a paw as soon as he sees me coming."

He reached over and gave the lady a thankful pat on the back.

The two men were ready to hit the road shortly after seven the next morning. Bo wanted to stay behind, which was manifested by his dancing around Marge like a purring feline.

The innkeeper was drying her hands on an apron with patterns of wild flowers, fading from the many trips to the washing machine. She looked at Karl, her voice more subdued than the night before. "I know I was a little rough–"

"Don't say another word," Karl cut her off right then, "I know exactly how you feel. But I have never met a more responsible lawman than your husband. I trust him and I ask you to do the same. And as he said yesterday, we're just going to ask questions. But," and with a wink in Amos's direction, "I trust you too, and therefore I leave it to you to explain it to Brenda."

The flying dishcloth, which Karl was barely able to duck away from, was her swift response to that last remark. Shoemaker picked up the rag, stepped into the kitchen and threw it in the sink. Then he walked over to the woman who had been to him like a mother when he truly needed one, smothered her with a heartfelt embrace, and whispered in her ear. "We'll be alright. Love you."

Marge said, more conciliatory now, "Can't say flattery won't get you anywhere. Anyway, since I understand you're also rejecting my breakfast this morning you might as well get out of here. And yeah, I assure you of one thing. The only male left in the house will be spoiled rotten."

Bo pushed his nose against her leg and received an enthusiastic rub-down.

"She's a handful ... with a heart of gold," Amos stated with conviction while he stuck the key into the ignition of his silver-grey Ford Explorer. "Not eating at home doesn't need to mean not to have breakfast altogether. But, don't worry, I told her I wanted you to meet the new owners of the old Betty's Luncheonette."

Karl looked at him and asked, surprised, "Anything happen to Betty?"

"Well, no. But she's now in her mid-seventies and figured it was time to get out. She has a daughter, married with two kids right outside of Greenville, South Carolina, where they found a nice retirement home for her. According to Marge – they talk just about every week – loves the upstate, the grandchildren and all, but still misses the Bay area here in Georgetown. Says needs to come back every three months to 'smell the *real* South.'

"But she couldn't have found a nicer couple to take over the diner. The new folks are in their early forties, I reckon, and have a little girl. Sweet little thing. The young woman runs the diner. Her husband works ..., I forgot, he told me. Anyway I think he travels a lot. But when he's here he helps out. Real nice guy. Likes to talk."

When they got out of the car, Karl glanced at the oak tree in front of the diner's only façade window and recollected the times when years ago he tied up Bo to that tree. That was after he and his canine had spent the first night in Georgetown.

The inside hadn't changed at all. The pale blue walls were still mostly hidden due to the many watercolor paintings by local artists. The same five round tables with the same chairs, leather seats, and the same five stools at the bar for the patrons who are either on a short lunch break or just like to chat with a neighbor or whoever is serving.

A boy in his late teens in cut-off jeans occupied one of the barstools and an elderly touristy-looking couple, their straw hats hanging over the back rest, feet in docksiders plus knee high socks, was sitting at a table near the window, sipping their beverage, he coffee, she a tall glass of iced tea.

A man who fit Amos Grimm's assumption with regard to age was balancing a ketchup bottle, a salt shaker and a red wooden box containing the sweeteners in one hand while pushing a cloth across one of the table tops with the other.

When he looked up to greet the new customers his eyes lit up when he saw the sheriff. "Hi Sheriff Amos, what a surprise." He rushed over and shook hands with Grimm, who introduced the two to each other. "Joseph, I would like you to meet a good friend of mine, a good friend also of your predecessor ... Karl Shoemaker. Karl, meet Joseph Hughes, one half of the luncheonette's new ownership."

"Nice to meet you, Mr. Shoemaker."

"Karl, please. And it's good to meet you too."

"I heard so much about you that after awhile I thought I knew you personally. As a matter of fact, I have been passing stories about you to visitors and shamelessly make them believe I was there. But, where is Bo?"

"You are too kind. Actually I have been leading an unassuming life, until I started to hang out with the guy next to me. And Bo knows better than coming along when he's residing in dog's heaven where he is right now."

"Marge spoiling him, I guess."

"Shamelessly."

"Alright," the sheriff cut in, "I am glad you two got to meet, but we also came here to have some of your, or better, Melanie's, special eggs-over-grits breakfast."

Joseph Hughes apologized and retrieved silverware and napkins from the bar and placed them on the table in the far corner. "This ok? Gives you some privacy in case you have to discuss the latest crime. Any news on that?" But as if recognizing that this was too forward a question he quickly and sheepishly said without waiting for an answer, "I'll give Melanie your orders."

Karl said to Amos after Joseph had left, "You're right. He seems to be a nice guy."

"Yeah he is. Now, let's talk a little about our program for today."

With a tolerating grin Karl accepted the casualness with which his companion had taken charge of his food intake as well as his time. He knew that this was yet another expression of Grimm's outstretched hand in friendship, southern-style. The sheriff had chosen him, not any of the detectives, to join him for this mission. Shoemaker felt good about that. Besides, the sheriff had once saved his life and also Brenda's. It was time to repay his friend.

"I pretty much know where the woman lived. It's on the beach side of Highway 17 off the Garden City Connector."

He stopped when Joseph deposited the steaming two plates in front of them. A low "Enjoy" was all he said before he withdrew.

Amos said, honest admiration in his voice, "The man has class. Now, I told Linus we would start asking a few questions in the neighborhood and find out if we can round up any relatives of hers. In the meantime he's to keep the press at bay."

"Is he okay with me being in on this?"

"Well, he's not the sharpest detective I ever worked with, but he is dependable. I can honestly say that. In other words, he is better at taking orders than giving them. He still has a lot of learning to do. In the meantime my reputation, whatever it's worth, is on the line."

After they were finished eating Amos left a ten and a five dollar bill on the table. Joseph Hughes was patiently waiting for the adolescent to dig up the remaining change from his pants pockets. He waved at the two, mouthed a 'thank you', before Amos and Karl had reached the door.

They took Highmarket to St. James to where Church Street turns into Hwy.17. When Grimm steered the auto over the two bridges and Karl watched the smooth takeover of the three imposing rivers and the Intracoastal Waterway by Her Majesty, the elegant Winyah Bay, masterfully disguising her deepest secrets, his mind took him back to that summer seven years ago when fifteen-year old Catrin Calhoun's body was washed ashore and found by a marine biologist in the murky marshes of the Hobcaw Barony.

"I think I know what is going through your mind right now. Sort of déjà vu, I imagine?" The sheriff asked with empathy.

Karl just nodded.

Amos understood and left his friend to himself and his memories, as different and wide apart as they had to be.

The traffic got a little heavier between Pawley's Island and Litchfield and grew to a steady flow when they passed Murrells Inlet.

The uniformed man stepped out of the gate house when the Ford Explorer approached. "Yes, Sir, how can–" he stopped for a second, when he recognized the former sheriff of Georgetown County. "Well, Sheriff Grimm, what gives us ... of course, you are here because of the murder of that young woman. Awful, ain't it?"

"Hey Sam, yeah it sure is. You retired from the police force before me, didn't you?"

"I did. But to tell you the truth, I worked harder in retirement than I did as a cop. The wife kept me so busy with errands to Wal-Mart, 'pick-up my gallbladder prescription from Walgreen's, clean the garage, take me to the Herbal-Society Meeting', I just had to find a way to get out of the house."

"I can understand," Amos agreed sympathetically. "Now, back to the deceased. We want to talk to some of her neighbors. You see the people every day, speak to a few here and there – you know of anybody she was particularly close to? Could save us some time."

"Well, Michelle Brown was just a great young woman, smart – she took evening classes at the university in Myrtle Beach, wanted to go to law school. Worked two jobs. She never passed this gate, coming or going, without exchanging a few friendly words with any of us here. Therefore, Amos, it's hard for me to give you names of people she was particularly close to. She was kind to everybody, and everybody liked her. But I don't want you to leave empty-handed. Michelle looked after an elderly lady who lives in the other part of Michelle's duplex on the first floor. You might want to start with her. Let me just look up her full name. Only know her by Miss Greta."

Sam stepped away from the car and walked into the gate house.

Amos looked over at Karl, obviously pleased. "At least we're not completely in the dark anymore."

"Margaret Snyder," Sam was back.

"That address is 213 Rose Hill Ct., right?"

"That's it. Round the circle, second road to the left, second duplex on the left again." Sam bent down a little to take a look at Karl.

Amos caught it and said, "By the way, this is Karl Shoemaker. Remember the Sal Salomon case seven years ago? The body of the girl in the Bay and the prostitution ring with foreign under-aged girls?"

"The lawyer bastard, son of the 'Honorable Senator'?"

"Yeah, and this man next to me delivered the SOB to us on a silver platter."

"The college professor from somewhere up north, north west, like Montana or somewhere around there." He leaned more into the car to shake Karl's hand. "Good for you to be here. Hope you two get this monster too before he kills again."

All the homes on Rose Hill Court were two-story duplexes, stone - fronted and in different shades of pale grey and beige, creating a calm contrast. Amos parked the truck in a space reserved for guests as it said on the sign in front of 213.

While the condo's façade could remind someone of a mockingbird's dull-grey belly, the person who answered the door was better compared to a warbler's conspicuous silvery-white patches on its wing and tail.

The elderly lady looked at them for two or three seconds, first through the peephole, then through the gap the chain, still engaged, allowed. The sheriff had kept his star for reasons like this one. Right away the woman's eyes caught the badge, but only after Amos Grimm introduced himself and his partner, and telling her the reason for their intrusion, did she release the chain.

"Mrs. Snyder—"

"Greta, please."

Grimm cleared his throat before he spoke again. Karl knew that the sheriff preferred to keep investigations as formal as possible — in complete contrast to his practice on a personal level.

"Well, eh, Greta, as I said, we are here to look into the murder of your neighbor, Michelle Brown—"

"You gentlemen must excuse me being so blunt, but I have been visited by police and radio people yesterday. I don't know more than I told them already."

"We understand totally. But maybe we have a few questions you weren't asked."

That seemed to make sense to her. She pulled the door wide open and her glowing face emanated from the anticipation to be of use to the authorities.

She led the two men into her over-furnished living room; most likely reflecting a time when more people shared the space. Greta recognized Karl's tallying its contents fleetingly and said, almost apologetically, "My husband died four months," and with a quick glimpse back at a calendar on the wall in the short hallway, "and twelve days ago – cancer of the pancreas. Took just five months from the time he was diagnosed to his, well, I call it his meeting with the Lord.

"I'm sorry. You didn't come here to listen to *my* story. Sit down, please, anywhere. Can I get you a cup of coffee? It's still hot."

Both visitors declined politely and after all had taken their seats in deep-cushioned easy chairs placed around one of two beech wood-stained coffee tables, Amos wasted no more time and launched his queries.

"How long have you known Michelle, Greta, and did you see her regularly or just from time to time?"

"Since she moved to the Reserve. That was a little over two years ago. I saw her practically every day, either leaving or coming. You see, she parks her car, a Volkswagen Beatle, yellow like a canary bird, with a green four-leaf clover painted on the right side, mostly in the same spot right under my window when she can. She visits – I still can't believe I have to speak about her in the past tense – well, she visited often, especially after Bill was gone. She would ask if I needed anything from the grocery store, she also checked on me when I —"

"Yes," Grimm side-glanced at Shoemaker and his rolling eyes told his partner *'this way we won't get out of here before supper.'* "So, you knew her as a helpful, concerned individual. Did she have a lot of visitors, maybe a boyfriend, relatives?"

"There was a young man who usually came on weekends. I teased her once or twice about him, but she kept insisting he was just a friend."

The elderly lady took a deep breath, and somewhat sheepishly, added, "I believe the reason she didn't want to talk much about him – I believe his name was Darren, yes, Darren Schloss – uh, well, he probably was already married. I have a niece who fell in love with a married man. He told her lie after lie. First he told her he was separated, then he wanted to make her believe—"

"Sorry, Greta, to interrupt, but let's stay with his connection to Michelle, if you don't mind. Although I fully understand. Daughter of my wife's cousin was showing off her engagement ring when she found out that she wasn't the only one her guy had made that commitment to. Plus he was married with three kids. Couldn't take the embarrassment – overdosed on sleeping pills.

"Now, you have any idea where this Darren Schloss lives?"

Greta thought about that for a moment. She struggled a bit getting out of the spongy armchair, succeeded, and walked over to a secretary that did not quite match the rest of the furniture in style and texture. It was probably a cherished heirloom the couple couldn't part with.

She picked up a chocolate milk-colored notebook and rejoined the two. "I received a phone call from him the day before yesterday. He told me who he was – I had never spoken to him until then – and asked me if Michelle was by any chance with me or if I had any idea where she was.

"He said they were supposed to get together later that evening, and he wanted to let her know that he had to cancel. He had left several messages and she wouldn't answer her cell phone. He asked me if I could check her apartment to see if everything was alright. We had keys to each others' places. Asked me to please call him back. He gave me his, this," pointing at a page in the notebook, "telephone number.

"I was apprehensive, didn't think there was something wrong with her car not in her spot. Another car was parked there instead. Maybe she had to do some shopping, or her car needed an oil change, there could have been a million things she had to do.

"And when I was about to open the door to her condo the UPS man yelled at me holding a fairly large package under his arm. Wanted me to wait for him before I closed the door again. He had to be making a special delivery, at that time of day. I let him go in first so he could put the box down.

"He made a few steps inside before he stopped, dropped the box and pushed me back out of the apartment. I had no idea what was going on until I heard him talk on his cell phone to the 911 person.

"And from what I read in the paper yesterday I'm glad I didn't see anything.

"By the way, her car was parked a few spaces further to the left, too far to the side for me to see it from my window."

"What time did you go over to her apartment, approximately, Greta?"

"There's nothing approximate about that. It was a few minutes before eight. I had to hurry. *Mash* starts right then and I never miss that show. Right after Mr. Schloss called me."

She gave Amos the notebook and the sheriff copied Darren's number into his own.

"Greta, you have been of great help and we don't want to take up much more of your time. What about relatives?"

"Well, she told me that her parents were killed in a hit-and-run accident several years ago. She has an aunt in one of the retirement communities in Murrells Inlet, another aunt and uncle somewhere west of Georgetown she spoke very fondly of, and a younger brother. I saw him once ... looked a little rough, if you ask me. He came to the door looking for her, thought she was with me. Michelle never spoke much about him. She called him Mikey. I have no idea where he lives."

They thanked the lady for her kind assistance and were about to leave when Amos turned around and asked her one more question. "Did you give all that to the deputies yesterday?"

"They only wanted to know about her relatives. So I told them about the aunts and the uncle like I told you. I completely forgot the brother."

"Thanks, Greta, we appreciate your time. We'll take a quick look at Michelle's apartment, but don't expect to find anything helpful. Our crew has already gone through it with a fine-tooth comb.

"And, of course, if you hear or see anything that you think could be of interest to us, call me, day or night." He heaved an inch-thick wallet from his back pocket which housed among other Amos-essentials a lonesome wrinkled card. He pulled it out, made a dilettante attempt to smooth it before he handed it to Greta.

She took the card, glanced over it and said, "I hope you find that monster."

"We will. Good-bye Greta."

As Amos Grimm suspected, the apartment didn't reveal any further clues other than what Tony Caparelli and the crew had been able to gather. The crime scene was still roped off, just in case some of the pictures gave rise to further inspection. As far as the rest of the flat was concerned, Amos and Karl still refrained from touching anything, for basically the same reason. Although no fingerprints were secured, "it's amazing what photos under a microscope can produce," the sheriff commented while they ambled through the remaining two rooms.

"Well, we have to leave a few things to our so-called specialists. Searching crime scenes is one of them."

Karl nodded in agreement and casually glanced at the spines of rows of books shelved in a corner bookcase that spread about three feet to either side. If nothing else, they might tell him if Michelle had some interest in subjects other than work related and which ones those were.

But he seemed to be out of luck. Medical and legal publications as well as textbooks from both faculties seemed to have served the aspiring professional woman as her dominant reading material.

A dedicated student, Karl thought to himself.

And he concluded that there was no point in staying any longer in a place where the most gruesome murder this small township had probably ever been exposed to, had taken place. He tried not to visualize the act and was grateful that the body had been removed.

He turned around to find Amos when his eyes caught the titles of three books that did not fit in with the others.

He picked up the books and read the titles:

West Africa Internet Governance Forum
Democracy in Nigeria
Poverty Eradication in Africa
The New African Faces

What is this all about? Shoemaker found this a bit odd. *Well, they could belong to someone else.*

He waved for Amos to come and take a look at them.

"Maybe she had a special interest in what's going on in Africa. But from what I've seen we can conclude that Michelle Brown led a very structured life, spending most of her time furthering her career, or careers."

The sheriff was satisfied.

Chapter Five

On the way back to the car Amos Grimm pulled out his notebook for the number Mrs. Snyder had given. "361-2934, and if my memory serves me right it'll have to be in the Little River area. Let's see what Darren is up to."

Not hiding his suspicion he added, "Probably tryin' to get out of Dodge if this hasn't happened already. Maybe the case will be quicker solved than I anticipated."

Shoemaker opened the door to the passenger's seat and in a mock-lecture reprimanded his older friend. "What about innocent until proven guilty?"

"Yeah, yeah, I know. But it's just a bit too much of a coincidence, don't you think so?

"Let's go over this. He calls Greta, tells her that he's been trying to get in touch with Michelle, but to no avail. Wants to let her know that he couldn't keep their date for later in the evening. It hardly takes the brain of good old Sherlock to make him a *person of interest*, and not that comedian Clarence Woodburn."

Karl injected, "Of course, that man is definitely a strong suspect. So strong even, that it's hard to believe someone could be so ridiculously obvious."

Amos steered the car back on the Connector, crossed 17 Business and continued until they reached the Bypass, where they turned north in the direction of Myrtle Beach. The former sheriff picked up his cell phone and dialed the office. "Olivia, darlin', how are you doing? Everything alright in the office?"

"Oh, hi sheriff, yes, everything is fine. We all miss you, though."

"That's sweet of you. You let me know if Linus doesn't treat you right, you hear? The reason I called – need to have you check out two addresses for me. First name's Darren, last Schloss; phone number 361-2934, our area code. Has to be Little River or maybe still North Myrtle Beach. We are on our way in that direction.

"The other one is a little trickier. The woman who was killed Wednesday, Michelle Brown, apparently had a younger brother. Goes by the name of Mikey.

"Go over to the courthouse and see if Ben Stein can help you with this. The man is probably in his early twenties, unmarried. Same last name, I guess. Call me when you have it. Bye honey, oh, wait, tell Linus to give me a call, too."

"Will do. Bye sheriff."

"Retired, huh?" Karl shook his head, smiling. "Could have fooled me."

"Well, I don't have to convince you, that our crew in Georgetown needs help. They didn't even ask Greta the most basic questions. We could have asked her a lot more ourselves, but I need to leave a few things to Linus and the detectives if they ever want to run the department by themselves. But I don't want the FBI putting their noses in our affairs like last time, remember?"

Karl nodded.

In Surfside they made a left turn onto 544 and after about four, five miles entered I31 following the sign directing them to North Myrtle Beach.

They were just about to exit where Hwy 90 was supposed to take them to Little River when the sheriff's phone rang.

"Just in time. What've you got for me, Olivia?"

"Schloss, Darren, Jr., 1785 Little River Neck Road, Little River, South Carolina."

"I know where that is. Thanks, honey. Did you get hold of Linus and what about –?"

"Yep, he's right here."

"Hi sheriff, what's going on?"

"Well, Linus, Karl Shoemaker is here with me. You remember him, don't you? Seven years ago; the Calhoun murder."

"Of course I do. Tell him I said hello. Maybe he can help us again with this new one."

"I will and he already is, helping us, I mean."

There was silence on the other end of the line. Amos grinned. "I also asked Olivia to find the address of the woman's brother. Did she have any luck? But if not maybe you can look into that yourself."

Olivia had not been able to go to the courthouse and he would check into that right away.

The sheriff disconnected the line and said to Karl, still with a sympathetic grin on his sagging face, a reminder that he had embarked on a healthier lifestyle too late for the flesh to shrink back into its proper place, "Well, Linus Thompson is as good an old Southern boy as they come, loyal to the core, follows orders to the tee, never complains. I could go on and on. But he's just no leader. He should have his deputies all over the area, searching for clues, her clothes for cryin' out loud.

"Thank the Good Lord that we don't have such violent crime that often in our county. Yet the times we were compared to Andy Taylor's TV town Mayberry are long gone.

"He was actually glad when I offered my help. That's not exactly the reaction of a well-together, self-reliant person, much less of a lawman. I worry about him."

"Alright Amos, I know you stuck your neck out for him. Just give him some time. He may come around," Shoemaker felt the need to get his friend off the subject. "But right now we should concentrate on Mr. Schloss. Are we still on the right track?"

"Oh yeah, we are going to leave this road here after a couple of miles, get on the Old Highway 17 which takes us straight onto Neck Road.

"If he is married, what Greta suspected, and me too, quite frankly, we might see the wife only. If that's the case we just ask her where he might be right now. Don't give her a reason; we just tell her that we want to speak to him."

Karl agreed. "You don't want to expose his extramarital affair, alleged, I should say, right off the bat, especially if he hasn't done it, killed the young woman, that is."

"Absolutely, besides, we could be looking at a colossal lawsuit. Now here we're getting off and start paying attention to the house numbers, 1785 has to be on the left."

The Schloss residence was a modest bungalow, with red brick sides and a wood-veneer front. The front yard gave the impression that somebody struggled to keep it up, but didn't quite succeed. Since the area was no more than at most three hundred square feet, the argument could be made that the owner didn't spend a lot of time there.

"Look at the mail box. I should accidentally run over it. We'd probably do the mail carrier a favor. But we came here to find out whether the man had anything to do with the murder of his lady friend and not why he's a lousy landscaper."

Karl nodded, emphasizing his agreement. "And let's not forget it."

When they approached the front door, other than the shades of two previous layers of paint that had resurfaced in various spots, an inconspicuous peephole caught their eyes.

"Haven't seen one of those since they closed down Sunset Lodge," Amos remarked with a grin.

"It's about him, isn't it," were the woman's first words after Amos had introduced himself and Karl.

"Please, slow down, ma'am. Is this the Schloss residence?"

She just nodded. Her face turned near-white; fear began to settle in her eyes.

Grimm noticed her apprehension. "We better go inside, before the neighbors start wondering. May we?"

She stepped aside and the two men walked inside. She led them into a small room on the left, halfway through a narrow, barely three-foot wide hallway. Straight ahead, behind a gothic-style open arch, was what seemed to be the living room. Why didn't she take them there?

After they had taken their seats in two armchairs whose corduroy covers showed an advanced state of wear and tear, the woman hesitated to do likewise. She was an unusually attractive woman. The high cheekbones, encased by a halo of blue-black hair that gently grazed her shoulders, gave this genteel face a classical Native American look.

However the jeans and T-shirt, a few shades lighter than their original tincture, appeared to have suffered the same fate as the meagerly furnished room and the exterior of the house.

"You said you were the former sheriff of Georgetown County," looking at Amos, trying nervously to toss a strand of hair out of her face. "You better tell me right now if your coming here has something to do with my husband."

"Ma'am, you have already answered our first question."

"What do you mean?"

"Well, unless your husband is in the house but doesn't want to be seen, we assume he's not here."

"You assumed right, he's not." She was still standing, waiting.

"Well then," Amos Grimm went on, "can you tell us where we can find him?"

"Of course, well, not exactly. He is a sales rep. Works for General Beverage Distributors, a wine and spirits company."

"I know them. They have their warehouse on the Bypass before you get to the Broadway-At-The-Beach complex. One of my deputies has a son who sells wine and beer for Preferred Beverages in Columbia. There are usually two groups, one for grocery stores. They call that "off-premise sales and—"

"On-premise," Mrs. Schloss interrupted. "Darren is in that second group, he sells wine and beer to restaurants, bars, and wherever people can consume alcohol." She spoke the last words with a noticeable degree of disgust.

"So, do you have any idea where he might be at this moment or which accounts he has on his calendar for today? All we want to do is ask him a few questions. He might know something about a matter we're working on."

"It's probably another one of his women-stories. What happened, did the husband catch them ... in flagranti, isn't that the word?"

The sheriff looked at Karl and for a nanosecond a flash of embarrassment seemed to scurry across the older man's wind-burned face.

"Red handed."

"Huh? Oh, yea, of course. No ma'am, we can't divulge that," reestablishing his composure with a fancy expression of his own, "at this moment. But we really would like to find out what he knows or saw."

"Well, let's see. Friday evening, he usually makes his last call at the *Golden Crown,* where in all probability he will have a couple of drinks, or three or four."

"Well, it's now one twenty five. Any idea where he might have a late lunch?"

"I don't know. I think that varies wherever he is during that time. You may want to try *Mama's Kitchen* on–"

Grimm butted in and said, "I know that place. Great oysters on the half shell. Mrs. Schloss, we appreciate your letting us come into your home and thank you for your courtesy."

Her response caught the two men by surprise. "Well, sheriff, it isn't much of a home and I wasn't all that friendly to you. But you startled me when you asked for him. I am constantly worried that one day he will be stopped by the police and lose his driver's license on a DUI charge. We need his income, as little as it is – he works on commission only – with me being laid off indefinitely."

"Mrs. Schloss," for the first time Karl opened his mouth. "Do you have children?"

"No, but Darren has two from his first marriage. A boy and a girl. They live with their mother and a future step dad. By the way, my name is Mary."

Back in the car Amos asked without diverting his attention to the road, "Well, what do you think of Mrs. Schloss, or should I say Mary Schloss?"

"Neglected, bored, and, as she admitted herself, scared stiff about their financial future."

"She was beginning to open up more towards the end, but in all likelihood would have had a nervous breakdown if we only as much as hinted on why we are truly looking for him."

Karl agreed. "She's trying to keep up the appearance of a normal household, just can't quite pull it off. The ill-kept yard, the paint peeling off the doors, the flea-market furniture – that's most likely also the reason why she didn't offer to sit in the living room.

"She probably has to do everything by herself and is just overwhelmed with it all, while Darren is having a good time with other women. She is a strikingly beautiful woman, and her numerously-washed, out-of-style clothes do not take a fraction of an inch away from that. I feel sorry for her."

"So do I, actually. Now let's see what we can rake out from the wine salesman – if we can locate him."

From where they were, driving east to Hwy 17 Business was only a short ride, but the traffic on the Ocean Highway, as it was proudly referred to by locals and visitors alike, was heavy due to the many traffic lights, back-to-the-office men and women, and the out-of-towners who were unfamiliar with the new bypasses, such as 22 and 31, which could make it a lot easier to get into and out of Myrtle Beach. Too bad they weren't able to take advantage of any of them since their destination was right on the business part of 17.

It was just about two when they passed the Myrtle Beach Library and began to look for a parking place, since *Mama's Kitchen* was just one more block away.

"Where are we going to find a place to park here with the cars bumper to bumper on both sides and every side street as far as I can see?" Shoemaker was anxious not to waste valuable time and miss their rendezvous with Darren Schloss. "Maybe I keep looking for a space and you go inside. We don't even know what he looks like."

Amos produced an innocuously superior grin, let the tires of the Explorer screech to stop right in front of a *NO - PARKING* sign that had an equally uncompromising addition stenciled into the bottom: *AT ANY TIME!*

With a wink at his partner the sheriff grabbed the blue light from behind his seat, placed it on the dashboard, casually turned on the flash and said, "No, we'll go inside together and we'll find out what our man looks like, if he's there."

"Some things will never change," and both knew what Karl Shoemaker was referring to. Seven years ago they were coming back from the Charleston Airport and Amos simply activated the siren and light after Shoemaker let him know that he was exceeding the speed limit by roughly twenty plus mph.

"Hi honey, I know we are late, but you think there's any chow left in the kitchen? To whip up a butter-drippin', sea-salt smellin' jumbo shrimp sandwich?"

"You aren't asking for much, are you, Sir? Uh, wait a minute, aren't you the—"

"Hush, sweetheart, we are also here to conduct a little business. And you might be able to help us.

The young girl's brown eyes lit up, as in *Maybe I have to do something important for the sheriff, or perhaps...*

"Does the name Darren Schloss sound familiar to you, wine salesman, works for General Beverage?"

"Of course," an obvious let-down feeling in her voice, "doesn't everybody? Every female, that is. Can't stand him. If you're looking for him he's sitting at the end of the bar – doing what he does best, drinking liquor and sweet-talking women into…, you know what I mean. Thinks he's a real Casanova. A creep, that's what he is."

"Well, thank you, thank you very much, uh, what's your name honey?"

"Jamie, Jamie Hendrix."

"Well Jamie, this is for you," handing her a five dollar bill, "you've been of great help."

Three tables were still occupied with diners. Two men in their late thirties, wearing fading-green hospital garb, were finishing their burgers at a corner table opposite the bar.

To the left of the arched opening three women were munching on their salads and acting as if they were enjoying it.

The table in the center, intended for a larger party up to a dozen hungry people, hosted just one couple. The two senior citizens were obviously way past their prime and so was their affection for each other. The man, who resembled the former sheriff of seven years ago, before the former Marge Baker entered his life and forced a nutrition-friendlier food regimen upon him, leaned a foot back from the table to accommodate for the potbelly. The woman, a gray handbag on her lap, sat opposite her husband looking lackadaisically at the *Georgetown Gazette* which he held in such a way that neither of the two could see the other.

The sheriff grimaced upon observing the pseudo-idyllic scene. "Now isn't that sweet. They even share the newspaper."

"I'm not sure they're consciously doing that," Karl added with a cheerless grin. They casually eased toward the back wall of the dining room and perched at one of three tables for two next to where the beech wood-stained bar ended in a softly curved right angle.

Jamie approached them, the look of someone privy to a secret all over her chubby-cheeked face, and announced in a voice that was closer to a whisper than conversational volume, thus making it that much more suspicious. "Winston, that's the chef, said he could scramble up a couple of jumbo shrimp sandwiches. Said on account of it being after lunchtime and all and," now for the next part she did hold her voice down even more, "you bein' law people, they were on the house."

"Now wait a—" the sheriff cut himself off. "Tell him we appreciate it very much. An unsweetened iced tea for me and a ..."

"Glass of water for me," Shoemaker ordered.

The sheriff leaned over to Karl, "I think we should tell our man at the bar that we want to talk to him before he realizes he's striking out with the barmaid and takes off. Uh, better yet, I'm gonna ask him to join us." He stood up and walked to the bar.

A minute or two later the sheriff was back with their 'man of interest' in tow.

Chapter Six

There could be no doubt in anybody's mind what was Darren Schloss's favorite pastime. While Amos introduced him to Shoemaker, Karl got up and looked at a guy in his early forties, maybe ten years older than his wife. At about six feet two he appreciably towered over the man from Wyoming. Dressed in a tailor-made navy-blue suit, yellow polka-dotted tie over a white dress-shirt made him look more like a US Senator than a wine salesman. However, the toothpick hanging suspended from his mouth cancelled that comparison.

"Look guys, this girl at the bar is about to leave for today and I was just about to talk her into trying some of our cordials and the Pinot Noir for which we're having a contest going. A sale here could mean two tickets to Paris, France, might be headed my way shortly. You don't want to prevent that from happening, now do you?" He angled a second chair from the next table, plunked down on the one that was already there and wedged one foot between the other's seat and the supporting crossbar underneath.

No shortage of conceit here, Karl thought, but didn't say.

"Who would the second ticket be for, Mr. Schloss?" The sheriff asked with an innocent look on his face and a quick glance at his partner.

"What do you mean? Uh, wait a minute. What is this all about? This has nothing to do with a speeding ticket I supposedly got by way of an automatic camera set-up. What do you really want from me?" The man's demeanor changed visibly from that of a brash hot-shot to a person who couldn't hide the uneasy feeling that was making his eyes shift rapidly from one side to the other. He pushed himself away from the table and was just about to get up when the sheriff grabbed him by the arm and motioned him to stay.

"Relax, Mr. Schloss. We need to ask you a few questions."

However, Mr. Schloss was no longer in the mood to accommodate Grimm's request and snapped his arm out of the sheriff's grip.

"Or we can do this at the station. We can come back with a written citation and force you, not ask you, to come with us. Won't make us any happier, though. So, your choice."

"Okay, have it your way. Now I'm anxious myself what it is you want to ask me about." He crossed his legs, interlocked his fingers and rested the hands on his thighs, staring defiantly at the two men. He had allowed his natural ostentation to return rather than admit defeat by following the lawman's orders. "Ask!" he said.

"Well then," Amos obliged, giving him a no-nonsense look. "For starters, how well did you know Michelle Brown?"

"The woman who was killed this past Wednesday? What makes you think I knew her?"

This guy is either the shrewdest con artist or just downright stupid, Karl thought to himself.

"That's not the answer to my question. Don't even try to play games with us. I'm asking you again. How well did you know her?"

Darren Schloss put one arm with a slightly perspiring hand on the table, the other over the back of the seat in an awkward attempt to project himself unfazed. He didn't succeed. "Alright, I knew her ... vaguely."

"Vaguely, huh? If you continue giving us the run around I'm going to tell you what we know. You called Ms. Greta Snyder on Wednesday evening and told her you couldn't reach Michelle and asked her to tell her you had to cancel your date for the evening. Why couldn't you call her later yourself? Needed an alibi? And don't give us another one of your *vague* answers. If I'm still not satisfied with your answers by the time our food arrives I'll be really mad.

"And to further discourage you from trying to outsmart us let me ask you if you didn't find it rather strange that we found you here?" The sheriff's eyes, unblinking, piercing, signaled the end of the small talk, a circumstance not unnoticed by his subject.

"Oh shit, you've been to the house already? I bet that bitch told you a lot of garbage. Yeah, that's what she does best, spreading lies around about me. But—"

"Stop it, right now," the sheriff struggled to contain himself. "Last time, Mr. Schloss, how well have you known Miss Brown?"

"We went out a few times, that's all. She was one of those classy types, very methodical."

"Were you intimate with her?"

"What do you mean?"

Amos shot another sharp flash across the table, stronger than words.

"No. She was too prissy, if you ask me. Think she was also catholic. Don't they have this weird thing, not to have sex outside of marriage?"

"That upset you?"

The salesman's assessment of his own masculinity hurled any thought of caution out the window. With a one-sided grin that gave away an immature chauvinistic mind of a most despicable degree he snapped back, self-righteously, "Life's too short to waste on things you can't get. Oh, here is your food, Sheriff Grimm. Don't want to upset you any further.

"And if you have more questions for me later that would have to be done in the presence of my attorney. And, by the way, I did not kill Michelle Brown. Why don't you ask her brother Mikey – always bugged her for money – where he was on Wednesday?"

With that remark Mr. Schloss heaved his gym-preserved body out of the chair and proceeded to exit the restaurant.

This time Karl opened his mouth for the first time. "Mr. Schloss, are you a hunting man?"

"I hunt deer occasionally, yea. What has that got to do with anything?"

"Nothing really, you need a special knife to clean them, don't you?"

"Later, guys," Darren Schloss ran the ball of one hand against the door and stormed out of the restaurant.

The shrimp sandwiches tasted delicious and the sheriff and Karl attacked them ferociously. When they were finished Amos left a ten dollar tip for Jamie and thanked her again. "Tell Winston I'll bring the crew here for our next department meeting."

And yet, the big gratuity couldn't quite pass over her disappointment for not being filled in on why they needed to see Darren. *After all, she was basically involved already, as, what did they call it on TV, an informant?* But the two had already left.

"I knew we had to get out of there in a hurry. The girl was just about to explode from an acute case of rubberneck," the sheriff muttered.

Many days this late in the year the weather in the coastal regions of the Carolinas was simply gorgeous. A gentler sun radiated a comfortable average of seventy degrees under pale-blue skies.

It was one of those days when the two stepped into the open. However, Mother Nature's generosity went pretty much unnoticed by them. The sheriff flipped the cover of his cell phone to expose the screen.

"Oh good, that's Olivia. Hope they found Mikey's address." He touched the number and the secretary answered in seconds.

"Yeah sheriff, you are lucky. Calvin Michael Brown, age twenty-three, lives on South Morgan in Andrews. You have to hang a left where 521, or Main Street, and Morgan cross each other. The number is 18 B. He's listed in the phone book. But I called Charlene Strickland at the courthouse to make sure I had the right one; she lives in Andrews."

"And what else did she say?" Amos asked good-naturedly.

"Well, she came right out and said, 'you mean Mikey?' You know she likes to talk—"

At that point Grimm started to roll his eyes. "Did she say anything we should know?"

"Oh yes, I think so. She said where he lived was not a real house but a, what did she call that again, uh, a detached garage apartment. And she kept rattling on and on about him being a real bum, never able to keep a job—"

"Did she also mention that he had a sister?"

"No, she didn't."

"Olivia, sweetheart, great job. One of these days I'm taking you and that lucky devil of a husband of yours to the Bay Restaurant for one of chef Boswick's specialties, the Santa Fe Chicken, or the Pirate Special, and a real Southern mud pie."

While he turned the ignition key to get his trusted SUV rolling he smiled softly, looking straight ahead. "It always pays off not to be stingy with a praise now and then. It seems to encourage people to work twice as hard afterwards. Olivia has turned into a fine young woman. Quite a change from the time we hired her as a file clerk. For an entire week she was horrified when the phone rang and nobody but her was there to pick it up.

"I remember one day, we were all in a staff meeting, when a woman called in and wanted a five-foot alligator removed from the backyard. Poor Olivia hurled out of the building to the Fire Department, which was at that time right next to us, grabbed the first firefighter she ran into, yelling, 'There's an alligator!'

"Kyle Hardwick, who did some farming on his daddy's land on Sandy Island, where the population of gators is exceeded only by that of the mosquitoes, politely spitting out a load of tobacco juice away from her, replied with all the hysterical agitation of a bear halfway through hibernation, 'Where at?'

'Right here,' Olivia hadn't caught her breath yet, 'in the back y—'

Then it dawned on her, and with a face as red as a poppy field, she stammered, 'in *her* backyard.'

"As I said, she's come a long way. Now, let's step on it. On the way we can decide if we feel like taking a ride into the country."

Shoemaker didn't quite follow. "What do you mean, 'ride into the country'? I need to take Bo for his afternoon stroll. This might be his last visit to the coast. And you know what?" He didn't look at the sheriff, didn't want him to see the sadness in his face.

"What, Karl?"

"I think he feels it too."

"Oh, yeah, I understand. Just thought you'd be glad to get involved again. Like old times. But the murder, like the one six, no seven years ago, just happened. So there will be plenty of opportunities for you to jump in. But I understand."

Instead of turning onto Hwy 501 to catch 701, which would have earned them a humble shortcut by avoiding having to go through Georgetown altogether, he stayed on Business 17. "Here's what we are gonna do. I drop you off at the *Inn* and go from there to Andrews. Gives me a chance to win a few points back at the home front."

"Well," now Karl felt a little guilty. "It's not as if you have to be there at a certain time. To my knowledge you don't have an appointment with the guy."

"Yes?" the sheriff elongated the one-syllable word, expecting an explanation for which he already knew the answer.

"Okay, give me forty-five minutes with Bo and then we ride to Andrews, together."

"Take as long as you need." And with a victorious grin Amos gave the accelerator an extra push and almost ran the red light at the intersection of 6th Avenue and Ocean Boulevard.

"Take it easy," Shoemaker's mock-reprimand was followed by "unless you're itching for a ticket.

"But let me give you my itinerary for the weekend already now before you book me for more of your extemporaneous excursions."

"It better includes a ride to Charleston."

Karl always marveled at the unconditional compassion and deep-rooted empathy Marge and Karl had bestowed upon him from the very first day he and Bo drifted into their lives.

"Now what do you think of Mr. Schloss, before we completely forget why we're here?" Amos returned, quite unceremoniously, their attention back to the subject at hand.

And Karl Shoemaker had no problems with that. He even accepted one of these sugar-laden lollipops the sheriff had started to swirl around in his mouth after Marge had put a ban on those 'ghastly' cigars she was picking up after him, half chewed or half burned, in the most unusual places. Told him if he ever came back with tobacco on his breath she would start shooting if he came within a hundred feet of the *Inn*.

"When he said, 'What makes you think that I knew her?' I thought that he was either the shrewdest con artist or the dumbest con man on earth. But I believe he's neither.

"His skirt-chasing activities simply show that he has no respect for women. Whether this despicable character flaw could reach to such a level that it becomes motivation for murder requires learning more about the man. The difference between his and his wife's appearance is striking. He appears to treat her like dirt. I don't have to tell you – I don't like him."

"Well, yeah, he's truly a fine work of art, if the medium I'm referring to can be used to create an art form."

Karl looked at the sheriff, sucked the last layer of the lemon–flavored lollipop before the taste would change to tapwater, wanted to say something, but didn't. After all, it wasn't the first time that Amos Grimm surprised him by getting a crude message across without uttering the words in kind.

They were passing through Murrell's Inlet when the sheriff mentioned, "Your question regarding the knife was interesting. Based on Caparelli's comments to the press, remember the zigzag shaped body wounds on the victim, we ought to check if certain knives could produce the kind of injuries he described. Have to get one of the boys to look into that."

Chapter Seven

Highways 17A and 521 join each other from their inception at the main intersection in Georgetown until the Sampit community where the first turns left in the direction of Moncks Corner and 521 in its new four-lane splendor takes the traveler in a beeline to Andrews, South Carolina.

Amos and Karl were just passing through that section when the sheriff tried to restart a sluggish conversation between the two. "Locals call this here the nine-mile curve, 'cause it's just about that far from Georgetown."

"Hm, okay." Karl's thoughts were still at the Recreation Center, where he and his trusted four-legged friend had journeyed to a little while ago. Marge had fed Bo as if she was preparing him for pulling a cart full of water melons to the Farmers Market.

"Well, what was I supposed to do? Throw it away after you two didn't show up? I decided I wasn't going to let the food go to waste. It's unchristian, anyway."

"And Bo agreed with you," he didn't even try to be serious. He brushed his cheek against hers, grabbed the leash and the man and his dog embarked on a daily ritual that had been going on for almost thirteen years of their lives.

The Rottweiler's advancing age had been showing its merciless presence in multiple ways. There were the obvious signs like the white whiskers, the increasing hollowness of the once vitality-exuding compact-body physique, or the loss of power in his legs, which used to allow him to jump out of the Jeep and catapult himself upon impact into the open like a wild cheetah.

But not long ago Karl noticed a new symptom, a symptom that had nothing to do with the canine's physical condition. More and more Bo preferred to be by himself, outside. On several occasions he had slipped through the fence around the back yard of their home in Wyoming and stayed away for hours, sometimes days. He always came back, though. But when he looked for him one evening in the thick woods behind the house, carrying a flashlight, he did find him curled up on a patch of soft pine straw peacefully asleep.

His veterinarian in Cody told him that being by themselves was indeed a practice of some dogs and a sure sign of the final stages in their lives.

The good doctor's repeated assurances that this was absolutely nothing personal – Bo had not developed a dislike for his master – but that it rather was an 'innate process that he has little choice but to succumb to'.

"You're awfully quiet." And with honest guilt on his face Amos added, "If you didn't want to come you should've let me know. Marge thinks already I'm coercing you into all this. And—"

"Amos, it has nothing to do with you. And I'm perfectly capable to say no, if I so choose. As a matter of fact I am honored, actually, that you are taking me along. I will make that clear to Marge as well. I'm just, well, it's kind o' personal. But I am okay, honest."

"Well, there's not much to talk about Andrews anyway. So, you just go ahead with whatever you were, eh, thinking about. It's obvious that I enjoy the company."

"So do I."

For the tough lawman he could be, there was an exceptionally sensitive side to Amos Grimm. Shoemaker gave his neighbor an assuring pat on the shoulder.

Yet, whether he wanted it or not, his mind returned his contemplations to his canine friend and their unique, almost unprecedented relationship. He was never in doubt that Bo's one and only goal in life was to please his master. And for a Rottweiler this meant to entertain, to question, and above all, to protect his keeper.

Although Karl was still wrestling with the inevitable – maybe Bo could hang on for another year or so – but ruefully recognized the egocentric manifestation such thoughts did provoke. And he felt guilty and sad for encouraging the canine to try harder, *you can do it, come on, catch the ball, good boy,* and all the ovations and thumbs up he often employed in an attempt to elevate the canine's enthusiasm and motivation. And Bo tried his best, always aspiring not to disappoint him.

There was his bravery, like when he didn't run away from the fire because Karl's late first wife and his daughter were still trapped in the house, or the time a two-year old Bo retrieved a sky-blue rubber boot in a small wooded area near Galveston, LA, that belonged to seven- year old Anne-Marie Beauchamp. With that in hand the police not only found the little girl, but were able to apprehend her molester shortly thereafter. Bo received a medal for his contribution in that case, which he is still proudly carrying around his neck together with his silver name tag.

Dark clouds were headed their way, aided by one of those late-summer gusts, announcing the arrival of fall, three weeks later than the calendar claims the change of the two seasons occurs. The weather in South Carolina can change faster than boxer Mike Tyson hit the canvas in his fight against Buster Douglas, but the people of South Carolina can always depend on steamy-hot and into overtime running summers.

"We might get a shower or two," Amos decided his friend had to snap out of whatever he was held hostage by. "When we cross the railroad tracks it's the second street. At the light."

The sheriff stopped the Explorer at South Morgan Street and let the light turn green.

"Now let's see. If I'm not mistaken that garage apartment is right behind Doc Hapegood's drugstore. Don't even know if he's a real doctor, but folks in the small towns around here take pleasure in elevating the status of people they find worthy enough. I once asked an elderly man from Aynor why he called the woman who did his tax returns 'Lawyer Clemons', he answered with a twinkle in his eyes, 'Gives the town a flair of sophistication.' Told me, that it might also favorably affect the outcome of his tax return. Country people may be a little slow to talk or to accept change, but they are certifiably no dummies. Oops, I almost passed our port of entry."

The russet two-story brick house with the number 18 stenciled in shiny black on the right side of the double-wide front door with two rectangular milky windows on either side was accented by a well-kept lawn, an island of a variety of blooming flowers, geraniums, day-lilies, petunias, and more they couldn't identify, cared for by a couple of ear-to-ear smiling garden gnomes pushing their tiny wheel barrows.

Grimm almost swallowed his lollipop. "Wow—"

"Hold it," Karl said. "Before you draw any conclusion and swing into the whitewashed driveway you might want to back up a little and—"

"Should've known better." Amos shook his head, pulled the lever into reverse and then turned into a pothole-riddled dirt trail. The warped plywood square with the number 18B clumsily penned on it was tossed into a huge thicket of briars, robbed of the post that was to keep it up.

The apartment was hidden behind more overgrown weeds and a wild wax-myrtle tree, set back somewhat further from the street than the tidy place to the left.

When the two men stepped out of the vehicle Karl said, not without disgust, "Hard to believe the people next door allowed this guy to let their property end up in such a state of dilapidation. That is, if they actually own the place."

Amos knocked hard on the raw pinewood door which revealed no visible sign of ever having been in contact with paint. No answer. He pounded the door a few more times, but to no avail. Karl started to walk around the building, but Sheriff Grimm waved him off. "No need to risk stepping on a rattler in this field of weeds. Hate to see run-down places like this. Let's try the folks next door. See what they can tell us about Ms. Brown's little brother."

"If his motorbike isn't leaned against the little tool shed on the right side over there, he must be out." The squeaky voice belonged to the lady who was craning her neck over the chain-link fence and turning her head in the direction of the two strangers. Her silvery-white hair looked like a hydrangea flower in full bloom. The sheriff guessed her to be in her mid to late seventies.

Shoemaker took a quick look at the small add-on which the lady had identified to be the tool shed. An undeterminable number of contraptions, all in various degrees of decay, rakes and shovels with broken sticks, or no sticks at all; pieces of an electrical cord run over a zillion times, lawn mower parts, mixed in with those from old Harleys, were scattered all over the yard. Karl, shaking his head in disbelief, just said, "No bike."

"Can I help you in any way?" the lady chirped, visibly pleased to have someone to chat with. And she wasn't about to let the new company slip away. So pleased, in fact, that she didn't even give the two a chance to answer. "The boy, Mikey, isn't as bad as people make him to be. He's a loner, doesn't really know yet what to do with his life. And he's so distraught, with his sister being killed and all. We are still in shock over this. However, if you talk to Kendall, my husband, he has a completely different opinion about him—"

"Ma'am," over the many years in law enforcement Amos had perfected the art of interruption to such a degree, that the person he had cut off didn't even recognize it. "Do you have an idea where we could find him? I'm Sheriff Amos Grimm, and this gentleman is Karl Shoemaker. We just wanted to ask him a few questions regarding his sister's death."

"Well, of course we don't check up on him, but the noise this motorcycle of his makes is literally deafening. If we want it or not, we hear most of his comings and goings. But why won't you come in, maybe Kendall knows where the boy is. So terrible what happened to Michelle."

Kendall was watching the news in the bright living room, which was the first room they were led into through an open arch behind the diminutive foyer. The voice of Bill O'Reilly filled the air.

"Think you can ask Mr. O'Reilly to go to a commercial so that you can turn and greet our visitors?" The woman's head turned in the sheriff's direction and with a wink and a sagacious smile that had evolved over decades of cohabitation, she said, "I may have to revert to my strategy, which has a one-hundred-percent success rate."

She tiptoed over to the side table next to where her husband was sitting and snapped the remote.

But the man was already up and reached out his hand to welcome the strangers. "Gentlemen, we are the Emersons, and this wannabe comedienne over here is my wife of fifty-four wonderful years, Mary Beth. And I'm Kendall."

Amos took a step to meet him and introduced himself and Karl.

"Of course," Kendall enthusiastically shook Amos's hand, "you're the sheriff. It's so nice to meet you. How could old folks like us be of help to you? But, by all means, sit down, please." He offered them to sit on the sofa alongside the wall next to the TV and his armchair.

Amos was just about to join Karl on the quilt-covered settee, when Kendall gently pulled his shoulder down and the sheriff plunged into the deep cushion of the host's favorite pre-bedtime back support. "It swivels," he said and slowly moved toward one of two smaller chairs framing a coffee table where he sat down.

Mary Beth had left for a short while and when she came back, she was carrying a tray with four tall glasses of iced tea and an equal amount of dishes containing chocolate-coated cookies. And while she placed each on the coffee table, convenient for all to reach, she left no doubt where those cookies came from. "Made them myself from scratch."

Southern hospitality at it's best. That and the fear of being alone. Amos Grimm felt equally great empathy and a heavy sadness for these wonderful southern folks. They belonged to a generation who welcomed friends and total strangers alike into their homes, trusting everybody and fearing no one. How much more would Amos have preferred to chat with both of them about topics they would have liked to share, their life journey, their family, and with a glance at the numerous pictures on the walls, on top of the TV, in between the books of the two shelves, grand and even great grandchildren?

But unfortunately they were not sitting in their living room only to exchange pleasantries. So many similar situations flashed by sheriff Grimm's mind, and slower than usual he proceeded to tell the couple the reason they had accepted their kind invitation.

"Thank you, Mrs. Emerson, —"

"Please, just Mary Beth."

"Alright, it's certainly a pleasure visiting with you fine folks, but as you probably have guessed, we came here to have a talk with Michael Brown. But he seems to be not at home. You got any idea where he might be? Does he have a job? He obviously doesn't spend a whole lot of time in his yard. That must bother you, I'm sure.

"My friend Karl here thought to label his compound untidy would be an understatement similar to calling Mother Theresa an okay woman."

Kendall smiled briefly and tried to de-hyperbolize the statement. "Yes, we understand what you're saying. Mother Theresa is one of the greatest saints after the Lord's Mother, and Mikey's place – you should see the inside, would make you puke – is a filthy dump."

The frown on Mary Beth's forehead disappeared after full credence to her favorite saint's holiness was reaffirmed. "We are at our wit's end with this boy, or man, I should say. But he completely changed after his parents had lost their lives in a car accident. His mother was my sister." The emotions were still too much for her to control.

Kendall reached over to hold her hand and said to her with loving grace, "Well, honey, I know you're still not over the accident and now Michelle's murder. And these two gentlemen understand that but they want to find Mikey.

"Let us tell them everything they want to know. Maybe they will find the butcher who killed her."

She shook her head. "This will not bring her back."

He shifted his position to face Amos and Karl again. "Sheriff, as much as we would like to I'm not sure if we can be of great help to you here. We see his motor bike at odd times, if we can behind all that overgrown weed and junk. He's not going or coming at regular hours. We actually see him face to face only when he comes over, bangs on the door, and asks for money. Hasn't paid his rent – we're asking twenty-five dollars a month – for this year. I would've long gone to the police, but Mary Beth feels she can't do that to her sister. Well, but now you're here."

"Yes we are. But not necessarily for the same reason you wanted to report him to the police." Now the sheriff was determined to move it along. "Karl and I have been all over the county the past two days, at least it seemed so. We saw Ms. Brown's neighbor, visited the home of her, well, don't believe he was her boyfriend, maybe a good acquaintance, and had a chat with that man's wife."

The slight lift in his voice at the end of that sentence had a visual effect on the couple. Both their eyebrows shot up in unison. It was Mary Beth, however, who spoke first. "Michelle? I cannot believe she would have anything, you know, romantically, to do with a married man."

"That's exactly what we felt after having talked to the two women. Her neighbor had nothing but praise for her and Darren Schloss' wife, well, let me say, had difficulties finding anything praiseworthy about her husband to report.

"We found and talked to Mr. Schloss later on and both of us came to the conclusion that his wife was too kind in her assessment. And he is definitely a person of interest to us. We'll keep a close tab on him.

"But back to Michael, or Mikey. Michelle's neighbor told us she met him once while he was looking for his sister. You told us that you don't know where he hangs out during the day, but did your niece ever bring him up in conversation? I can just assume you had a good relationship."

"The best. And yes, she was always worried about Mikey. As I said before, he isn't all that bad. He seems to carry a defiant chip on his shoulders ever since the accident. And now with his sister … oh my God, you don't think he had anything to do with that …?" The lines in her face appeared to have deepened and the color faded while she was talking.

Amos remembered the many times in his long career when he had to give parents or grandparents any kind of bad news about one of their loved ones, or, as in this case, hint at a potential involvement in a homicide. He felt sorry for her and quickly tried to throttle her fear. "We have absolutely no knowledge if he had anything to do with Michelle's murder; so far we know of only two persons who had visited her, and Mikey is one of them. What we want right now is to ask him where he was Wednesday late in the afternoon and if he can tell us more about his sister's daily routine.

"By the way, do you know where she worked?"

"That we do." Kendall Emerson, welcoming the fact that they were able to be of some help after all, stated without hesitation, "She worked in the hospital in Georgetown. We saw her there once when we had to take Mary Beth there for her annual, what's the name for that, anyway, for her annual physicals. She said she worked there and in the one in Murrell's Inlet. As a social worker. Now, whether she actually worked for the hospital or for the Social Department, I couldn't tell you. She was also taking evening classes to become a lawyer. At, what's the name of that college in Con—? Think she also worked a few hours at a law firm as a trainee. Isn't there a name for that? Para something; honey, do you know the name of that law firm?"

Mary Beth shook her head. "No I don't."

"That's fine, Kendall. We can easily take it up from here. Should you find out a bit more about your next-door tenant, we would appreciate giving us a call." He gave him his business card.

Both men thanked the couple for their kindness, promised they would do their best to bring the perpetrator to justice and left.

"Well, what do you think we accomplished here?" The sheriff asked when climbing back into the SUV. But before Karl could say anything he answered his own question. "Not all that much, I'm afraid. Then again you don't want to scare'em off, not on the first visit, anyhow. But I bet you, the minute Mikey shows up Kendall will be on the phone. He's not as protective and forgiving of their nephew as Mary Beth. I can always bring out a deputy to be on the look-out for him if we don't hear anything in the next couple of days.

"We also will be able to dig a bit more into Michelle Brown's life when we know exactly who she worked for."

Karl agreed, but added, "Leaves just one question for me to ask. With all this in place, what do you need me for?"

The answer to this would come sooner than either of the two anticipated.

Chapter Eight

The evening sun conveyed her retreat by way of the sprinkling of flaxen rays working their way through the dense mixture of loblolly and longleaf pine tree-forests when Amos Grimm and Karl Shoemaker emerged from the confines of Andrews and set about their cruise-controlled easy ride back to Georgetown.

"What the hell are you talking about? People around here open up rather spontaneously to strangers even if they don't speak their language." Looking straight ahead, his gotcha- smile hiding from his co-pilot, the sheriff added, "If you know what I mean."

Shoemaker let his left elbow dig into Grimm's ribs, returned the deceptive smile and said, "Yeah, I know what you mean. What the heck, you know I'm with you all the way. Just put me to work."

"We'll have to split up from now on, anyhow. Whoever had something to do with the murder isn't gonna wait for us. If one of our two suspects falls into that category he may be looking for another residence by now, if he hasn't done so already. "So, who do you want to drop in on next?"

Karl's answer came spontaneously, "Next I'm taking Bo to the Bay Restaurant. I'm sure he would like to leave a few of his liquid landmarks here and there as well as sniffing the ones left earlier, before returning to his favorite corner in front of the bay window, letting the rest of the world pass by. Didn't get to see Bobby last evening. I could ask him if he's done anything more about that ridiculous accusation by the plastic surgeon, what was the man's name again?"

"I forgot. Quite frankly, I forgot about the whole thing. Yeah, it'd be good to ask him if there's any development in that, you are right, ridiculous accusation."

"And tomorrow I am going to Charleston," Karl carried on.

"You are? I forgot that too; just kidding. Well, back to *our* case. Darren Schloss, what motive could he have had?"

"What comes to mind first would be that Michelle cut off the affair, if it ever was one. Remember, she told Greta he was just a friend. But if she did ditch the guy that could have disrupted his ego trip beyond repair."

Amos unwrapped another lollipop, strawberry-flavored, and offered one to Karl who declined with a smile. Shoemaker still remembered the day when the sheriff replaced those stinking cigars, per Marge, with the sweet taste of candy — cold turkey.

"That would be the most obvious one, of course. You think there could be another reason?" Amos asked.

"Not at this point. And there is no basis for speculating without knowing more about their relationship."

"Very well, then how about Mikey? Greta said she saw him only once, but I have the feeling he visited her more often."

"His situation is obviously a different one. To judge from his living quarters, and we don't even know how they look inside, it's no stretch to make the assumption that he's not swimming in money."

"Ain't that the truth," Amos affirmed, giving his lollypop another lick. "Wouldn't be surprised if he owed money to a lot more people than the Emersons. Not only is he way behind his pitifully low rent, he also seems to have no shame to ask for more handouts. Kendall had obviously a lot less sympathy for him than Mary Beth.

"Well, women are usually more tender-hearted and forgiving then men, anyhow. And I bet you she's been slipping Mikey a few Andrew Jackson's from time to time behind Kendall's back."

They'd just arrived at the nine-mile curve again when Amos looked at his rear view mirror. "I have a good notion to pull this guy over. Must be going seventy-five."

No sooner had he said this when a black pick-up truck sped by them and the shot made the sheriff lose control over the vehicle and the Explorer landed on its side just about thirty feet into Hwy 17 Bypass.

The emergency physicians in the Georgetown Memorial Hospital were treating sheriff Amos Grimm with professional swiftness. Half an hour later, one of them, Dr. Allen Lowell, pushed himself through the door with his right shoulder while trying to slip off his surgical gloves. He briefly scanned the emergency room, recognized Grimm's wife and asked her to follow him.

In a tiny examination room the physician, a middle-aged man with a bushy mustache, the beginnings of a modest expanse around the midsection, asked pale-faced Marge to sit down in the only chair in the corner, lifted himself on the plastic-covered bed and said calmly, "Mrs. Grimm, first of all, your husband is going to be fine."

This statement produced an audible sigh of relief from the still shaking woman. But knowing there was more coming Marge sat quietly, her eyes riveted to the man's face.

"There were two things that saved his life," the doctor continued. "His shatter-proof windows to be number one. We know that from Dr. Shoemaker, the gentleman who was with him. He told us that according to the impact the bullet would have in all probability hit the sheriff in the area of the left temple."

Marge's eyes burst wide open, panic-stricken, and with both her hands covering her mouth the muffled words "Oh my God" filtered through as a whisper of terror.

Dr. Lowell, who had decades of experience in dealing with the turmoil and anxiety of his patients' loved ones, immediately gave her some comfort in the reassurance that the sheriff was okay. "And don't let all the bandages upset you. He was banged around pretty good. He obviously lost control of the car, which, under the circumstance, was to be expected. Lots of bruises, cuts, a few ribs may have cracked. We'll have to keep him here for, well, two or three days to make sure the trauma hasn't triggered anything else. We can't rule out a small concussion, though."

But the doctor added, encouragingly, "Your husband, Mrs. Grimm, is as tough as nails, if you allow me such a cavalier profile, and in the end he will need lots and lots of TLC, which only you can provide. And I have no doubt you will.

"He also has a healthy sense of humor, to which I was a witness not long ago. I was going into and he was coming out of the gym in Pawleys Island. I asked him if he had a good workout. Without a moment of hesitation he said,

"Well, yeah, if it weren't for that I wouldn't give this place the time of day.

"And you know the first thing he said when they brought him in?" Dr. Lowell didn't wait for an answer. "He said, 'Just in case I can't talk you out of keeping me here overnight, ask my former bride to bring my pillow.'"

Marge choked when she heard that and a tender smile joined two lonesome tears. "And I thought he would have asked for a bunch of his lollypops. But this is much sweeter," and both chuckled at the pun.

"Oh, thanks for reminding me." The physician lifted his index finger. "Almost forgot. I told you before that two things saved his life. We found some strange lacerations inside his mouth, but couldn't figure out where they came from. So I asked a nurse to check on Karl Shoemaker, who was lucky enough to be thrown out of the truck and land on a patch of grass away from the highway. Outside of a few abrasions in his face and a couple of stitches it took to close a minor flesh wound on the left upper thigh he's unharmed."

"I'm so very glad to hear that," was all Marge was able to say while gripping one particular bead of the rosary in her lap a little harder.

"Yes, and when the nurse came back she had the answer to our puzzle. Apparently Dr. Shoemaker tried to pull your husband out of and away from the vehicle when he noticed the sheriff choking on something. He opened his mouth and found the tip of a little stick way back between the tonsils belonging to … you know what."

"One of his lollypops!" Marge gaped at Dr. Lowell, and moments later appended, "He … could, or would have suffocated?"

Dr. Lowell nodded just once. "But it didn't happen. Thanks to his friend who was prudent enough to extract the little devil without further damage…and I'm convinced what you're doing right there," pointing at the rosary in her lap, "had a lot to do with it as well.

"But now I have to go back and see what my colleagues are doing."

"Doctor Lowell, thank you so much for calming my nerves a bit. I thought I'd lost him. But you need to let me see him, and Karl, too."

"Well, he'll be sedated. But they should be taking him shortly into another room. I'll have a nurse take you there whenever they've moved him, and she'll also have Dr. Shoemaker's room number. But remember, don't be too disturbed by the amount of Band-Aids they wrapped around various parts of his body. This always looks worse than it is." The doctor got up from the bed, walked over to her and gave her a reassuring hug.

The following morning Karl and Marge were sitting at the familiar kitchen table where they had so many stimulating discussions more than half a decade ago. Today, however, the mood was subdued. Marge hadn't touched her bacon enriched bowl of grits and Karl was making a listless attempt to finish a roll he had spread with strawberry jam.

Marge's mental pendulum kept swinging from praising the Lord for His intervention that averted more serious injuries to blaming the two men – completely indifferent to the fact that there was only one of the two present – for not heeding her warnings. "I used every persuasion I could think of to keep you from getting involved in this murder case, or homicide, as he would be quick to correct me. But did you listen? The two of you are running neck and neck as far as thick-headedness is concerned. I'm particularly disappointed in you. I hoped at least *you* would be smarter."

"Now wait, Marge, I totally understand your anger, but we have no proof as of yet, if the shooting yesterday had anything to do with the murder or our investigation into it.

"And let's be grateful he's going to be alright. You heard what the doctor said this morning. They just want to keep him over the weekend for some more observations."

"Well, maybe you're right," Marge said, repressing her indignation as well as she was capable of at that moment. "Don't get me wrong. I don't want to be ungrateful to the Lord. It's just that everything inside my head keeps spinning around when I think what could have happened. The window; Amos always has the windows rolled down. 'The fresh air will keep my mind sharp,' he says. But even the closed window wouldn't have saved him if you hadn't pulled out that popsicle stick out of his throat. And for that—"

"Marge, please, whatever is spinning around in your head didn't happen. And you heard Doctor Lowell this morning rule out anything worse than a mild concussion. Amos will be as good as new, you'll see.

"Now I'll have to get my butt out of here. Told Brenda I'd meet her at nine. At least I have an hour to prepare myself for the wrath that is coming my way down there."

"Yeah, what did she say when you told her? Can't believe she let you get by without giving you a piece of her mind."

"She didn't say anything."

"What?" The innkeeper squealed.

"I didn't tell her yet. Didn't want to spoil our reunion. We haven't been apart this long since we got married. I figured there would be plenty of time after, eh, well ..."

"You mean you haven't told her?" But realizing what Karl just said or was about to say the sweet compassion returned into that beautiful rosy-cheeked face of hers. "Then what are you waiting for? Don't let that pretty girl wait. Knowing her she's already tryin' to climb up the walls. Give her my best, and tell her she has my permission to give you a tongue-lashing that will make you shake in your pants.

"Just look at your four-legged monster here. He hasn't a care in the world. And don't you fuss with me. He's gonna stay with me." She lifted her finger and Karl knew there was nothing he could do to change her mind.

"But I'm sure you're going to the hospital—"

"So, what does that have to do with anything? I noticed that he doesn't mind being left alone. More so than when he was here last time. Both of us are senior citizens. So it shouldn't come as a surprise to you that we get along so well. It's that and the two pork chops that show up periodically in his bowl."

Karl shook his head in thankful amazement, threw another glance at Bo. Satisfied with his companion's reaction to being the subject of their conversation – supine, left front paw blanketing one ear and eye, in other words his typical leave-me-alone position, he gave Marge Grimm a grateful hug and made a few steps toward the door when Marge urged him not to speed and wished him a *particularly* wonderful reunion … displaying a benevolently ambiguous smile. Karl turned around one more time and the innkeeper murmured, more to herself, "The world can't be that bad when grown men still have the capacity to blush."

On the South Santee Bridge, shortly before Georgetown County relinquishes road and land ownership to its bigger counterpart of Charleston, Karl Shoemaker realized with regret that yesterday's incident would overshadow his date with Brenda. She would be shocked that he got himself immediately involved in another murder case. But he couldn't possibly have refused Amos's invitation to come along. The man had saved his life once. And Brenda had adventurous blood running through her veins also.

The shooting, on the other hand, was a different matter. A cold shower ran down his spine as he imagined how much worse that episode could have turned out. Thank God that Amos would be alright.

But who was behind this? Had it, as Marge suspected, something to do with their snooping around into Michelle Brown's fatal stabbing? Maybe Mikey had followed us. But according to Kendall and Mary Beth he just owned a motorcycle. Well, he could have gotten hold of a car in a bunch of different ways. Most likely he is an addict and therefore on the prowl twenty-four seven for more of that stuff. Somehow he found out that we were trying to see him and didn't like it. If that were the case the sheriff would have to seriously push him up right next to Darren Schloss on the suspect ladder.

Yeah, Darren, the playboy. He was more than just irritated when he stormed out of the restaurant yesterday. A lot about this man was show and showing off. The girl, Jamie, confirmed that without them asking for her opinion.

Now that they had established their first contact with the two suspects …, well, in Mikey's case only indirectly so far, they would have to take them to task again. But how with Amos out of the loop for at least another week?

The first thing Karl would suggest to the sheriff would be to have a deputy for each of the two suspects and put a tail on them. Monitor their daily activities.

Well, from the looks of it, his visit wasn't shaping up the way he had hoped for. Amos retired, what a joke.

And then there was Bo's ongoing strange behavior. The canine was almost fourteen years old. He had been giving him medication for the arthritis in his hind legs and spine. But according to the vet his problems seem to be more neurological than physical. Even on the baseball field at the recreation center his moves and reflexes could at best be described as lethargic.

Maybe the veterinarian was right. But that was an assessment Karl wasn't ready to accept as of yet.

He couldn't imagine how difficult and painful this transition had to be for Bo. Right then he decided to show more understanding for his canine friend's struggle with his own life's intricacies. No more scolding if he spent a night in the woods or for the few accidents that had turned up in a few places inside the house recently.

And as if talking in the presence of Bo's alter ego he steadfastly validated his resolution: *From now on I'll show you how much you mean to me, how much I appreciate your having been my faithful companion for so long.*

But now, if you excuse me, I'm going to have a rendezvous with the most beautiful woman I know.

Chapter Nine

Brenda had rented a neat one room efficiency apartment in one of the side streets off East Bay. Karl Shoemaker steered the Jeep into the cobble-stone-paved street named Fisher's Wharf by the antique looking sign at the corner that housed a clock-repair shop.

She had described him the place, praising its charm, the two Palm trees reaching up to her second floor window and that he could find it in his sleep. That the number was eleven, the townhouse a pale-green hue, and the first floor occupied by the customs brokerage firm *Schneider and Farnsworth* were unnecessary details.

When he stepped out of the vehicle, grabbing the five yellow and crimson long-stemmed roses, he felt like he did the first time he laid eyes on Brenda in the Bay Restaurant more than half a decade earlier.

His blood circulation picked up speed as he found the front door unlocked, probably left so by a brokerage employee, and hurried up the squeaky wooden staircase to finally arrive at the door of apartment number Two. The bell responded to his touch with a soft ding-dong and Karl's excitement had reached the boiling point. What would she be wearing? The new pink silky negligee he had given her for their fifth wedding anniversary? A naughty smile flashed across his face when he recalled the atmosphere of glittering rapture, reminiscent of the eighteenth century French art form of rococo. The tenuous garment was subsequently always referred to as the *robe de chambre*.

She must not have heard the ring. He tried it again, longer now. *No matter what she's wearing as long as I can wrap my arms around her slender body.*

Still no reply. *Where the...*

He tried the door knob to rattle the door. She was probably still asleep. Had a long session at the Medical Center. The door was open and Karl stepped inside. But there was no one throwing her arms around him. With rising concern he scanned the tiny room, threw the flowers on the table. The kitchen sink was clean, the bed empty. He opened a door on the left, a closet full of clothes. On the opposite side a door lead into a bathroom with the toilet in front. The plastic shower curtain drawn.

And from behind it a deceptively husky voice eloped: "Hello sailor!"

Brenda extracted three crisp slices of rye bread from the toaster, shaking her hand each time. "Now, what do you want to see or where would you like to go? I know everything about Charleston. What I didn't know before or had forgotten I learned while I was here." It was her subtle way to get her husband out of bed.

After a few hours of sleep – finally, Karl Shoemaker let the aroma of fresh coffee hug his nostrils. "I'm getting too old for this. We have to make some changes ..."

Brenda looked at him, her head tipped to the side, as in *what are you talking about?*

"We just won't stay two weeks apart anymore."

"Two weeks, three hours and thirty-five minutes," she corrected him, smiling. "And wasn't this better than meeting at the Cracker Barrel in Mount Pleasant?"

They both laughed at the comparison.

But it didn't last, it couldn't.

Karl knew he had to confess to Brenda what had happened in Georgetown. Slowly and deliberately he got out of bed, one leg at a time, and moved over to his wife who looked at him with apprehension.

He gently pushed her down in one of the two chairs, gave her a kiss and said, "I love you."

Then he proceeded to tell her about the murder in Garden City, Amos' and his interviewing one of the suspects, waiting a second, and – he had to swallow once before he could say it – the shooting.

Neither of them spoke a word for quite some time. Pale-faced and straining for composure Brenda asked, "How is Amos?" But before Karl had a chance to tell her that the actual shot had missed him, she got up and rushed to the telephone on the wall next to the refrigerator.

"Marge is probably still in the hospital," he said, suggesting she might try there first. But Brenda had already dialed and was holding for Marge to pick up with her back facing her husband. Marge was home and the conversation was carried for the most part on the other end with Brenda uttering only one or two-syllable sounds.

When she finally began to speak in complete sentences, her voice returning to its normal pitch, Karl knew that the conference between the two concerned women was not only coming to an end but that his friend indeed was going to be okay.

His own fate would be an entirely different story, of that he was sure. But the inevitable wrath didn't come, at least not in a manner he had expected.

Brenda made the one step back to her chair, sat down and rested her forearms on the table with one hand on top of the other; all the time her unblinking eyes fixed on his.

Karl watched her collected movements with amazement. Was this the calm before the storm?

"Don't ever do this again," was all she eventually said. Still no screaming or yelling, not even a raised voice.

"But what could I do?" Karl threw his hands up in the air. "Amos had asked me to go with him. Wanted to interview a few people in the victim's neighborhood. From there we tried to find the two guys that came up during the questionings."

And while he said this Brenda was shaking her head. "You still don't understand, do you?" Noticing Karl's confusion she continued, "I'm not talking about this. I understand that you agreed to go with the sheriff. As a matter of fact, I would've been disappointed if you hadn't. What upsets me, and I don't care if Marge keeps trying to convince me of your noble intentions, what upsets me is the fact, that you didn't tell me about it.

"Sweetheart, I am your wife. And I intend to be involved in everything you do, *when* you do it. Don't you understand that?"

"Of course I do." Karl Shoemaker heaved a huge sigh of relief. "Marge was so mad at Amos for even looking into the murder, since he had officially retired. But he was just trying to help his replacement, who, based on what I heard, just isn't capable, or let's say ready, to tackle a major case like this one. She threatened to call you too and I had a hard time to keep her from doing so.

"And Brenda, not in a million years did we think that someone would take a shot at us after we had just left the nicest people you can imagine, the aunt and uncle of Michelle Brown and her brother. He's next after the first guy we saw, the only other suspect we have so far.

"But you know what upsets *me* now more than anything?"

"What's that?"

Brenda's quizzical expression triggered the edges on Karl's mouth to lift slightly into what could be taken for a cautious smile. "That we may have put the success of our weekend together in serious jeopardy…and it had started so great."

"It doesn't have to be. Amos will be alright. Marge said the doctor told her he would hold him for two more days, just to play it safe. But he's completely conscious, so much so, that he asked Marge to bring him some decent food. So there is really no reason why we can't have a good time here in Charleston. There are so many places I want to show you.

I have a surprise for you, another one. You should have seen your face when I opened the shower curtain this morning.

"Anyway, let's get out of here soon and put the murder case on hold until, well, until later. Then we can rationally discuss how to proceed with the case."

Karl's body froze. "We?"

"Yes," Brenda gave a quick nod. "It's déjà vu, Baby."

The weather couldn't be more accommodating for a stroll through the City of Charleston, a.k.a. 'The Holy City' for its many churches. To the Roman Catholic Shoemakers this title was, of course, slightly over the top. Another title given to the city, and strongly supported by Brenda, was 'Cultural Capital of the South'.

But Brenda was not about to dwell on semantics and said, "Let's just write this off as an enormous stretch and let me give you instead the true reasons the city is famous for, its history and charm."

And at about twelve-thirty Karl and Brenda left the apartment to embark on their self-guided tour of one of the most fascinating places in the Deep South.

Before stepping down the narrow staircase Karl turned back and said, his brows furrowed, "And there is something I want *you* never to do again."

"I'm listening," Brenda responded with vigilance.

"Never to leave this door unlocked, especially when you're inside."

"You didn't complain about it earlier."

He gave her a pat on the butt and paced down the squeaky steps. "Let's go. Can't win this, anyway."

Pointing to the cobblestones, Brenda admired the ingenuity of those citizens who lived in Charleston more than a hundred years ago. "Though they are hell for cars, but then again, they weren't around then."

Knowing that Karl wasn't familiar with the city at all, she immediately appointed herself as the tour guide. "Since we're so close to the Waterfront Park let's walk there first and then back east to the Battery."

"Ah, the famous Battery." He took hold of her hand and the two crossed the street that led into the park where they could hear the waves hit the wall under the boardwalk with rhythmical regularity.

They passed people relaxing on the many benches along the path. Students were lying on the tree-shaded grass cramming a few more facts into their brains before a looming test. Some of them, so Karl noticed with an indulgent smile, seemed to be paying more attention to their neighbor of the opposite sex than to their books.

Brenda pointed to the pineapple-shaped fountain at the park's western part, "where in the summer kids and an occasional unabashed grown-up take refuge from the scorching heat under the sprinkler's refreshing water."

Before they made a u-turn she pointed to the nearby cruise ship, one of many that docked there to pick up vacationers with destinations like the Bahamas, the tropical islands of the Caribbean, or the West Indies.

Karl caught the yearning look on her face and said without hesitation, "One day, one day we'll be on one of those too."

They reached the tip of the peninsula close to noon with the sun generously pouring out her glistening rays upon the seagull-white canvases atop of a dozen sparkling sailboats.

One of the plentiful benches placed between the Atlantic Ocean and the row of stately columned mansions was chosen by the two sightseers as the perfect spot to rest and get lost for a short while in the splendor of life prior to the Civil War, appropriately named antebellum.

Well, that lifestyle disappeared as did their daydreams. And it was Karl who caused the frown on Brenda's face when he glanced over to the cannons on the battery and said, hiding his grin, "If only you guys hadn't been so gung ho about getting out of the Union—"

"What are you talking about?" Brenda's head jerked around, momentarily speechless. Then she saw the amusement in his eyes, landed a short punch to his stomach, followed by an extemporaneous smack on his cheek and said, trying to sound serious, "You better don't talk like that to a real Southerner, if you don't want to join Amos in the hospital. People around here still have strong feelings about that period."

"I'll keep that in mind, next time I meet a *real Southerner*, which seems to happen more and more infrequently every time we come down here."

They both decided in their own minds to stop that kind of unproductive chit chat and turned to something more tangible, food.

They got up and ambled through the narrow streets flanked by skinny stucco houses with wrought iron rails around dwarfish balconies.

"They say the ironwork was done by slaves from Barbados." Meandering casually as if without aim Brenda led Karl to a cozy little restaurant on Queen Street. "Where do you want to sit, inside or over there?" She pointed to a table for two at the right corner of this open-air anteroom; behind the peaceful trickle of water released by an artfully ornamented fountain whose time-tested copper exterior had succumbed to a cobblestone-grey.

"Baby, this is our table."

And Brenda wasn't disturbed by her husband's rather brief approval. She had learned over the years that Karl always chose few words when most people found themselves in exuberant outbursts of their feelings.

And his squeezing her hand a bit firmer while ushering her to the place without waiting for a hostess to do that only confirmed what she already knew.

They were so absorbed in one another that they gave their orders to the surprised young waitress without surfing the menu; a tomato based soup with a ham and cheese sandwich for him and a large plate of Caesar salad for Brenda.

Entranced – as always, when he looked into her eyes – the tender fern-green seemed to liberate an unusually intense sparkle.

The waitress brought the two decafs they had asked for after they had finished eating. Karl had resumed admiring the woman sitting across from him, silently promising her never to stop loving her and always protect her when someone vaguely familiar came out of the inside part of the restaurant. Karl frantically tried to remember the man's name.

But before he succeeded, the man, mid-forties, five ten, hundred sixty pounds, clean-shaven, thinning sandy hair, waved and rushed over to their table. Visibly pleased he greeted Karl, who had barely gotten out of his chair, with a firm handshake. "Hello Karl, so nice to see you."

Just at that moment it came back to him. "Oh hi, Joe. What are you doing here? Scouting a few rare recipes?"

He chuckled and turned to Brenda. "I'm Joseph, Joseph Hughes."

Shoemaker had to admire Joseph's quick reaction to his faux-pas. Hughes saved him from further embarrassment by introducing himself to Brenda.

"Yes, eh, Joseph, this is my wife Brenda. We were just enjoying our coffee. Why won't you join us, I mean if you have the time?"

Hughes accepted the invitation and angled a chair from another table.

"You are the new owner of Betty's Place, right? Marge told me about it last week."

"Well, Melanie, my wife, signed above the dotted line," Joseph corrected her with a conceded smile. "No Karl, I wasn't after recipes for the Luncheonette. Just picked up a few items from Sam's; always trying to save a buck. I heard about this place here from one of our patrons in Georgetown and thought to check it out while I was in town."

"We liked it here so much that we didn't even take the time to see how the restaurant looks inside," Brenda said.

"Well, you have to find out before you leave. Modern décor made of classic teakwood. You don't find that too often."

They chatted for a while longer with Karl and Brenda listening for the most part to Joseph's further rendition of the Queen Street Restaurant's interior and his plans to take his wife here for their wedding anniversary.

Eventually he slowly lifted his body out of the iron chair and said, "I think I'd better head back to Georgetown and help Melanie get ready for the evening regulars. Are you guys going back tonight or will you be spending the weekend in Charleston?"

"Well, Brenda has to stay here until Wednesday. But I think I'll have to go back tomorrow or at the latest Monday morning. Need to look in on Amos," when he saw Brenda's 'don't start this' look too late.

Falling back on the chair didn't take the newcomer as long as it would a diamondback rattler to deliver a fatal strike. "Yeah, I didn't want to meddle in your investigation. But I heard about the shooting this morning at eight o'clock from a guy who seemed in need of a cup of strong coffee. We open at nine-thirty, but I felt sorry for him. Put on a fresh pot for him. And he told me that the sheriff was in the hospital. Is he alright and how—"

"Well," Shoemaker was ready to answer that part and applied his experience from hanging around lawmen on numerous occasions for whatever else Hughes wanted to know, "he will be fine, but you understand I am unable to say anything about the case while it is still open."

A tinge of red rose from the neck into his face, and obviously a bit embarrassed, Joseph apologized, wished them a wonderful weekend and left.

Karl wiped his brow and shook the imaginary beads of perspiration off. "Sorry I asked him to join us."

"Well, it was the polite thing to do. He seems nice, just a bit too talkative for my taste."

"Well, where were we?"

"You were looking into my eyes," Brenda whispered with an endearing smile.

They spent the afternoon visiting more sites, like the Old Exchange on East Bay, which is considered to be one of the three most historical buildings in the city.

Brenda proudly resumed her post as her husband's private tour guide. This way Karl found out that George Washington had dined here one evening. He didn't tell her that he just read on the tiny sign on the brick wall, that the year that happened was 1791.

"Did you know that South Carolina was the 8th State to ratify the Constitution?" Not waiting for an answer, he didn't have one anyhow, she went on, "They needed nine States. A month later New Hampshire came up with enough votes and thus validated the United States Constitution."

Not exploring the Provost Dungeon underneath the building would be like eating spaghetti without the tomato sauce. The dungeon had been opened to the public as a museum of sort. She allowed him to read, hear and watch how criminals were dealt with within these dark cells two and a half centuries ago.

They also visited a few of the grand colonial homes where tourists were allowed to walk through.

"Many of the older houses in Charleston are haunted by ghosts." Brenda said this with exaggerated seriousness. "Particularly around Halloween the papers are full of reports containing claims of door knobs turning, footsteps, doors opening and closing, rushes of air as if someone is walking through, drifting shadows. Yes, Charleston has its share of ghosts."

"Keep that up and you won't be able to sleep tonight."

"I'm not worried about tonight. I have someone to protect me."

Just at that moment Karl's cell phone rang. He opened the lid and recognized the number on the screen. "It's Amos." He punched the green button and said, "Amos, how are you?"

He stayed on the phone for about ten minutes and reported the conversation to Brenda after he had disconnected the call. "Okay, here we go. First of all, Amos is going to be fine. Marge will pick him up tomorrow morning, if the old warrior doesn't jump ship earlier – like someone else I know."

"I wasn't shot at," Brenda's counter came in defense of her checking herself out of the hospital after having been beaten unconscious while they were working on the Calhoun case.

Karl shook his head, smiled, and continued the rendition of his conversation with the sheriff. "The truck apparently was stolen."

"The truck where the shot came from?"

"Yes. But guess what, the pickup had been impounded."

Brenda was momentarily dumbfounded. "You mean the truck was stolen from the county pound?"

"That's what he told me. And the reason he thinks it was snitched is that the owner, a truck farmer from Pleasant something—"

"Hill, Pleasant Hill."

"Yea, that was it. Anyway, the man's truck broke down after he had made a delivery of thirty pumpkins at Walmart. He had to leave it on a busy section of 701, where it immediately became a traffic hazard, went back into Walmart to make a call. A highway patrol trooper called the office where Linus Thompson made the decision to have the truck towed.

"Olivia, the secretary, reached the farmer at the store and let him know that he could pick up his Chevy truck at Joe's Wrecking Company. And if he did that right away the penalty would only be twenty five bucks."

"How did he plan to get it out of there if it didn't run? And how did the thief—"

"His son in law is a free-lance mechanic – Amos said that was just a fancier word for unemployed – with all the tools of the trade on the bed of his Dodge Dakota. The two arrived at Joe's Wrecking Company around four. By the way, the farmer's truck was basically brand new, under twenty thousand miles. He later said he had just mailed the third payment to the finance company.

"The son in law found the problem rather quick, it had something to do with one of the computers or sensors; Amos didn't exactly know what it was. It's not important, anyhow.

"After he finishes he gets a call to look at a car in Carvers Bay and takes off. The farmer marches to the office to find out if there is any paperwork to be filled out or signed. He knows Joe Grubbs and the two chat for a few minutes. And when he comes out—"

"The truck is gone," Brenda finished the sentence for him. "If the aftermath hadn't been so dreadful this sounds like a typical local prank by some teenagers with too much time on their hands. Did they find the truck?"

"This morning – in front of Joe's Wrecking Co."

Brenda refrained from making any further comments to this bizarre story and firmly stated instead, "More of that tomorrow. *Our* date isn't over yet."

And the weary sightseers allowed the waning sun to chaperone them to the elegant Carolina's Restaurant on Calhoun Street for a romantic dinner.

Chapter Ten

At ten on Sunday morning the Shoemakers had enjoyed a deliciously hearty breakfast – oven-heated sour-dough rolls, butter, a wide selection of sliced sausages, prosciutto, strawberry preserves, hot coffee with cream.

A soothing contentment elevated by a full stomach joined forces in opposing Brenda's request for Karl to get out of the chair and put on some decent clothes.

She stepped behind him and slung her arms around his shoulders. "Don't you want to find out what I had in mind when I promised another surprise yesterday?"

"Oh yeah, I'm sorry."

"Ok, whatever we haven't seen yesterday we'll cover today."

Karl mumbled with the chin on his chest, "Oh no, more sightseeing."

Brenda smiled.

And so did Karl after he had comfortably plunked on the bench of the horse-drawn wagon of the Old South Carriage Company looking condescendingly down at those poor walkers, dragging themselves along the sidewalk like a pregnant dachshund.

The young coachman, dressed in the uniform of a revolutionary war soldier, let his passengers settle down on the bench of the carriage. Then he gave the horses, a stout white and his sandhill crane-gray partner, the sign to move by giving the reins a quick tug.

For the next two hours Brenda and Karl allowed the slow and easy ride to carry them back to the time when this modus of transportation was the privilege of Charleston's high society.

And after they were dropped off at the Market Place Brenda sprung another surprise on him. "Now we walk back to *my* place, get the Jeep, and drive to Mount Pleasant."

"What's in Mount Pleasant?"

"Boone Hall Plantation. One of America's oldest working plantations. Crops from cotton and pecans to peaches, strawberries, tomatoes and pumpkins have been grown there for over three hundred years.

"Today every restaurant that has a reputation to defend will be represented and show off a dish of their choice. You'll find there the greatest variety of Southern culinary cuisine you've ever seen."

And after Karl admitted his limited knowledge of southern cooking, she added less enthusiastically, "Then I'll send you grudgingly back to Georgetown ..." She hesitated for a moment before completing her thought. "And if all goes well, the three of us shall embark on our long return trip Wednesday, or Thursday at the latest."

"Yeah well, if you, however, want to be in Georgetown for the *Wooden Boat Show*, we'll have to stay over the weekend, which would mean you'd miss the *Cody* Stampede the following Friday." Karl exhibited a mischievous grin, knowing full well that Brenda wasn't fond of one of the most popular sports in Wyoming.

And she proved her abhorrence for that, in her mind, 'inhuman exhibition'. "I remember that boy, or young man rather, who's been brain damaged ever since he was thrown off and hit in the head by one of the bull's hoofs.

"It was all over the papers and on the evening news. And I feel very sorry for him. But, if you ask me, I think anybody who engages in a *sport* like that one, has to be brain damaged before being ejected and hoofed by the animal.

"And *I would* like to be here for the Boat Show, though, if it's alright with you. You would enjoy it, I'm sure of that."

"Fine with me," Karl replied, nodding his head in a generous gesture, whereas in reality he was happy she wanted to stay a bit longer for this ever growing, fun-packed event. Even if he subtracted half of what he had heard from Lois Catbury, it sounded exciting.
"Just fine with me."

It was already dark when Karl and Brenda reluctantly said their good -byes. By that time they had tasted just about every color of food known to man, and Karl apologized to his digestive system for placing such a heavy burden on its organs.

When he arrived at the *Inn* his glancing eyes registered right off two changes from when he had left yesterday morning. Amos was back, but Bo was missing.

Marge saw immediately the concern on Karl's face before he had a chance to properly greet his hosts and check on Amos Grimm's condition, "Well, first of all, Bo's alright. I felt so bad for him that there was nobody who would take him out for his morning and afternoon stroll, with Amos in the hospital and all.

"I called Amy at the Bay Restaurant. But she couldn't spare anyone. A large group of female golfers had just arrived and she would need every waitress, kitchen help from the chef to the dishwasher and bus boy. She herself was operating the hostess stand. But the sweet girl she is, she offered to come herself as soon as someone could seat the customers.

"Then I had a brilliant idea. Trace Meehan, our neighbor on the B & B Bakery side, has a fenced-in yard. So I took him there. The problem is he doesn't want to come back inside. I finally brought him water and food. He seems to be alright, just wants to be by himself. He misses you, that's what it is, I'm sure."

"Hope you're right," Karl mumbled to himself, concerned, but not surprised. *"I wished I could help him."*

He went over to Amos, who, casually garbed in shorts and T-shirt, was munching on peanuts, which he expertly flung into his mouth with his right arm, while the left was resting in a sling, bandaged from shoulder to below the elbow. "Amos, are you okay?"

A little slower than usual the sheriff turned to face his friend and that's when Karl noticed the Band-Aid over the left eye, across the cheek and chin. "Don't look that worried. I'm okay. They plucked all the grain of sand and whatever doesn't belong there from the face. Now go and look after your dog. We can talk later."

Bo was lying under a big holly bush in the far corner of the neighbor's tiny backyard on a thick bed of pine straw separating the shrub with its crimson berries from the grassy part of the enclosure.

The canine looked up at him, but unlike the customary stormy greetings he stayed where he was, seemingly content with his situation. There was no excitement, none of those unbridled, yet so cherished jumps which on so many occasions had both of them rolling on the ground and the squabble wasn't over until Karl's face had received a comprehensive dog bath.

Karl squatted down to gently stroke the canine's neck and ears. "What's up, old boy? Need anything? More water?" But the blue bowl, decorated by countless tooth marks, was full. Bo lifted his still imposing head just enough to retrieve the milk bone from his master's open palm, of which Karl always kept a few in his pockets.

"Will check on you in a bit." He left the chewing animal behind, reaffirming his resolution to do his absolute best in allowing his companion the freedom to experience the conclusion of his life's journey in its intended manner, dignified and proud.

Karl found out very quickly that the sheriff didn't take Friday's shooting too lightly.

"I've been taught to restrain myself and show a reasonable amount of tolerance when someone does me wrong. But shooting at me, drive-by or otherwise, raises my blood pressure to an unsustainable level," he told Karl Monday morning during their ham and eggs breakfast. "This means we have to get our behinds in gear, pronto."

Shoemaker threw a quick glance in the direction of Marge, who had been peculiarly quiet, but didn't say anything. *Let's not rock the boat,* he wisely thought to himself.

"I'm going to check on Bo, see how he survived the night in his new bedroom. And if I get him up we'll go for a short walk."

Bo had moved further into the corner, where he had dug himself a four-foot long and almost one foot deep cavity, making him totally invisible until one stood almost in front of him.

The milk bone in the outstretched hand of his master seemed tempting to the laboring dog. But it took him a few minutes to heave his aching body out of the hole, and Karl knew from observing Bo's mysterious behavior as of late that retrieving the milk bone was just the tip of the iceberg.

The real reason for making the increasingly harder effort to secure his footing was a more pressing one. Slowly, a little wobbly, the canine chose a cluster of camellia shrubs in the other corner of the yard to take care of that kind of business. Bo had always been extraordinarily discriminating when choosing his bathroom. There was nothing much to choose here, though.

On his way back he stopped in front of Shoemaker, waiting for him to hand him his treat, and when that didn't happen, he returned to his makeshift bed with his head down.

Karl had tried to lure Bo into following him by moving back toward the gate in the chain-link fence, waving the bone back and forth.

It almost broke his heart when he realized that this playful teasing didn't work anymore. He followed Bo to his newest exile, gave him the milk bone, and stayed with him. The canine was now resting on his side with his eyes fixed on his master.

"I think I know what you want to tell me," Karl's compassion for his beloved four-legged friend was overflowing. And through misty eyes, on his knees, he kept on gently stroking Bo along his back, the exposed side and legs. "You want to tell me that your new behavior is not only strange to us but to yourself as well. But don't fight it. There are higher forces at work here which you can't control. It will eventually lead to a permanent state of peace and complete harmony within."

When Karl finally and with great effort took his retreat, walking backwards until he reached the gate, he said a silent prayer asking God to grant Bo a pain-free and comfortable retirement and added his promise to do everything in his power to help in making this happen.

Amos was still sitting at the kitchen table. With the breakfast removed Karl found him jotting down something on a yellow legal pad.

"Oh, you're back. I made us a list of what we have to do, whom to see, and so on."

Karl braved a shy glimpse in Marge's direction. She stood in the sectioned-off kitchen, called working station by her. In addition to the customary hardware it also housed a number of smaller gadgets, invented to lighten the housewife's workload.

"Sometimes they do," the innkeeper told him once. "But often all these juicers, egg slicers, and bread making machines are the result of a last-ditch attempt by a husband to do better than a gift certificate from Walmart."

Her uncharacteristic silence evoked a queasy feeling in Karl Shoemaker's stomach.

"The first thing I have to do is go to the office, well, we might as well go there together, and tell Linus Thompson that I need Caparelli. He's a pretty sharp guy. Has good insights when it comes to asking the right questions. Uh, you ready?"

Karl, slightly perplexed by the sheriff's display of such a sudden urgency, responded after a brief moment of hesitation, "Well, yeah."

"We already lost a lot of time, and I don't want the Feds coming down again for something we should be able to take care of ourselves."

He got up, grabbed a light, cocoa-brown jacket, walked over to Marge to give her a fleeting kiss. But when his wife turned her face away Karl knew that there was more to Amos' hasty exodus than his worries about Federal interference.

"What was that all about?" Karl asked the sheriff when he took his place on the passenger seat of the Ford Explorer after convincing himself that Bo was alright.

Amos turned the ignition key with a long sigh. When the vehicle gradually picked up speed he made an attempt to answer his friend's question. "Well Karl, I've been in law enforcement for all my adult life. It's just in my blood. I know I've promised Marge to step down, and basically I've done it. But when a heinous crime occurs in my jurisdiction I can't let Linus Thompson call the shots. Not yet, anyhow."

He steered the Explorer into Highmarket Street, risked a quick glance at his friend and said, "Marge has to understand this."

"She does, Amos. She's just worried. *You* have to understand that too."

Olivia stormed out from behind the glass window to greet the boss with a spirited embrace before she backed off on account of the strap that kept his left arm close to the body and the Band-Aids covering his face. Several 'Hi Sheriff' and 'Welcome back' emitted from open-door offices and cubicles.

After introducing Karl to Olivia and three of the four detectives, Amos ushered Karl Shoemaker in the direction of the sheriff's office, which he had relinquished to Linus Thompson a few years ago.

The door was closed. Grimm pressed on the gold-plated handle after a casual courtesy knock, opened the walnut-stained pinewood door without waiting for an answer and found an unsuspecting Linus Thompson hurling his feet off the midsized desk, throwing a couple of files, his cigarette lighter and cell phone on the floor in the process.

"I want to say 'Relax, Linus', but that would mean to resume your prior position."

Linus hurriedly picked up the files, put them back on the desk, swept the lighter and phone into his pants pocket and pushed his lanky body to meet the visitors.

"Shouldn't you still be in the hospital, Sheriff?" he asked, trying to get the blush in his face under control.

"Uh, hospitals make me nervous. Get less sleep there than at home. Besides, it looks worse than it is. Mostly superficial. I told you that Karl was here, didn't I?"

The two shook hands and Linus invited them, with obvious discomfort, to take seats at the small table in the corner. Amos' smiling face was looking at them from everywhere. Amos with different governors from both parties, Amos and a few of his detectives, Amos with the Republican Senator, Amos and the Democrat Senator, with Mayor Livingston, dignitaries from the business community, sports, with more hair and less chubby, with less hair and more chubby, on official law enforcement meetings, on fishing trips, hunting with the late former Senator Strom Thurmond, when, according to the date on the plaque, the latter was still in his prime, the mid-nineties. Dozens more were spanning his entire career from a young detective to his wedding to Marge Baker. The photo, showing the couple and Father Connelly in front of the altar, was captioned *My greatest accomplishment.*

"Well, don't look at me. I didn't plaster the walls with all those pictures. This man here had a lot to do with that." The sheriff threw his head in Thompson's direction.

"Guilty as charged," Linus concurred, relieved that the conversation was shifting away from a potentially unpleasant encounter.

But to think the sheriff could easily be sidetracked would be a mistake as was evidenced by his opening remarks after they had taken their seats around the time-honored table, affectionately referred to as the *(K)night Post* by the detectives for the many late hours they had spent here, devouring the remains of the day's bagged elk (i.e. hamburgers and French fries), downing earthen one-liter mugs of *Met* (i.e. eight-ounce glasses of iced tea), and planning strategies for the pre-dawn launch of the next crusade in defense of the Christian Church (i.e. flipping a coin who was to investigate the break-in of one of the silos on the Johnston truck farm in Dunbar, or who had to go to the County jail and question R.B. Febben, why he was peeping into Marie-Louise Klummerstein's, age ninety-one, window, and whether to meet at nine-thirty or ten for breakfast at the Grits Factory in Pawleys Island).

"Well, Linus, Clarence Woodburn didn't do it, so it's a little early to celebrate." But the sheriff's sarcasm was always short-lived and left no lingering grudges behind. "Where's Caparelli this morning?"

"At the courthouse. I'd asked him to see if he could find anything on your guy Mikey. Rob Clemens from the *Gazette* knew – don't ask me how – that y'all had been to Andrews to check on him. He asked me if I had talked to you already."

"Robbie is a bona fide pain in the ... But he has a good head on his shoulders, you've got to give him that. Linus, call his dad at the *Ice House* and tell him that I'll be missing the next Rotary meeting and ... ouch—" The bad arm's elbow had slipped off the armrest.

He grimaced for a brief moment, before he continued. "And tell him that I would appreciate it if he could persuade Robbie not to bring up Mikey in the paper. He listens to his daddy. The old man still chips in with the boy's tuition at CCU. Just call the—"

There was a knock at the door.

"Come in," Linus hollered in the same direction.

A man, a couple of inches under six feet, black curly hair, dark blue sports coat over a beige shirt with the top two holes unbuttoned, jeans, stepped in the room, looked at Grimm, blew out a lung-full of air, and rapidly approached the sheriff with both arms outstretched to give him a regardful embrace. "Holy shit, Sheriff, should you be out of the hospital already?"

"No, but I'm glad you're here. Want you to meet Karl Shoemaker." And facing Shoemaker, he said, "Karl, this is Sergeant Antonio Caparelli. If you want to stay on good terms with him, don't ever call him *bambino*."

Karl chuckled and shook hands with the shorter man.

They all sat down and the sheriff didn't waste any more time. "Toni, you just came at the right time. I was about to ask Linus to see if he could let you help us in the Garden City murder case. The entire force might be involved before this is over.

"The killing happened last Wednesday. Don't have to tell you that we've got to get our act together. The perpetrator could already be in South America, for all I know.

"Alright, we have a few suspects, two, actually. A philanderer from Little River and the victim's brother from Andrews. If one of those two committed the crime we're lucky. But as we all know, investigations usually lead to more persons of interest.

"Furthermore we should keep the people in mind who have been helpful, Greta Snyder, her neighbor, Darren Schloss' wife Mary and the Emerson's in Andrews. Just in case any of them has remembered another detail.

"Also the farmer, whose truck was temporarily stolen," lopsided grins and shaking of heads over this episode, "his son-in-law as well as the guy who runs the wrecking company.

"I suggest that you two pay the elusive Michael Brown a visit and Karl and I will snoop around Little River to check on the situation in the Schloss household. The couple might be a bit short of domestic bliss.

"Now, Toni, what did you find out at the court house? How does his résumé stack up?" And turning to Karl he asked, "Is that the way you pronounce that?"

"I'm impressed," the professor answered with a smile.

Antonio Caparelli was obviously excited for having been chosen to be part of the investigation. He had joined the Georgetown Sheriff's Department about eighteen months ago leaving New Jersey, a five-year old marriage and a boy of two behind. "Well, Sheriff Grimm, it doesn't portray a squeaky clean choir boy, that's for sure. However, whether several petty theft convictions, one for cocaine possession, and bunches of bar brawls – all misdemeanors, by the way – could lead to murder, remains to be seen.

Chapter Eleven

Amos and Karl were on their way to Murrells Inlet in search of Michelle's aunt Gwendolyn Brown. Olivia had given them her address, after she had dialed the number listed in the AT&T phone book. And Mrs. Brown was gracious enough to postpone her grocery shopping so she could see the sheriff. She lived on 1012 Wicklow Drive.

"That's in the newest section of Murrells Inlet, behind Home Depot," Grimm said after they had passed North Litchfield.

It seemed to Karl as if his friend was saying this just to say something. "You are still thinking about the domestic predicament you're in. Am I right?"

"Well, it just bugs me that she doesn't understand that I have to do this. The people gave me a moratorium until we have found a capable man to take over the department. I wanted, and I still want that man to be Linus Thompson. Although I'm beginning to have my doubts that he'll ever get there.

"So Karl, I can't let those people down. It's as simple as that. A grisly murder has been committed in my county and the killer is still on the loose. This is one area where my otherwise very rational wife chooses to be stubborn as a mule." He steered the Escort to the left at the fork where Bus 17 and the Bypass part company. "We're almost there. But how did Brenda react when you told her about the shooting?"

"Well, can't say she was thrilled. But the real reason why she was mad was different from Marge's."

"What do you mean, different?"

"She not only wanted to know right away what was going on, she insists on being part of the search, well, alongside you and me, of course." Both twisted their heads toward each other and the look of alarmed astonishment on the face of the driver compelled Shoemaker to immediately add his own theory in an attempt to avert further strain on his friend's already pressured cardiovascular system. "I don't want her to get beaten up or put herself in harm's way, nothing even remotely dangerous. Although that might be easier said than done with Brenda. But I see no problem for her to talk to some of the potential peripheral informers, well, for example, the lady we are about to see now. Women can sometimes better relate to their own kind."

Grimm didn't respond right away, but it was obvious to Karl that he was digesting what he just heard. And while he one - handedly turned the car onto the Bypass of Hwy 17, he said cautiously, as if he were about to release a long kept secret, "I wonder if this would work with Marge."

"Of course it would. As long as you're honest about it; that you really need her for whatever it is you ask her to do. She'd smell a dirty trick in less time than a flying hockey puck could rearrange your face."

That analysis prompted a contorted expression on the sheriff's face that said, "What the hell are you talking about?"

But instead he slowly shook his head and grumbled more to himself than to his partner, "I fought tooth and nail against putting female police officers on the street, much less in an investigative capacity."

Shoemaker realized that his friend's old-fashioned principles, though rooted in the highest respect for the opposite sex, were unfortunately completely out of touch with modern public opinion. "Amos, welcome to the twenty-first century! And I think we just passed Wicklow Drive."

Amos Grimm used the good arm to jerk the Explorer around, grimaced at the strain it had on his shoulder, and piloted the vehicle into Wicklow Drive. Number 1001 marked the beginning of a stretch of pastel-colored row houses. Five houses down the street on the opposite side a yellow-orange hue sported 1012.

After the car stopped Karl reached over and pulled the key out of the ignition before the sheriff got to it. "I'm going to take the helm from now on."

There was no protest.

A striking beauty opened the door before they had even reached it.

She smiled softly at Amos' question if she possessed ESP. "Not many people drive past my house. It dead-ends around the next bend. So I figured it had to be you. Well, please come in."

She ushered the visitors through an unlit corridor all the way to the back of the house where the brightness of a completely glazed-in sun room forced their eyes to adjust to the new condition.

"Should I take some of the blinds down?" The five- ten lady, pitcher of iced-tea in hand, asked in a warm alto tone of voice.

Both men indicated that this was not necessary.

She pointed to the table on which two glasses had already been deposited. As the visitors took their seats on the snowdrop-white wicker chairs Mrs. Brown filled their glasses before joining them. Her less than shoulder-length hazelnut hair framed a set of equally colored eyes, a tiny nose, and rosy cheeks. The few fine lines draped around the edges of eyes and mouth in an otherwise baby-smooth face were the only indicators that she might be closer to fifty-five than a decade younger.

It took even an old veteran like Amos Grimm a few awkward moments to remember the purpose of their visit.

"I am Gwendolyn Brown, and you must be Sheriff Grimm."

Amos presented his badge and introduced Karl as his friend and partner in the investigation. "As our secretary told you, we would like to talk to you about your recently murdered niece Michelle and her brother Michael or Mikey, as he's called by the people who know him."

Mrs. Brown looked at Amos and asked him, a trace of sadness on her graceful face. "What do you need to know, or should I tell you what I know about them. I'm afraid it will be too little to be of help to you."

"Sometimes a seemingly trivial observation turns out to be the missing link. So, why don't you go ahead first and we'll see how far that'll get us. Okay?"

She appeared to be seriously eager to help. "Fine with me. Well, I am Michelle's aunt on her father's side. Paul was my brother. Have you seen the Emerson's?"

Amos gave an affirming nod.

"Well, then you have heard more about Mikey than I would be able to tell you. I haven't seen him, let's see, since he was rushed to the Georgetown Memorial Hospital after a drug overdose. And that was, if my memory serves me right, five years ago."

"Do you think he could be capable of murder?" Grimm knew that whatever her answer was to that question would be meaningless, but he wanted to give her a feeling that her opinion was important.

"My knowledge about my nephew's recent past is sketchy at best, and is based primarily on infrequent calls from or to Mary Beth in Andrews or what I read in the paper after committing one of his lawbreaking activities.

"But to answer your question I have no idea how far he would go to satisfy his addiction. Because that's what it is all about, I think.

"He was always kind of shy. As a boy he came to see me often. His parents lived on Prince Street in Georgetown and I was renting an apartment on Queen. He always struck me as if he felt neglected at home. It is true that my brother Paul in particular was very fond of Michelle. Whether that was picked up by the youth, who knows? But children are very observant in those matters. However I can assure you, both, my sister-in-law and Paul were so ecstatic to have been blessed with a girl and a boy that they gave them the same name. I have been baby-sitting, still do for neighbors and friends, and learned quite a bit how careful parents have to be in making sure that their kids feel loved by them — equally."

There's more to that woman than her good looks, Amos thought to himself. *Time to find out how she feels about Michelle.* "I think you're right. To underestimate the keen perception of kids has the tendency to backfire.

"Now let's move on and talk a bit about your niece, who was murdered in a most heinous rage, as it seemed."

Gwendolyn's expression changed instantly. The horror of what happened to Michelle last Wednesday reappeared brutally fresh on her mind.

Amos ignored Shoemaker's scolding glance. The way he looked at it, there were no plausible rationale that could belittle an action equal to or worse than the savage practices of the beasts of the wild when fighting for their survival.

And Gwendolyn Brown seemed to agree with him after she had regained her composure. "Heinous rage, that's what whoever did this must have harbored inside. And that is exactly what I do not understand."

Amos raised his eyebrows signaling 'why'?

"Because I couldn't imagine that anyone who knew Michelle would be capable of harming her, much less in such an, as you said, animalistic way."

"Does that mean you believe the perpetrator didn't know her?"

"Well yes, that would be my explanation. Michelle was the most helpful, humanitarian person I know, or knew, rather.

"Last year I had a bicycle accident. A man with double the legal limit of alcohol in his blood threw me off the bike. I spent an entire week in the Waccamaw Hospital. Michelle heard about it through her work there."

"Wasn't she a social worker?" Amos broke in.

"Yes, she was. She also was in her second or third semester of law school. And she volunteered several evenings a month at the Georgetown or Waccamaw Hospitals. I don't know how she did all this.

"But what I wanted to say, not only did she visit me every day in the hospital, she also took care of chores in the house here, like watering the flowers, placing the garbage outside, feeding my cat, well, you get the idea what kind of a person my niece was."

Amos agreed. "That's the picture we also received from the Emerson's and Mrs. Margaret Snyder."

"Oh Greta, yes, Michelle brought her here once. Very sweet lady."

Suspecting that he couldn't get more than an overwhelmingly positive character description of Michelle Brown from this well meaning lady he asked her a few more questions about possible acquaintances.

"Did she ever mention the name Darren Schloss to you?"

"Yes, she did, but not favorably. As if, well, for a lack of a better explanation, as if she just couldn't get rid of him. And, yes, he seemed to get a little impatient with her."

"Impatient?"

"Yes, I think he wanted more from her than she was willing to give. She also felt he was married, although he denied it."

Grimm looked at Shoemaker, grinned and said, "We do know the answer to that one, don't we, Karl?"

Karl just nodded.

"Did she have other friends, from college, work?"

"Not that I know of. Besides, where or how would she find the time for any kind of relationship with that kind of work load?"

"You got a point there, Mrs. Brown. We thank you for the tea and your time. I hope we can come back if we feel you may be of further help."

"Anytime, Sheriff, Mr. Shoemaker, and when you do come back, call me Gwendolyn. One more thing, if you talk to that Schloss guy, ask him about the letter. Michelle thought he was pretty nervous about a foreign letter he had received when they saw each other the week before she got killed.

"Well, that could have been about anything. Most likely something dealing with his philandering habits. Come to think of it, she did tell me that he had spent a year in the Peace Corps. Maybe in South America? Anyway, just thought I let you know."

Amos obviously didn't intend to give this letter too much attention, but nodded affirmatively when Karl suggested they have another word with Mr. Schloss.

Amos picked up the phone before Karl had turned the ignition key. Turning halfway to Karl he muttered with a coy grin, "Let's find out right now where we can find our Don Juan." He punched the seven numbers and waited for an answer, which came momentarily. "Hi honey, you busy right now?" No answer this time. "Well, I need you to do me a favor."

Shoemaker looked up in surprise. *He wouldn't be talking like that to Olivia. He's actually already making a pitch to rein in Marge. Pretty shrewd by the old fox.*

"Look, sweetheart. We can't go on like that. I know you're mad at me, but we do need to find the person who slaughtered a young woman. Her relatives and neighbors have nothing but good things to say about her. She was holding two jobs and went to law school in the evening. From what we heard she did not deserve to be killed, much less in such a gory way."

She must have started to say something because Amos was quiet, except for an occasional "yeah", "right", or a convincing "I understand, honey".

"Look, we have to find this guy, his name is Darren Schloss. The number should be in the phone book. I don't believe he's at home, but his wife probably knows where we can look for him. He's a liquor salesman."

Another pause, followed by "Too risky. I don't want to have to explain all this to Olivia. You see, we can't identify ourselves to either one of them. By now he knows that we're after him and most likely has given the appropriate instructions to her if the sheriff's office asks for him. That's why I want you to call his house. If a man picks up, just say, 'Sorry must have the wrong number' and hang up."

Pause, then "You can do it. Well, listen, please. If she, her name is Mary, answers, you say that you're the owner of the Beer and Liquor Stop in Bucksport. Darren was supposed to have brought you a case of Manischewitz yesterday, and that you've tried his cell phone but he didn't answer. If she could tell you where he might be now. But let her give you his cell phone number, just in case you had it wrong.

"I know that's a lot to ask of you…yes, I know you don't want to have anything to do with it…and you don't *want me* to have anything to do with it. Okay, okay, call me back if you learned anything…I'm good. Still hurts when I move around too fast, but Karl is driving. Love you."

Then he quickly disconnected with a huge sigh. "Well, let's have a sandwich. There's an Arby's right over there in front of the Holiday Inn."

They both got one of the establishment's deluxe sandwiches, the magniloquent adjective presumably hinting at the freshness of the bread and sausage and the inclusion of a drink of one's choice. Both decided on decaf.

After they had tacked on some of the condiments to their trays they settled down at a corner table.

"Well, what do you think?" Amos looked at his friend expectantly.

"Think about what?" Karl had no clue.

"Will she do it?"

"Will she …oh, you mean will she make the call? Hard to say. What was her reaction, or should I say revulsion when you tried to smooth-talk her into it?"

Amos' lopsided grin gave away his own doubt.

"First of all," Karl ripped a large paper napkin off the metal box and wiped some excess mayonnaise off the corners of his mouth. "Marge is smart. That might be against us in this case. But she either saw right through your scheme and is mad as hell at you for thinking she would fall for that, or she saw right through your scheme and felt a kind of compassionate pity for you and your conciliatory attempt, as transparent as it might have been."

"And who's the one who suggested that *scheme?*" Amos shot back in mock indignation.

"Well, I go for the latter, if that makes you feel any better."

Marge had just returned from church where she had lit a candle in front of the statue of Mary. She did that often, asking the Lord's Mother for her intercession on behalf of a person she knew needed help, a sick neighbor, one of her grandchildren's first school day, or for peace in the world.

The man she always included in her prayers was just at that moment stepping out of the sacristy. Father Connelly would never interrupt someone who had come to say a silent prayer in the sanctuary of the church. But the priest knew that Marge Grimm, one of his favorite parishioners, always liked to have a private chat with him, impart a few of her concerns, mostly health issues, children, or simply the ups and downs of daily life.

So, as always, he kept himself busy until he heard the familiar squeak of the worn hinges upon the return of the foot bench into its upright position. The clergyman caught up with Marge in the middle of the church. "Hello Marge." The elderly woman turned around, smiling at Father. She was visibly pleased to see him and with just a nod slid into the next pew when Father Connelly pointed in that direction with a wave of his hand.

Keeping his warm baritone voice low, he asked her, "For whom did Our Mother have to intercede today? Nothing wrong with the children, I hope. Amos still on the mend?"

Marge Grimm faced her priest with a serious expression on her face. "No, the young'uns are fine and, yes, Amos is doing well also. In fact, he is actually doing so well to be working already."

The experienced pastor recognized the cynicism in her last remark. "Am I on the right track sensing that you are unhappy with Amos working this soon after his release from the hospital? And if I am right, I most certainly agree with you."

"Father, it's not so much that he's working, it's what he's workin' on." She retrieved a tissue from underneath her sleeve and touched the corners of her eyes. "You've heard about the murder of the young woman in Garden City, haven't you?"

"Uh, yes, of course, awful. Now I understand. He is trying to find the person who did this. But I thought he had retired, at least semi. And you think the shooting had something to do with this? The paper didn't say—"

"Well, we had all these wonderful plans. He even promised me a cruise to the Caribbean." The sadness in her eyes intensified. "And you can bet the entire Sunday collection that the shooting and the killing are connected."

Father Connelly suppressed a smile. He knew full well that his faithful parishioner was too upset at the moment to be funny.

"Well, Father, what I really asked the Lord's Mother was not so much to pray for Amos' safety, but to help me to stop being so uncontrollably angry at him. He broke his promise.

"He tried to explain, but nothing made sense to me. Surely not worth losing his life over. Said his replacement wasn't ready to handle a major case like this one. Didn't want the FBI come down here again, like the time the Calhoun girl turned up in the Bay. And he didn't want to take the fall if Linus messes up. Amos stuck his neck out to convince County Council to let Linus succeed him."

Father Connelly had listened patiently before he spoke with great compassion. "My dear, good friend, it seems to me, that Mary has already answered your prayer."

Marge looked at him, surprised. "I don't understand. What makes you say that?"

"Well, you see, at the start you were mad at Amos because he, as you said, broke a promise. But then you listed several reasons why he felt he had to take over again. Sounded to me as if they were beginning to make sense to you. The anger is slowly being replaced by understanding. Wonderful, isn't it?"

It's not as easy as you make it sound, Father, Marge thought to herself, but said, "Well, thank you, Father."

"Don't thank me, Marge." He nodded in the direction of Mary's image. "Thank her!

"There is no one I know whose heart is filled with more love than yours. There is no room in it for anger."

Climbing up the wide steps leading to the front door of the *Inn*, still absorbing the true meaning of her conversation with Father Connelly, her fuzzy mind was directed to the large black bundle blocking the full length of the entrance.

"Bo am I glad to see you. It's about time you came back." She bent down and gave him a rigorous rubdown, then had to step over him to reach the keyhole and open the door. "Let's go inside and whip up something good for you to eat. You must be famished."

Not without putting great strain on his legs, front ones first, then the hind legs, one after another, was Bo able to lift his weighty body and follow Marge inside.

Right away she filled the first dish she could get hold of with water. "You know what? I'm going to pour some of this meat stock over the chops. Makes them go down easier."

And while Bo was lapping up the water the phone rang. She saw it was from Amos.

"Well, Lord, they say you work in mysterious ways. I guess you want me to make that call," Marge conceded after she had placed the receiver back on its base.

Amos and Karl were munching on their sandwiches when Amos' cell phone started to vibrate in his pocket. "Bet you it's her." And with a victorious smile he pulled it out and opened the cover.

He shook his head and answered the call. "Tony, can you talk freely from where you are? ... Good, then just talk a little louder. I'm gonna put the phone on the table so that Karl can listen in."

"Got you. Well, here's the scoop, guys. I'm sitting in the palatial Great Room of Calvin Michael Brown, Esquire."

"Where's he?"

"In the bedroom. Don't worry. He can't hear me. I plugged his ears. Also cuffed him."

"What?" The word escaped the sheriff's mouth loud enough for two middle school-aged kids, the only other patrons in the place, to abandon their intense *Playboy* perusals, with an annoyed look on their acne-sprinkled faces that said 'Stop that. Can't you see that we are studying?'

When the sheriff became aware of the boys he repositioned himself in a way the juveniles could see the badge on his chest and the holster with the gun around the shoulder inside his unbuttoned jacket.

And before Caparelli could finish his question "Sheriff, are you still there?" the two had the restaurant to themselves.

"Yeah, we're here. Why in God's name did you have to put the cuffs on him? Did he get violent or something?"

"No, as a matter of fact he was high as a kite when we got here. Thought we were bringing him some weed."

"Alright, but was it necessary to—"

"Just hear me out, Sheriff. It turned out to be a little more complicated than just the dope. When we squeezed ourselves into the trailer through the half-foot opening it almost took our breaths away. There is literally not one bare inch in the entire place. If I hadn't just swept a two-foot high pile of empty beer cans, dirty clothes, coupon papers, parts of a carburetor, and zillions of more junk stuff off the only table I'd have had nowhere to sit down."

Amos whispered into Karl's ear, "Tony can't report anything without dramatizing it. Well, he's Italian."

"I was just about to throw a few more things to the heap when I noticed a plastic folder with some papers in it. I took the papers out, bank statements, bills, an Inpatient Survey from the Georgetown Memorial Hospital, and more, kind o' documents, you know.

"But guess what name was on all of them?"

"I don't know, Toni, tell me."

Karl detected a tinge of irritation in Amos' voice and smiled.

"Sam Osborne!"

"Do I know him?"

"The man who owns the truck."

For a brief moment Amos and Karl looked at each other, both dumbfounded. The sheriff cleared his throat as if this had been the reason for the delay of his response. "That's interesting alright. Where is Linus?"

"I sent him, uh, I mean we thought he should let Mr. Osborne see the papers and ask him if he indeed kept them in his truck. Linus called a little while ago, he's on his way back, and said that the farmer did keep those papers in his truck. Said there were also two twenty-dollar bills in with them."

"Okay, Tony, as soon as Linus is back come straight to the jail with Mikey. We'll meet you over there."

"Ten-four."

"Oh, Tony, good job."

Amos threw the rest of his sandwich together with the empty cup into the disposal bin. Karl grabbed what was left of his and both stomped out of the restaurant.

Back on 17 Bypass Amos said, not hiding his excitement, "Schloss might not even be at home or his wife may not know where he is. Mikey is more important. Now we have proof that he was driving that truck last Friday. Well, circumstantial, anyhow. If we get him to sing, which should not be too difficult – just keep him in the jail house for a couple of days without his drugs. Then we let him tell us that the farmer's truck was indeed the vehicle out of which we got shot at."

His phone buzzed again. He picked the device up, saw who the caller was, and said, "Oh hi honey."

"I almost gave up," Marge sounded exhausted.

"Yeah well, I was talking to Caparelli. Had some encouraging news."

"Well, good, because I can't give you anything close to that."

"Really?"

"Your 'party of interest', isn't that the correct investigative jargon?"

Amos smiled. "Perfect."

"Well, Mr. Schloss seems to have flown the coop. Mary hasn't seen him since last Friday. She seems to be a nice person. I feel sorry for her."

"You did great, sweetheart. Thanks a lot. I'll be home early today. Karl and I are on our way to the jail to talk to the victim's brother."

"Be safe, both of you."

"We will."

To Karl he said, "As I suspected. Darren hasn't been home since Friday."

"You know what? I think I can handle Mikey by myself. Maybe you should stick your head in the Bay Restaurant. Marge told me that Bobby had asked about you. That reminds me. Tomorrow is the hearing. You know, the one about the kid who tried to break into the cash register and then slipped on the wet floor."

"I was kind o' hoping you would suggest that."

Chapter Twelve

It was one of those evenings in October when the temperature had dipped low enough for the air-conditioning system to take a well deserved rest.

The chance to receive a new assignment kept the Enforcer wide awake for the better part of the moonless night.

Tomorrow morning he would meet with the delegate of his African employer. It would be another one of many proud moments for him. With the elimination of the young woman in South Carolina, the mission called XP 012 was close to completion. With no lingering complications.

His continued success had finally paid off. He was now the most sought after enforcer for one of the world's most ruthless conglomerates, whose dealings included extortion, identity- and grand theft, pedophilia, human trafficking, running one of the largest narcotics rings known, with huge farms in South America and Indonesia and a network of dealers that would dwarf the Mexican cartels, the Thailand Factories, and the recent merger of five splinter groups in North Korea put together.

He stared at the clothes hanging neatly on hangers inside the double-door wide closet. He had already selected his attire for tomorrow's meeting, steel-grey sport coat and slacks a shade darker, white starched dress shirt under an indigo-blue tie. The mandatory black notepad as well as an ashen toupee and a matching moustache, this one somewhat shorter than his favorite black one, were laid out on the dresser, reflected in the three-piece mirror behind them. A few more changes to his face in the morning would accomplish what, like a chameleon, he had been practicing as long as he could remember; never to show his natural physiognomy when on the job, even when meeting people from within the Organization.

He was not one of the foot soldiers, he was the Enforcer, the one to be called upon at the final stage of a project, and only then when his skills were needed. And his skills comprised the no-frills elimination of individuals or groups of people that the leadership considered to be in the way of either finishing their intended goal or posing a threat in getting there.

He couldn't think of anything else that he could have forgotten or overlooked. A few more days and he could leave this town for good. Maybe his next assignment would take him back to Africa. He would like that.

There were no safety concerns in that part of the Black Continent. Ruthless greed on one side and the ravages of poverty on the other canceled each other out.

After he turned fifteen he was considered a grown man. Although Biafra had been reunited with the Mother Country, and official military warfare had ceased, tribal hostilities, particularly in the Capital City, had not. If anything, they had intensified.

That was the time when he came to the conclusion that his pick-pocket times were over. But the lack of anything even close to a formal education was not the only obstacle in landing a real job. His lifestyle didn't exactly make for a favorable résumé.

One opportunity to earn some money on the up and up came in the form of a huge parking lot in front of a supermarket and a clothing store with the meat market next to it. Here all the aspiring thieves reversed their rolls. They competed with each other for the job of watching the vehicles of the shoppers, wealthier citizens and expatriates.

However, the able juveniles had to face strong competition in the presence of the hundreds of lepers in their soapbox carts. With the base of these small wagons close to the ground they were able to display astounding mobility by using their cloth-protected, mutilated limbs to push themselves around. That advantage plus the added sympathy of the shoppers gave those guys the edge. He hated them and he hated the expatriates. That was not the career path he had envisioned.

The man twisted his mouth into a wicked grin when he reminisced what happened next. The Monsoon season had been more vicious than he could remember and the downpours flooded the streets of the city with merciless regularity.

That day was a particular nasty one. The torrents were running on both sides of the pothole-riddled thoroughfare. And it was here where his life's path took yet another turn. For the better, he knew. Just like the second voice had promised.

For the street kids this was another, more profitable time of the year when they could make good money, without having to worry about getting caught. On the lowest part of the Ibadan Road, a stretch of about hundred yards, there could be up to seventy automobiles on any given day stranded with water working its way into the interior. The boys sloshed through the water as fast as they could. Usually a nod of the head by the driver in the direction of two of the lads closest to him sealed the deal. Then the elected youngsters began to push the stalled vehicle to a point where the vehicle's wheels could muster enough traction to move on without further manpower.

A couple or more bills changed hands and the rescuers waded back to where another customer might need their assistance. The reason that the pay was usually good and no pay extremely rare had little to do with the honesty or integrity of the car owners, but rather with the severity of the inevitable penalty. Cars with a flat tire or two, inflicted by a machete-like weapon, could be seen days later, stripped of just about every piece that could be removed before a tow truck showed up …and that could be days.

A slowly moving black sedan had caught his eyes. And since it was still in motion none of the boys found it necessary to intervene. Right away he noticed the banner mounted to the driver's side of the hood.

Either a diplomat or a Government official, he spoke to himself with increasing curiosity. Rapidly he waded into the muddy water and thrust his back against the trunk, using the remarkable strength of his legs to prevent the car from stalling.

The driver finally maneuvered the car with his help to higher and dryer ground. And when he walked around the automobile, the heavily tinted window on the driver's side slid down about six inches. A hand reached out, holding two or three bills - not just one pound ones - and waved at him to get them. "The Minister says 'o şe' (Thank you)."

He grabbed the money and watched the Minister and his driver dash off eager, as it seemed, to make up for the disruption. He was just about to fold and stuff the bills in the back pocket of his faded denim shorts (a present he made to himself, when the store clerk wasn't looking) when something fell out from within the pound notes. Thanks to his well trained reflexes he caught it before it fell on the smutty, wet road. A business card. Looked like the ones his father had. Too bad he couldn't read, English in particular. Just a few words of Yoruba, Hausa and Ibo. He turned the card around. There was something written, in Yoruba language:

Meta Loco Babatunde (see Luca Babatunde)

He had heard that name more often than he would have liked to. The Police Commissioner of Lagos. He had the reputation of mercilessly enforcing the law, his own. Many of his street companions were serving jail time of five or more years for stealing produce from the market vendors. And rumors had it that the great majority of those juvenile delinquents wouldn't survive long enough to ever see freedom again.

And as so many times before he was forced to consult the voice inside his head. But it wasn't the one he wanted to listen to, the one who always encouraged him to go forward, to disregard those nagging exhortations that occasionally succeeded to fight their way to the surface of his conscience. But instead it was precisely that one, the voice of all the beleaguering warnings he used to be so afraid of. And the voice entered his dream, friendly, but firm:

Remember me? You used to call me your voice of reason. I am actually much more than that. But let's leave that for right now. You haven't been listening to me. There would have been so many opportunities for you to be taken care of. I told you right after you had begun to roam the streets of Lagos to go to the British Embassy. The people there were actually looking for you. Under Secretary Collin Thatcher himself made numerous attempts to find you. But you didn't take my advice to turn away from your lawbreaking conduct. But it isn't too late yet. There is still time. Go to the Embassy. They will send you to the school for the children of British Embassy personnel. Your transgressions will be excused because of the horrific situation you were thrust into. Too many children have been left with very few choices.

I am again pleading with you to make three turns:
Turn yourself in to the Embassy
Turn to your Maker (I am sure you know who that is)
Turn away from your path of destruction and ask for forgiveness

Do this and I promise you that your life will change for the better. And I will be with you for the rest of your earthly life – and save your soul.

To go to the Police Commissioner will eventually elevate you into an even more dangerous arena, one from which you won't be able to escape on your own.

The event left a calming, soothing sensation around his heart, for which he had no explanation. What did the voice mean by 'to save your soul'?

But he didn't have enough time to make sense of what he was just told, because, as always, the second voice instantly broke in. And the familiar upbeat sound hit his inner ear, rasping, clothed in authority.

I hope you're not that ignorant to fall for that trash. What a waste that would be. Didn't you survive unscathed under my tutorship? The Commissioner will probably send you to the Chief of Police. Only very qualified applicants will get the chance to be hired for the police force. Once accepted the opportunities are limitless.

You are not going soft on me again, are you? Until now you made your living with taking money from people who had more than you in the first place. Although you don't know it, you practiced in a small way what will be known in times yet to come as wealth redistribution. Only then the stealing will be done by the governments.

But just wait what you can do in this field as a member of the Police Department. There's one thing you have to do right away, that is to improve your reading and writing skills. You have taught yourself admirably. But you need to take a few courses to catch up. Once you have accomplished that I'll tell you to read the writings by Charles Darwin. No need to talk to you about that now. Too early, you wouldn't understand.

As an officer in the Police Department you will get the training to perform more rewarding tasks than what you have done so far. In due course I'll steer you to the right people. Just don't be afraid when you're asked to do things you might find a bit peculiar at first. These are people you can trust; they are under the guardianship of some of my associates.

Was it his imagination or did he actually hear a rumbling chuckle accompanying that last remark?

Go and do what the Minister offered you to do, because if you don't you will be on your own. I cannot help you then any longer.

Like the time before, he was drawn again to the second voice. Although he still wondered about the first one, the remark about his soul, the secure feeling that had engulfed him like a warm blanket.

Yet the second voice left him all psyched up, ready to tackle the unknown. He stubbornly dismissed the fleeting moment when he feared that all these promises could be a setup. What if he went to the Police Department, showed the business card, and instead of being ushered to the Commissioner's office, he were swiftly and unceremoniously fitted with a shiny set of handcuffs?

Well, as it turned out they weren't a setup. The attractive receptionist in a fashionable crème-colored business suit didn't exactly usher him to the Commissioner's office. But she stepped around her desk and walked with him to the corner where she told him in a refined West-African English that the Commissioner's office was at the end of the corridor on the left side. Her shapely figure on top of a couple of remarkably long legs didn't escape his emerging interest in the opposite sex.

The clerk looked at the card, and with a knowing grin gave him a piece of paper containing instructions where to go. The building he was directed to was about a mile and a half from where he was and closer to the River Niger, and even closer to the City Jail.

Now the smirk on the clerk's face began to make sense to him. Were they throwing him in a cell, of whose conditions he had heard horror stories from the few lucky jail breakers? Seriously contemplating to break away now before it was too late he remembered the last words of the voice, *if you don't you'll be on your own. I cannot help you then any longer.*

His strange attraction to the persuasive second voice gained the upper hand again and this decision did land him in the jailhouse, but not in a cell, not as a prisoner, but as a prison guard.

In this capacity he learned in three months more about the almost unlimited power of authority – even among the lower wage earners – than during all his teenaged years on the streets. And it took him less than that to take advantage of some of those wicked methods himself.

He helped for example three inmates to escape in exchange for fancy clothes and monthly cash payments for one year, and, just in case a need arose in the future, free girls.

After six months of fine tuning his skills in the acquisition of a myriad of profitable schemes, he found himself on the streets again. As a traffic cop.

He looked at the digital alarm clock on the nightstand next to his bed and couldn't believe that he had wasted most of the night tossing and turning, mulling over his life story, his accomplishments, hopes for his future, instead of trying to get a solid stretch of deep, sustained sleep.

But whenever he reached this point in the recollection of his career he couldn't help but also retrieve some of the more memorable escapades while on the beat.

The River Niger separates the downtown area of the city from the suburbs. The linking bridge is arguably the heaviest traveled thoroughfare in the entire West African region. Around-the-clock traffic comprises legions of businessmen and Government employees with different agendas and destinations.

He was assigned to a veteran cop, whose better than three years on the force had a great influence on doubling his meager salary. One of those lucrative tricks was actually a lot easier than most of the methodology and started with one of them directing the traffic on the city side and the other on the opposite end of the bridge. Prior to taking their positions they agreed on what kind of cars they would stop. Sometimes they would choose all BMWs, another time all dark-blue sedans, and so forth. And only cars with drivers, whose affluent owners usually carried a fatter wallet with them. Of course, foreigners were preferable, since that group was most vulnerable when caught without identification.

Now, when a vehicle that matched their pick of the day approached his location wanting to enter the bridge to get to the other side, he stopped it for running through the red light, or for any other concocted violation – notwithstanding that the light had never worked as far back as he could remember – asked for and retained the person's passport. He then told the confused individual that he could pick up his passport at the police station after having paid his fine.

When the car reached the other end the second cop would wave the driver to the side. This time it was for a routine check only, as the officer assured him. And the passport was a foreigner's only means of identification. But of course, that's exactly what his buddy asked to see. The end result was always the same. A substantial amount of cash had to change owners before the vehicle could move on.

The same procedure was applied with automobiles exiting the bridge on his end. Only this time the reward landed in the Enforcer's pocket.

A mean smirk flashed across his facial features as he recalled the many befuddled, confused and angry people, trying to make him understand what just had happened to them.

And once a month the two cops would pay a visit to the station where they collected a percentage of what the clerk had demanded from the car owners for the return of their passports.

The system worked brilliantly. Whoever had knowledge of someone's wrongdoing would never report this to the authorities, but instead employed another widespread method called blackmail. That meant that he and everyone engaged in these practices had to look over their shoulders to make sure no one was watching what they were doing.

He figured there were no more than two hours left before he had to get ready for the meeting. Unable to force his mind to come to rest he just let it drift into a time he fully expected would be revealed to him tomorrow. A higher position in the WAIS–West African Intelligence Service–perhaps? That would most likely be a desk job in Abuja or Lagos. He liked the high esteem he would be held in by the men and women under his leadership. Surely they would choose him to train the next enforcer. And with the prospect of that happening he finally drifted into an abbreviated sleep before the unyielding alarm clock called for action.

Chapter Thirteen

Karl arrived at the County Courthouse at nine forty-five fifteen minutes before the hearing was scheduled to begin.

He picked up the car keys, loose coins, and his watch from the tray after he had passed through the security check. He walked over to the elderly gentleman who sat behind a small desk with a sign on top that read INFORMATION. He was directed to the third floor and room number 312.

Cautiously he opened the massive door, but after a peek inside the chamber he proceeded with more confidence past the heavily occupied rows. He took a seat in the second one, which was completely empty, a condition it returned to as soon as the six foot three police officer bent his imposing upper body down and gave him a no-frills message. "You can't sit here."

So much for the ring-side view. He got up, felt that everyone was looking at him, although no one was, and approached a bench, where a man in his thirties, lots of sparkling stuff dangling on his chest, moved his legs to one side, thus enabling Karl Shoemaker to squeeze by him and find a seat.

While they were waiting for the judge to arrive, Karl Shoemaker wished he had left the Bay Restaurant a bit earlier last night. But he was glad to have seen Bobby who spent some time with him before his lawyer, a slow-talking southern gentleman by the name of Sam Marquette, gently latched on to his elbow, trying to maneuver the restaurateur out of the bar.

"Think we should go over some of the stuff for tomorrow with Curtis over here." With a nod over his left shoulder he pointed at the man behind the bar. "Make sure he still remembers what happened." The last remark was accompanied by a friendly smile.

Curtis Wilson motioned to a short, pear-shaped man, who immediately squeezed his expanded midsection through the opening at the end of the bar and with a cartoon-like grin signaled to the four customers in front of him that he was ready to be at their service.

After Amos had dropped him off at the *Inn* with the message for his wife that he wouldn't be late, Karl went straight to the neighbor's yard to see after Bo. He had made himself a mental note to clean up the area and close the cavity that served as the canine's makeshift bed. But Bo was not in it. Where could he have gone? Karl walked over to the fence and checked it for openings where Bo might have been able to slip through. No way, not even a rabbit would be able to penetrate an enclosure as tight as this one.

With each step towards the *Inn* Shoemaker's concern gained strength; and almost fearing for the worst he burst into the lobby and called for Marge before he could see through the open kitchen door. And there stood the Innkeeper, her eyebrows raised. "What's the matter? Amos alright?"

"Uh, yeah, he's alright." Then he saw him, being caressed by a girl. He guessed her to be between eight and ten, a year or so older than his daughter Cookie was, at the time she perished in the fire. The picture in front of him made his stomach feel queasy and it took extraordinary effort on his part to elude reliving that crushing event a dozen or so years ago.

"He just dropped me off, and went on to Andrews. Said he wouldn't be late. But, what is going on here?" There was Bo, on his back, playfully pawing at the little girl's long hair and accepting her gentle strokes on his exposed belly. That carefree position, which came with a complete abandonment of his otherwise so well guarded dignity, had always been for his master's eyes only.

Now the child turned around and looked at him with a pair of hazelnut eyes as large as Brenda's special star on their Christmas tree in Wyoming, so it seemed to him. But those eyes as well as the rest of her fairytale-face stared at him with suspicion, as if she were afraid of being scolded for having done something she shouldn't have.

Marge stood there, smiling, eager to decode the mystery for him. "Well, this beautiful little sunshine here is Charlotte, Charlotte Carson. She is Joseph and Melanie's daughter from the Luncheonette."

She turned to Charlotte and said amiably to her, "Charlotte, this is Dr. Shoemaker, Bo's daddy."

Cautious, perhaps even more fearful after she was told who Bo belonged to, she said with what came out almost as a whisper, "Nice to meet you."

Karl walked over to the bay window where she had kept her crouching position. Bo was still lying there in all his undisguised splendor, his mouth wide open, paws bicycling in mid air. Shoemaker squatted next to Charlotte and reached out his hand to her. "Charlotte, you can call me Karl, okay?" She nodded, keeping her eyes fixed on his. "Now tell me, how did this dog make it up here when I couldn't get him to even lift his head out of his cave earlier this morning?"

She lifted her shoulders so high, that they almost touched her ear lobes, still looking straight at him.

Marge, who had been watching them with affection, said, "Melanie, her mother, came by to ask me for the recipe of a southern style chowder. She thought it would be nice to add a warm soup to the menu with the colder months approaching. And while she was jotting down a few notes Charlotte stood around with nothing to do. So I asked her if she liked to visit Bo in Mr. Meehan's backyard. And lo and behold, it couldn't have been more than five minutes when she was back — with Bo in tow. Now what do you have to say about that?"

"I'm speechless," Karl looked at her, and then back at the girl, flabbergasted.

A sudden restlessness jolted his thoughts back to the present. Everybody was getting up and the judge took his seat in the middle of the bench at the far end of the chambers. He seemed to Shoemaker a bit young for carrying such a big responsibility. But that concern was rendered completely unwarranted when he began listening to Judge Kenneth Robertson's precise and methodical instructions to the accused as they were lead into the chambers by police officers one after another.

Since most of the defendants pleaded guilty, the judge asked them a few questions. Had they been consuming alcohol within the last seventy-two hours, which could possibly impair their ability to think clearly? Or were they aware that a guilty plea would result in the judge's right to give them the maximum sentence even if the prosecutor had asked for less.

With keen interest Karl watched bond hearings, learned about different types of bonds, the grave consequences if they were violated, sat through cases of attempted and executed burglaries, with or without arms, several dealing with possession of narcotics, when two things happened: The judge's call for a lunch break and Shoemaker's sudden awareness that neither Bobby Moore nor any of his friends, the Stammtisch crowd, his lawyer, Curtis, the bartender, were present.

Maybe civil cases would be heard after lunch. But he decided to find out for sure and walked over to a lady who carried an armful of files to the prosecution desk.

She looked at him quizzically after he had posed the question, then said, "Oh no, civil cases are heard by Judge Grayson two rooms down the hall."

A little embarrassed Karl thanked her and left in search of Judge Grayson's chambers, hoping he hadn't also broken for lunch already.

The uniformed female officer positioned in front of the door flicked her head in the direction of the room when she saw him coming as in 'Just go on in'.

Pretty casual, Karl thought and returned the invitation with a nod of his head as in 'Thank you.'

Contrary to the first chambers this one was a lot smaller. The black robed elderly gentleman, the Honorable Judge Thurgood Grayson – according to the gold-framed sign in front of him – was listening to one of two lawyers, facing him from opposite sides, pleading a case for her client.

In his attempt to slide as unnoticeably as he could into the first vacant spot, Shoemaker's eyes were riveted to the happenings in the front. And only after he felt reasonably sure that he hadn't disturbed the proceedings, he ventured to glance around the surprisingly bright room despite of the appropriately dark furniture. That's when he saw them, Bobby, his lawyer Sam Marquette, the bartender and chief witness Curtis Wilson, in the first bench behind the bar. In the next two rows Karl recognized some of the Stammtisch guys. There were Mayor Jim Livingston, Charlie Bradford, the editor of the *Gazette*, Henry Jones, his buddy, the real estate broker, and a bunch of more people he didn't recognize; all huddled together like a small band of conspiratorially charged partisans.

Then Karl Shoemaker caught a glimpse of three persons sitting next to each other in the third row, a fact that brought an amused smile to his face, their presence, however, he didn't find surprising at all. The gray-haired distinguished man in black was none other than Father Paul Connelly, flanked by Lois Catbury, who most likely was about to face the longest speech ban she ever had to endure during her waking hours. And Karl thought the female next to Lois was probably the cleaning lady Vanessa Simmons.

The judge ordered the defense attorney to deliver additional documents asked for by the plaintiff to the office of the law firm Hadler, Simpson and Schoen and that he would set a new date after he had heard from them.

Obviously hoping to finish the next case before the lunch break, Judge Grayson's warm baritone voice announced the next case, "Mr. and Mrs. Jacques Sutton versus Robert Forrest and Amy Kristine Moore Enterprises dba The Bay Restaurant.

"I understand Mr. Ballister is representing the plaintiff?"

"Yes, Your Honor. Right here." The person who rose up at that time was a man in his mid - sixties with thinning hair, dye-altered into a pine-straw auburn, a bit too much loose flesh in the chin and neck area, dressed flawlessly in the work clothes of a jurist, from the navy-blue pinstripe suit, white shirt under a crimson tie matched by the visible triangle of the kerchief to the black thin-soled footwear.

At that point Karl noticed the people sitting in the first row right of the center aisle, the pew Mr. Ballister had just left. He could only see the backs of a man, a woman and what had to be the Sutton's adolescent son.

"Your Honor, my clients feel entitled to a restitution of five thousand dollars from the Bay Restaurant for causing physical and emotional harm to their son."

"And what exactly did the Bay Restaurant do to cause that kind of harm to their son, Mr. Ballister?" the judge asked.

"The floor was wet, but there was no sign warning the public to that effect. Bradford Sutton slipped and suffered a severe laceration on one leg below the knee in addition to the days-long trauma initiated by the whole experience, Your Honor."

"I understand the boy was in a great hurry; in such a hurry, actually, that he didn't notice the cleaning lady mopping the floor. Why was he so anxious to get out of there?"

"Well, he was obviously afraid of Mr., eh, Wilson, who basically accused him of stealing. Not paying much attention to who and what was in his way."

"Hmm." Judge Grayson took a deep breath before he said, "How big was the laceration, as you called it? And how long did they keep the boy in the hospital?"

"They released him that day."

"Do you plan to use any witnesses, counselor?"

"Yes, your Honor, I would like to call the victim, Bradford Sutton and his dad, Jacques Sutton. If it pleases Your Honor, I suggest for you to question the boy first."

"Well then, let's go ahead." He waved his hand at the small group on the other side of the aisle and said, "Young man, would you please step forward and stand next to your lawyer?"

A gangling figure emerged from the threesome and with one hand in his pocket dangled toward Mr. Ballister.

Karl thought if his face revealed the same color as his neck, the boy's self-assured body language was at odds with his state of mind.

"Alright, Bradford, need to ask you a few questions. You listened to your attorney who asked for a substantial sum of money from your employer for physical and emotional pain you allegedly sustained from taking a fall on the floor in the lobby of the restaurant. Do you agree with that assessment?"

"Yes, uh, sir."

"Why were you in the restaurant at that time of day? Did anybody ask you to come in?"

"Uh, no." Bradford looked for help from his lawyer, but didn't get any.

"You ran away after Mr. Wilson spoke to you in the area of the cash register. Why?"

"He accused me of trying to open the cash register."

"Well, were you?"

The judge repeated the question when the boy didn't answer.

"No."

"So you slipped on the wet floor and tripped over the broom, eh, the mop. Is that right?"

"Yes."

"As you were lying on the floor, Mr. Moore, Mr. Wilson and Mrs. Simmons treated your injury. Is that right?"

"Uh, yes."

"Did you think they were unnecessarily rough on you?"
"Well, it hurt."
"You may sit down." Then he asked Mr. Ballister to approach the bench. And after a short communication among the two the attorney returned and glanced over to the two adults on the left, shrugging his shoulders as in saying *'nothing I could do.'*

In a furious attempt to get his say in the matter Mr. Sutton left his seat and stormed over to his lawyer. "What's going on? I am the second witness. I have a right to be heard."

"For God's sake, sit down." Ballister hissed at his client.

"I'm gonna have a word with that judge." He shoved the lawyer away from him who was desperately trying to hold him back.

Sutton made two steps in the direction of the bench when the restrained, yet unambiguous voice of the Honorable Judge Thurgood Grayson sliced through the eerie silence of the courtroom. "You make one more step in my direction and I'll have you in handcuffs faster than you can say *sorry*.

Temporarily stunned, Sutton retreated ... backwards.

Waiting until the plaintiff had again taken his seat next to his family the judge returned to the proceedings without wasting another minute.

"Well then, I think I am going to have a little chat with Mr. Marquette here."

Sam Marquette got up, prepared for the judge to query him.

"Mr. Marquette, what do you have to say to what Mr. Ballister and the alleged victim just stated?"

Sam Marquette stepped forward and halted on the opposite side from where Mr. Ballister still stood. "Well, Thur ... eh, Judge, here's what actually occurred. Mr. Wilson, the bartender of the Bay Restaurant, present here today, entered the restaurant at around three-thirty that day, earlier than usual because he had an appointment with a liquor salesman. He has a key to the back door. He expected the establishment to be empty with the lunch crowd and the staff usually gone before three. That's why he was taken by surprise when he caught sight of Bradford, the bus boy, who habitually didn't stay a minute longer than he had to. And—"

"Where was Mrs. – wait a minute – yes, Mrs. Simmons, at that time? Did he see her too?"

"Not right then. You know the layout —"

"Never mind that, Sam. Just answer my question."

"Well, Mrs. Simmons was around the corner in the lobby, Your Honor, and since he came in from the rear of the building, he couldn't see her from there. But the boy in front of the cash register was in plain view to him."

The judge asked, "And what exactly did Mr. Wilson see and do after he had seen the young man standing there?"

"I would like to have Curtis Wilson himself answer that question."

"Fine."

Curtis got up, and since he had been occupying the aisle seat, proceeded to march straight forward towards the lawyer, alternately tugging and fidgeting on his shirt-sleeves and the lapels of his lizard-green summer blazer. He just didn't feel all that comfortable in the role of a witness. He halted next to Marquette where he let his arms hang loose, then hooked his thumbs over the top of his belt buckle the size of a small tool box; a desperate, yet not quite successful attempt to calm his nerves.

The judge recognized Curtis' uneasiness, and came to his rescue by referring to his military service, after noticing the VFW label on the lapel of his jacket, "Which one, Mr. Wilson," tapping his own chest, "Korea or Vietnam?"

It took the barman a few seconds to follow the meaning of the judge's question, but then his face brightened and with considerably more confidence and an undeniable lift of pride answered, "Both, Your Honor."

"Mr. Wilson, we thank you for your service."

"Thank you, sir, your Honor, Sir."

Smiling faces all around, or at least from the left side of the aisle.

The judge cleared his throat before he returned the discussion to the subject matter.

"Well now, Mr. Wilson, we learned that you entered the restaurant from the back when you saw Bradford Sutton standing at or in front of the cash register. Is the young man present here today and if so would you point him out to me?"

Curtis obliged.

"Now, in your own words tell us what precisely you saw him doing."

"Well, the boy didn't hear me coming in. Since he had no business to be in the bar area, particularly at this unusual time, I got curious and approached him, you know, kind o' tiptoed until I was right behind him."

"Alright, you're there now. And what is Bradford doing?" The first signs of the judge's impatience appeared in the form of deeper furrows between a pair of bushy eyebrows.

"He was pushing buttons and trying to pull out the drawer which only works with a personal number and a password. I asked him about that, because to my knowledge only Bobby, Amy and myself have access to that code."

"What happened then?"

"He took off like a rabbit."

"Now, Mr. Wilson, I read in the brief I received from Mr. Ballister that the cash register was brand-new and the staff referred to it as 'the computer'. Was the register in its appearance so similar to a real computer that the boy could have confused it as one?"

"Quite frankly, Your Honor, I don't think so. It just has a keyboard like a computer for typing the amounts and names. And from that information it prints the tickets. There's no internet, or e-mail.

"And besides, I overheard Bradford on several occasions boasting to the waitresses that he had his own account with Charles Schwab and did all his transactions with them on-line. I do seriously doubt that he didn't know the difference between a real computer and our cash register."

"Thank you, Mr. Wilson. Before I let you go answer me one last question. Did the drawer you mentioned earlier contain cash money?"

"Yes."

Curtis returned to his seat with relief written all over his face, as if he had just finished an important interview.

Judge Grayson on the other hand was ready to move on and told Mr. Marquette, "Let's now get to the situation pertaining to the wet floor."

As with Curtis Wilson, Sam Marquette suggested having the eyewitness, Mrs. Vanessa Williams, answer his questions.

The judge gave his consent.

After Vanessa had an encouraging hug from Father Connelly and a thumbs-up from Lois she moved with confidence to the front as if thinking, *as Father told me, I'm just goin' to tell the truth.*

"Well, Mrs. Simmons," the judge skipped the preliminaries, not to lose the flow of the hearing. "You heard Mr. Wilson say that Bradford, in his words, 'took off like a rabbit' after he had confronted him."

"Yes Sir, Your Honor!"

"Well, and here's where you come in. Just tell us what you saw."

"Yes, alright. I was mopping the floor in the entrance hall. On account of the fact that many people move back and forth in that area, some don't wipe the shoes off before comin' in, you know, I have to clean that floor more often. I do the dining room and the bar on Sundays when the restaurant is closed. But of course the waitresses sweep the dining room in between—"

"We understand, Mrs. Simmons. What time was it when you did this?"

"You see, I don't drive any more. And when I have to clean up during the week, Ms. Amy picks me up. I don't live far from the restaurant, on Screven Street. On Sundays I just walk. Usually right after church. Sometimes even later, when one of the children has asked me to come for dinner."

By now the judge's body language was a mixture of mild frustration and *oh what the heck. Let the lady speak. She didn't ask to come here in the first place.* "Go ahead, Mrs. Simmons. Do you know about what time it was when Mrs. Moore picked you up two Thursdays ago?"

"That is what I was about to tell you."

This time Judge Thurgood Grayson barely suppressed a smile at her rebuke.

"Ms. Amy always picks me up when everybody is gone. And I usually have close to an hour before it gets busy around there, you know, for supper. Mostly she wants me to just mop a certain spot, but I always think, *might as well do the whole front, s'long's I'm here.*

"And when that happens, it's always between three and four o'clock."

The sigh of relief coming from the bench could be heard in the last row.

"Alright. Now, did you see the boy when he bolted around the corner?"

"I heard him screaming before I even saw him. But you got that right, Your Honor; he sure was in a hurry to get out. Tripped over my mop and buried it under his belly. Tore the dang thing right out of my hands. I fell backwards and my rear end missed the water bucket by less than the diameter of a possum's tail."

The ensuing giggles and chuckles were stopped in their tracks by the sound of the gavel by which the judge demanded order in the courtroom – with a disguised grin on his face.

"And how long did it take for Mr. Moore to arrive? I understand that Mr. Wilson called him right away."

"Not more than a minute or two. He was upstairs."

"And did any of you or the two men handle the boy a bit rough as he claims?"

"Your Honor. He was still screaming so ungodly fierce, that none of us dared to even touch him. Every time Mr.

Bobby asked him where it hurt, he pointed to different parts of his body. And when we finally saw the small tear on his lower leg we fetched the medicine chest from behind the hostess stand, rubbed some antiseptic around the wound, put a Band-Aid over it and wrapped the whole shebang with more bandage at least three layers thick.

"Then the two took the lamenting youth with his *life threatening* illness to the hospital.

"And if you ask me, Your Honor, that's just about the same as if you carried a chicken to the vet because the color of her egg shells had changed from white to brown."

With his gavel in the ready-mode the judge excused the witness. "Thank you, Mrs. Simmons. You have answered all my questions," and turning his head sideways in the direction of the bailiff, mouthed the words, "and then some."

Back to the witness, he said, "You may take your seat now, Mrs. Simmons. I'll have to go over a few notes and will be back shortly with my verdict."

It didn't take the judge more than ten minutes before he was back with his ruling. "It is in my judgment that the plaintiffs were unable to prove neglect on the part of the accused concerning the wet floor as well as the immediate medical treatment he received from the defendants. The cleaning of the floor did not have to be announced by a sign or anything else since no staff member or patron was expected to be on the premises at that time of the day.

"And the documents from the hospital, from which Brandon Sutton was released the same day, called his injury a minor laceration. And there was no mention of an emotional trauma. Case dismissed.

"This is my official ruling. But I want to have it added to the record that I have a nagging suspicion that the underlying crux of the story is of a more sinister nature.

"When I asked the youngster if he was trying to open the drawer of the cash register he said, "No". This was in direct contradiction to what Curtis Wilson said, a man well known in the community with an unblemished reputation. I don't think I have to remind anyone present that lying to a judge is more than a misdemeanor under the criminal justice system."

Then he got up, turned to Bobby and emitted the two words, "Robert Forrest?" His mischievous smile could not be seen by anyone in the audience since the judge had already turned his head and was leaving through the door behind the bench without another word.

Chapter Fourteen

Karl waved at the group around Bobby and left the court house by himself. He wondered what his friend might be doing now. Would he want to sue the boy and his father, who most likely was the instigator of those absurd accusations in the first place? Well, probably not. Bobby was just too good-naturedly laid back. 'There're more important things I have to deal with than messing with an adolescent and his stuck-up father,' would be his sentiment.

While he was walking to the car his cell phone rang.

"You miss me?" Brenda's sensuous voice reached his ear before he even said 'hello'.

"Sorry, ma'am, you must have the wrong number," he answered in a lousy southern vernacular imitation.

The silence on the other end lasted a nanosecond. "Wait till I get my hands on you."

"Oh yeah?"

They both decided that that was idle twaddling enough and proceeded to discuss when Karl was to pick her up. Brenda had to turn in one last paper the next day and would be able to leave MUSC around two.

"Maybe we can have a late lunch at the Blossom Restaurant on East Bay. Weather permitting, and it should be in the low seventy's tomorrow, we might be able to sit outside. They have a cute little courtyard."

Karl got in a few comments pertaining to Bobby's hearing; that it had gone well for him, and the accusers made to look like fools. "The judge was sharp as a tack, well prepared and he had a keen sense of humor, the dry kind."

But for the most part it was his wife who did the talking. Karl didn't mind. As a matter of fact he couldn't get enough of this bubbly voice of hers, so full of enthusiasm and excitement.

"Alright then, you know where to pick me up?"

"I do."

"Two o'clock?" Brenda left nothing to chance.

"Count on it. And, uh, yes, more than you ever could imagine."

"What are you talking about?"

"Missing you."

Karl was in a good mood when he turned on the engine of the Jeep. In such a good mood actually, that he successfully manipulated his brain to shove the investigation of the ugly murder in Garden City to the far corner of his mind.

Instead he reflected that he would see Brenda tomorrow, that they would enjoy their last days in Georgetown together, topped-off by the upcoming and so much talked about *Wooden Boat Show* on Saturday.

Maybe he could squeeze in a few more things before they had to embark on their week-long trip back to Wyoming. And that meant also returning to the challenging task of navigating scores of marginally motivated college kids through the tangle of Germanic grammar.

But his good buddy and colleague Stewart Bramble was taking his classes. Forever could he not talk to or think about Stewart without revisiting the most horrible tragedy of his life – the death of his wife Linda and his eight year-old daughter Carolyn, pet-named Cookie by everyone. Both of them had not survived the fire that ultimately burned the house to the ground. Bo, the puppy, their latest family addition, had to be removed from the blaze by force to which the scratches and multiple lacerations all over the firefighter's body, including his face, bore undeniable witness. That was one of many reasons why Karl became so attached to this brave canine. Over the years he could recall many more examples of Bo's unflinching loyalty to his master.

I hope he'll be more cooperative this time and accepts my invitation for a walk to the beach. And if he isn't I'll call on Charlotte. That thought produced a kindhearted smile on his face.

While Karl was in the courthouse the on-and-off retired sheriff Amos Grimm had summoned Linus Thompson and detective Antonio Caparelli for a meeting in the sheriff's office.

Styrofoam cups, half full with cold coffee, yellow notepads, and the articles serving as cigarette suppressants, two of Amos' popsicles, Caparelli's chewing gum, and the two items that kept Linus from going off the cliff, a giant Herschie's chocolate bar – and a pack of Marlboro Light, only for emergency –, adorned the top of the center piece of the *(K)night Post.*

"Well, guys," drawing the raspberry-flavored lollipop out of his mouth, Grimm opened the meeting. "We made some progress. Brown admitted yesterday that he stole Sam Osborne's truck. Problem is he claims that he doesn't know the person who put him up to it. Said he found the reward, three twenty dollar bills in a plastic bag with a two-trips worth of cocaine under an oil drum on the left side of his trailer after he got back from returning the truck. When I asked him how he got back from Georgetown to Andrews he just shook his head, 'Hitchhiked.' I have no problem with the last part." Grimm added with a dry chuckle.

"If he murdered his sister, how does the shooting at us fit in?"

Caparelli voiced his opinion. "If this had anything to do with the murder he would have to have heard from someone that the two of you were coming to Andrews to check on him. Who could that have been?"

"Jesus, sorry, am not supposed to use the Lord's name in vain by order of my wife. Anyway, we saw a bunch of people that day. Let's see, Greta, the lady who found Michelle, Schloss, his wife. Wait, Darren Schloss, the womanizing liquor salesman. Of course, he could have told him.

"Did he know him?" Caparelli asked cautiously.

"At least he knew of him. He mentioned him to us when we interviewed him in *Mama's Kitchen*. Fits nicely, almost too nicely."

With the chocolate bar gone Linus was playing with the unopened cigarette pack. But his temptation was quickly stopped in its tracks when he saw the sheriff's warning eyes aimed at the coffin nails, Amos' favorite description since he himself had stopped inhaling them.

Linus Thompson, loyal to his former boss, and greatly appreciative for Amos to have taken the reins in this investigation, took the opportunity to offer his own observation, one more akin to his rather unadulterated understanding of the law. "How's that sound? Right behind Joe's Trucking is an empty lot. Belongs to four brothers. At least they're all on the deed. Joe Grubbs has been wanting to buy it from them but they can't get their ducks together. Think if they hold on to it longer they can ask for more money. No luxury condominiums will adorn that area any time soon with Joe's Wrecking on one side and a junk yard on the other. The whole place is overgrown with weeds, so much—"

"Where are you going with this, Linus?" Amos' patience was beginning to wear thin.

"Well, hear me out. The weeds are so overgrown that you can't see the shack from the road that's smack in the middle of the property. And that shack has seen its share of shady deals between some of the more notorious scoundrels of the city.

What if Mikey was one of them last Friday? And when he leaves, possibly with the dope Tony found in the trailer, he walks by the truck, always looking for an opportunity, and sees the keys. Jumps into the truck and drives to Andrews. When he gets to the trailer he catches sight of you and Karl walking around the mobile home or by peeking through a window of the Emerson house. Hides somewhere out of sight and waits until you leave."

Caparelli is not convinced. "Why would he shoot at the sheriff?"

Amos lifted the index finger of his right hand, as in 'let me answer that.' "I asked him that last night. He seemed to ponder over that for a moment, but his answer was crisp and unambiguous. 'Had a phone call.'

"He was a bit more hesitant when I asked him if we could verify the call and that we would have to do this using his phone. He handed it over eventually, probably cursing himself inwardly for not stomping on it a few times. I asked Olivia to trace all his calls from Friday on. Maybe we're lucky, but I'm not holding my breath; unless Clarence Woodburn had something to do with it."

He and Caparelli snickered at this unlikely scenario while Linus' eyes shifted uneasily from one to the other before he lowered his head in an attempt to hide the embarrassment.

In a fatherly good-natured gesture Amos Grimm grabbed the neck of the younger man with his fleshy paw and said, "Don't sweat it, Linus, worse things have happened to the best of us.

"Now why don't you check with Olivia and see if she found out something while Tony and I keep our fingers crossed."

Linus jumped up, obviously relieved to escape further discomfort, and left the room with a purpose. Detective Caparelli strolled over to the coffee machine, grabbed the half-empty pot and poured another round of the tar-black brew.

"What do you think? We need a break, Tony. Need to know if Mikey has anything to do with the murder of his sister, directly or indirectly."

Linus returned with a computer sheet in his hand. "Brown received eight calls since Friday and placed himself two, one to the Emerson's and the other to a woman in Walterboro. Of the eight incoming calls, let's see, seven came from the same woman and the remaining one was placed from a hospital room. Olivia checked all of them. The woman in Walterboro claimed to be Michael's girlfriend. Olivia said she sounded completely out of it. Slurry speech. Told Olivia to have him call her, immediately. Mrs. Emerson let her know that Mikey's phone calls always sounded like a broken record. They're invariably a plea for money."

Linus Thompson displayed a congenial grin before he continued. "She also told Olivia to make sure to give you her love and for you to stop by any time. She assured her that she'd keep a full badge of her special chocolate cookies on hand for you."

"Lovely people," Amos injected with a smile on his face as well. "Now, what about the hospital call?"

"Well, that's a strange one. Olivia called that number and when no one answered she checked with the nurse's station and was told that that particular room had been empty Thursday and Friday. And the call was made Friday at four fifteen in the afternoon."

"Well, I'll be ..." The sheriff and Toni Caparelli looked at each other, mystified.

"But let me just finish my thought right quick," Thompson said. "When Mikey saw you in Andrews, he knew you were looking for him. He had a record, was a known addict, probably stoned right then. He waited until you left and followed you.

"And the rest is history. It may not have happened that way, but I thought at least we shouldn't rule out that Michael Brown did this on his own and the theft of the truck and subsequent shooting at you and Karl Shoemaker might not be linked to the murder in Garden City."

"We can do that. He could be innocent as far as the murder is concerned. But I cannot believe he did all this by himself. The phone call, for example, why from a hospital room? The caller obviously didn't want his call to be traced. The payment. What for? If you ask me, it was for shooting us or at us, as it turned out.

"If Michael Brown was as stoned as you suggest, Linus, he must be an excellent shot. Remember, he was aiming at a moving target out of a moving vehicle. Also, would he be willing to kill for sixty bucks and a tiny bag of cocaine?

"No, but I think we have to keep him in the pool of suspects. Maybe he didn't murder his sister, but he could very well have been an accomplice to whoever did it, particularly if that man was Darren Schloss. Michelle had dropped her brother's name occasionally in connection with his money problems.

"Maybe he overheard her talk to him on the phone; about other matters which could have given Schloss an opportunity for blackmail.

"Anyhow, Tony, I think you should again go over to the jail and see if you can get more out of Mikey. He's got to be hidin' stuff from us. Ask him how well *he* knows Darren. Apply some of your fancy interrogation skills, stretch the truth but don't break the law."

The detective, showing a half smile around his mouth, agreed with a nod, "Understood."

"And Linus, I know you have enough on your plate—"

"Uh, sheriff, Robbie Clemens from the paper called for the umpteenth time. Wants us to give him a progress report on the *homicide,* as he put it. Couldn't put him off any longer, so I agreed to see him at two o'clock. I'd prefer it if you could make the time and talk to him, though."

"No, Linus, you can handle the guy. He's just doing his job. Can't really blame him for that. I didn't see anything in the paper today. His dad must have had a word with him.

"Since he knows that we have been keeping an eye on Mikey, tell him he's definitely a person of interest. We feel confident that we'll have an answer to his strange behavior shortly. And when that happens we'll let him know."

With this Amos Grimm got up, made a few steps to remove the stiffness in his legs, turned back to his men and said in perfect Brooklyn-Southern-Italian, "We're having spaghetti Bolognese, can't miss that.

"Give me a ring the second something new comes to your attention."

Chapter Fifteen

In his suite at the unassuming Hampton Inn on the outskirts of Atlanta, Georgia, the Enforcer was wrapping up his personal hygiene. He thought of topping it off with the night-black moustache, but decided against it.

At exactly seven – forty five his cell phone rang. After he heard who it was his uncontrollable anger became evident immediately in the form of an ugly reddish hue creeping up his burly neck. Barely could he restrain himself from shouting into his mobile. "Didn't I tell you never to call me? And when I say never, I mean it."

He listened for not more than a few seconds before he barked, "I don't care if things are heating up down there. When I told you never to contact me, which part of 'never' did you not understand, you moron? I gave you that phone to be available to me at all times. And if I ever can't get hold of you I'll hunt you down – and that will be the end ...of you.

"Now, since you are already on the phone you might as well tell me why; and it better be good. You have thirty seconds. Go!"

"Who told you that?" The Enforcer cut in as soon as he thought he'd heard enough. Then he disconnected the line after he got the answer.

He truly hated the interruption, forcing him to grab his coat, looking himself over, from his flawless hair piece, matching tie and pocket kerchief to the glossy shoes, and leave the suite.

He was supposed to meet his superior at the Ritz Carlton on the corner of Peach Street and Morgan at nine o'clock. The traffic was very heavy in downtown Atlanta this time of the day. And the last thing he wanted to happen was to be late for his meeting.

After he left his rental car, a black BMW, with the valet-parking attendant he entered the lobby at seven minutes before nine, which gave him a sigh of relief.

"Could you please give me the room number of Mr. Samuel Okune?" he asked one of the liveried desk clerks.

"We cannot give you that number, Sir. However I will be happy to call him for you."

This made the Enforcer slightly irritated, but he was not about to cause a scene.

"May I tell him who is asking for him?"

"James Foley."

The clerk dialed a number, spoke to the person at the other end, hung up and turned to the Enforcer. "Mr. Okune will be coming down shortly, Mr. Foley. You may want to have a seat over there." He pointed to a group of armchairs grouped around a huge glass-topped round coffee table.

'Mr. Foley' thought *'might as well'* and settled in a chair from which he could keep his eyes on the elevators. He grabbed one of the magazines from the table, one with a beautiful woman on the cover. At least judging from her scantily covered upper body she showed immense qualifications to be the spokeswoman for the silicone industry.

He was flipping through the pages with adolescent fascination when a shadow covered part of the glossy photo of another model. Slightly irritated he looked up and into the broad face of no one else than Loco Babatunde, the Police Commissioner from Lagos. The man was wearing a native Nigerian *riga*, multi-layered, multi-colored, and a chocolate-brown Asa-Oke cap on his head.

Babatunde stared at the Enforcer for a little longer than the latter felt comfortable with, then glanced at the magazine, exposed a perfect, pearly-white set of teeth, and said, grinning, *"Sannu da zuwa. O t'ojo meta."*

The Enforcer jumped up and greeted the man with a polite embrace. "Yes, too long," he responded, likewise in Yoruba language. He had seen the former Commissioner only two times in his life, and both times when he was supervising prisoners and Babatunde still the Police Commissioner.

"When I saw you the last time you were still a *yaro* (a boy), and now you are a *mutum* (a man). Let's go to my room where we will have more privacy."

The younger man followed Babatunde, whose slightly bent-forward shoulders displayed the first signs of an advancing age.

He was still trying to digest the new discovery. The former Police Commissioner was now his boss. Yet with admiration he remembered the man's ruthless and uncompromising pursuit in keeping order in the City of Lagos with the help of his own personal interpretation of the law.

Babatunde's freelance philosophy had made a lot of members of the police wealthy. All methods of bribery and extortion were tolerated. As a matter of fact officers, who, through clever maneuvering, had successfully come to a nice chunk of hush-money, oftentimes were promoted. One of those officers, whose rank was elevated, explained to him his good fortune. He had managed to nicely supplement his income by forcing a wealthy contractor to make monthly payments to him, with a stern promise that he would make a report to the chief of police accusing the builder of having used inferior concrete for the foundations of some of the buildings for which he had obtained government contracts.

And when he asked him if he had any proof to back up that accusation, the officer looked at him in disbelief, almost stunned by the naiveté of his question. 'Of course not,' he said, 'but I am sure he has used inferior materials ... at some time or another.'

And when he asked his opinion why this was rewarded with a promotion, the answer was both puzzling and at the same time inspiring. 'The Commissioner likes it when his people take things into their own hands and show boldness and guts.'

And it wasn't long after that conversation when he himself landed his own coup that caught the attention of Loco Babatunde, who passed his name to the leadership of this secret organization. From then on he was promoted rapidly until he had reached the ultimate honor within the WAIS, the title of Director of Foreign Affairs. While he had to keep himself punctiliously informed about the status of each operation he was assigned to – through coded e-mail communications – his true task comprised the swift elimination of anybody who might be a danger to the successful completion of the project. His self-appointed title of 'Enforcer' precisely fit the job he had been carrying out with steadfast pride, underscoring the thought with a wicked grin.

Loco Babatunde had already been in charge of the WAIS when he was officially still heading the Police Department. His predecessor's life in the underground organization was aborted when he tried to enter the Côte D'Ivoire by an assassin from a rival enterprise doing business along the Gold Coast. Since the existence of these criminal establishments was quietly tolerated by the governments of these countries, oftentimes even supported by high ranking members, an assault on their lives could reliably be traced back to a competing faction.

The suite which 'Mr. Okune' had checked into was one of the most luxurious ones the hotel had to offer. There were two adjoining bedrooms. *'Why so extravagant when he's all by himself?'* The Enforcer thought to himself, shaking his head. A lavishly stocked wet bar flanked one wall of the main room backed by an equally long mirror. A bunch of plush armchairs and two couches in a soft shade of navy-blue with pictures of scantily clad females gave the room a more sensuous appearance than the businesslike atmosphere Babatunde most likely had intended to create. But then again, Africans had their own peculiar ways to conduct business.

The former Police Commissioner invited him to take a seat in one of the armchairs, which made the five ten tall Enforcer almost disappear. He noticed that his boss had not followed suit, but instead, proceeded to swing one of his legs over the armrest of one of the chairs opposite him. Now he had to look up at him, which, for the first time, awoke in him a touchy feeling of apprehension.

Chairman Babatunde, as he was referred to by the informed few within the WAIS, had added several new ventures to the organization's activities. While some of the old stuff was still happening – a few years ago several low level hoodlums were able to slip through the screening process and gradually sidestepped their covenants to the organization by engaging in dealings contrary to the new objectives of the WAIS – they had been stopped for the most part; the old fashioned way. The stakes had been raised considerably under his leadership.

The Chairman, who had first-hand knowledge of his visitor's reputation, had been carefully briefed with regard to his performance. Not once had this man refused or even hesitated to accept even the most dangerous assignments. And it was precisely this complete lack of interest in the purpose of the commission or in the fate of the victims that had made the Enforcer so valuable and at the same time perilously close to overshooting the mark.

There was something eerily sinister about the man sitting across from him. Right now his face was blank, absent of any sign of tenseness. The *Chairman*, no stranger to corruption with all its necessary dirty matters of minor importance, recognized immediately some of the character traits of the typical psychopath. The sober recollection of the byname 'Psycho', given to the man back home with a strange mixture of admiration and fear, prepared him just in time to proceed cautiously.

He allowed his body to coast imperceptibly into the softness of the chair's seat and said, "You have done a very good job for Mission XP 012, *aboki*."

"Thank you," the Enforcer replied in English, trying to get Babatunde to do the same, since his knowledge of Hausa was not very good.

"There is one thing, however," the *Chairman* continued in perfect Oxford English, "the elimination of the young woman in South Carolina was, it seemed to me and to others involved in the case, unnecessarily severe. We do not want you to use that method anymore. Plunging a Fulani-style machete into a body is not our way. I wonder why you did this? It showed emotion, a weakness in our business. It must have taken you too long. You could have been caught. And I am not sure the woman knew a lot, if anything, about our plans. But that's *ruwa,* sorry, water under the ...?"

"Bridge."

"Yes, thank you. But from now on we have to be very careful. You know our weapon of choice – with silencer.

"Well, in the past you have never been informed about the final goal of a project you were assigned to. But because of the importance of this one I shall make an exception."

And Babatunde went on briefing the Enforcer on what the WAIS intended to accomplish, the current status of the project and what and who he needed to keep a watchful eye on. "We are satisfied to have accomplished what we intended to, so we can, how do the Americans say, wrap it up soon. Besides, it's becoming too expensive for us." He uttered the last part displaying a loathsome grin.

After this was completed and the *Chairman* had assured himself that there were no questions remaining he turned to his subordinate, a superior grin on his face, and announced almost ceremoniously, "*Sai gobe tukuna za mu tashi.*" (But we shall not start until tomorrow)

Then he clapped his hands twice and from each bedroom appeared two ebony-skinned girls in their early twenties, with legs of undeterminable lengths despite their western style miniskirts, slowly and seductively approaching the two men.

Another one of those peculiar African ways, 'Mr. Foley' thought. But he found nothing wrong with this one.

On the way back he tried to go over some of the points of the meeting in his head, that Babatunde's criticism was wrong and uninformed but had left no lasting impression on him, anyhow. His skin was made of elephant hide. Babatunde's unequivocal statement, that no informant was to survive any WAIS project, told him *what* he still had to do, but even Chairman Babatunde could not decide over the *how* this had to be done. He checked his reaction at that thought in the rear view mirror and chuckled, pleased with what he saw.

He was rehashing the point he had made in defense against one of the former Police Commissioner's accusations when the soft ringing in his ears announced the first voice, a voice he didn't want to hear. The soothing effect the tenderness of the sound had on his euphoric state of mind also aroused his nervous system, which brought on a furious tug of war from which he was unable to free himself without the help of the scratchy utterances that inevitably followed.

So, the lines are drawn. You have to make a decision whether to go along with Mr. Babatunde's orders or turn away from your senseless string of sadistic acts.

Either way, you probably will wind up dead, anyhow. But the death here on earth is no comparison to what will happen to you thereafter. The One who sent me knows that you never had a formal religious education. And that's what I am going to give you until your time here on earth comes to an—

Right at that moment an earsplitting static temporarily drowned out the voice, and he almost ran the car into a wall of a viaduct on the Interstate Highway. "See what your religious education does to me?" This was the first time he had the nerve to talk back to the first voice.

That wasn't me. It won't be the last time. The enemy will do everything to break us up. It's up to you to listen to him. The world sees in you a criminal, and, if you ask me, correctly as one of the worst kind.

Eventually your arrogance will be your downfall and you'll get caught. Prepare yourself for the world's punishment for your atrocities.

I have told you this since your petty theft crimes in Lagos: You have to repent and ask God for forgiveness. That will not protect you from your earthly punishment, but if you turn away from this evil lifestyle of yours, you might be able to evade eternal damnation. They call you a psychopath, and they might be right. But we know that you are perfectly able to distinguish between right and wrong.

Ask God for help. Christians call that prayer. He will listen. The decision is yours. It is also your decision to continue listening to the lies of your coach who is anxiously waiting to speak with you. If and when you elect to cut the ties with him, you let me know. I will give you a Name that makes him cringe. But you have to want it."

And when the Enforcer didn't respond to this invitation the voice came back. *I am signing off now.*

The gentle rustle that caressed his ear while the voice was trailing away reminded him of the time when the pre-monsoon winds grazed the leaves of the big paw-paw tree in the yard behind his parents' house back in Lagos. But he was given little time to dwell on the innocence of his early childhood under the protection of his devoted mother.

And he almost welcomed the shrewd determination in the rawness of the other voice that was waiting impatiently to penetrate his eardrums. At this time a sickeningly foul odor filled the interior of the car. Yet strangely this didn't bother him. In fact he was equally eager to have the second voice bring him out of this state of confusion. And gradually that familiar feeling of belonging did return, a belonging that had bestowed on him an unconditional loyalty to this invisible creature.

So, with his sweaty hands tightening their grip on the steering wheel, his mind and body on high alert, they all melted into one fortress-like advocate for the causes of the underworld whose depth still eluded his imagination, but remained a constant subject of his exploratory pursuits.

Hogwash! Smart of you not to give in to that trash talk. Babatunde, who like many more of the leaders is also under the tutorship of our army, will make sure that you stay on track and out of harm's way. And, by the way, don't think for a second that Chairman Loco Babatunde would have come this far by himself.

I know that you are still shaken up whenever the other side is trying to make you change your ways. They talk to you about their version of afterlife, what a farce. Just think about it. What fun is it to live a life of deprivation and sacrifices? It is the here and now that counts. There's nothing after you die. So why play according to someone's rules that exist only in the minds of fools?

Look at the leaders in the world? Are they so squeaky clean as they profess to be? I don't think so.

Instead it is all about money for them, and the power that comes with it. And if you do it right, the money will follow and you too can bathe in the glory of invincibility.

You have been a good soldier for the organization; with a blind trust toward those who gave you orders. You didn't even ask what your services were supposed to accomplish.

That's part of your personality. You take pleasure in hurting people without even knowing them. That's what the people label psychopathic behavior. However contrary to their condemnation the complete lack of remorse for one's actions is precisely what we are looking for in our chosen humans.

But now, after the briefing given to you by Chairman Babatunde, you know what XP 012 is all about. He has not told you, however, what your assignment will be after you have completed this one.

By now the Enforcer was approaching the entrance to the Atlanta Airport and had to concentrate on the exit for the Avis Rental Car Return.

I'll come back later; the voice had read his mind.

After he had parked the car in one of the Avis lots he proceeded to the terminal. He soon found out that his plane was delayed by at least one hour. He went to one of the bars in the Departure Area and ordered a Scotch on ice. But before he could lift the stubby glass to his lips the voice was back.

This stuff dulls your senses. You have to be alert at all times.

Anyway, after this assignment you can decide to retire or accept another commission. If you do decide to quit the compensation will allow you to live how and where you want.

Now the Enforcer was eager to get his questions in before the voice disappeared. "I'm sure you were listening to the other voice earlier. Which name was he referring to, the name that would make you cringe?"

The sound waves of the ensuing screech raced through his ear canal, hitting the cochlea with such a force that the neighboring receptor cells couldn't prevent him from losing his balance. He fell off the bar stool and it took him a few frightening minutes before his equilibrium returned.

Chapter Sixteen

Karl was up very early that Wednesday morning. And his excitement caught even Bo's attention. Until now still soundly asleep, he lifted his head and stretched out his ears, letting his dark eyes follow his master's every move.

Ever since Charlotte had so easily persuaded him to follow her back into the house from his self-inflicted exile, the aging dog was again spending his time inside the *Inn*. It goes without saying that this gave Marge Grimm the greatest pleasure since her soft-crusted apple pie won the first prize in the 1995 Pee Dee Pastry Contest.

"What do you say, old boy, are you ready to take a ride with me to Charleston and pick up Brenda?"

There were a few familiar sounds the perceptive canine picked up on right away. Not without effort, surely not painlessly, one by one, did he straighten and stabilize his legs. And with his tongue hanging out of his mouth, head tilted, Bo let Karl know, that, yes, he was ready.

"I just don't like it," Marge complained. "Amos flying all over the country, and now you are taking my good friend here away, leaving me all by myself."

"Well," Karl turned his head away from Bo and suggested to Marge, sounding as if it was already a done-deal, "why aren't you coming with us? We are only driving to Charleston. Brenda suggested a restaurant where we will have lunch and then we come right back. And tomorrow, we are all are going to pick up Amos from the airport in Myrtle Beach, okay?"

"Well, aren't you the perfect charmer?" And on the tenderhearted innkeeper's face reappeared her endearing smile and more spontaneously than she was known to be she added, "I like that idea, I really do. Thanks, Karl."

The trip to Charleston was highly entertaining for Karl Shoemaker. Marge kept feeding him with alternating hilarious and tragic anecdotes, tales and legends from and about the Low Country. There once was a preacher in Awendaw who revealed to his flock during a Sunday worship a dream he had the previous night. And in that dream God Almighty himself appeared to inform him that the next time he needed a ride to Charleston (the preacher employed the hitchhike method to get around on account of not possessing a driver's license), he should accept the third offer to take him there.

As it so happened preacher Hieronymus Hardgrave felt that need the very next morning. Standing right next to the wooden sign whose fading inscription invited the indifferent traveler with a stern warning:

WORSHIP WITH US
IT COULD BE THE LAST CHANCE YOU GET

He couldn't prevent the redness from rushing into his face when Raymond Washington, the man who took care of the three azalea bushes and the patches of grass on the otherwise earth bare ground in front of the church, and regularly gave the preacher a ride in his nineteen seventy - eight Chevrolet Impala, drove up.

He waved for Raymond, who steered his noisy vehicle into the yard as soon as the Reverend came into his view, to keep on going. But good old Ray didn't immediately comprehend what that meant. So Hardgrave yelled at his befuddled parishioner that he was catching another ride.

He was about to step back into the shadow of the building, to be hidden from the next driver, just in case another parishioner had to be denied the privilege of giving him a ride.

But it was only after he had to disappoint Lucille Witherspoon with the same prophetic excuse, when a Dodge pick-up truck, which had seen its best years during the Eisenhower administration, came to a screeching halt. A thick dark beard covered most of the driver's face. And his clothes, a dirty, unidentifiably colored T-shirt, jeans ripped as if they had been through a shredder and shoes that didn't match. The man motioned for him to jump in.

Certainly that was not the transportation Reverend Hardgrave had expected. But with a heavy sigh he uttered under his breath, "Lord, You surely work in mysterious ways."

"Well," Marge took a quick look over to where the celebrated McClellanville Diner used to be, now under a different name and ownership, before she went on. "Some kids found the clergyman in a swamp off Hwy 17 in Sewee hiding behind an old Atlantic White-Cedar tree" – she turned to Karl for effect – "without a stitch of clothes.

"The 'kindhearted' bearded man had escaped from the Georgetown Jail. And in desperate need of a set of decent clothes the hitchhiking preacher was the perfect answer, almost as if God Almighty had put him there.

"Over the years that story took all kinds of different endings, but I think we'll just leave it right here."

There were more stories, lots of them. And by the time they had reached the ramp leading to the Arthur Ravenel Bridge spanning the Ashley River from Mount Pleasant to Charleston, the innkeeper was still raving about the legendary general of the Revolutionary War, Francis Marion, better known by the turf he preferred to mount his attacks from, the Swamp Fox. "There are probably more towns in America named Marion than gas stations between Georgetown and Myrtle Beach.

"The English hated him. Accused him of racism, raping the Cherokee women, fighting dirty, and whatever more. But I think they were jealous of him because he had beaten them in so many battles. And when a few years back that movie 'The Patriot' came out, which, I have to say, may have defended his warfare tactics a bit too eagerly, the papers in London called him a terrorist, for cryin' out loud."

"Yeah, I saw that one. Mel Gibson, right?" Karl injected, fascinated and amused by his older friend's enthusiasm.

But she wasn't finished yet. "The movie may have whitewashed his methods but in the eyes of every South Carolinian that man was a hero. Hereabouts he's hailed as the forerunner of the …, gosh, now I don't remember the word for that, sounds like one of our close relatives."

"Guerrilla, guerrilla warfare, maybe?" Shoemaker tried to help her out, inwardly grinning at her unwavering support for a man from Georgetown, who died some two hundred years ago.

"He became a State senator after the war," followed by an aggressive nod that Karl interpreted as meaning, "Southerners were always proud of their brave men who fought for their freedom and for the one of future generations."

In between her rummaging in the past she didn't miss a beat in leading Karl to the visitors' parking lot.

Bo only lifted his head when his master turned off the ignition, let down all windows and said to him, "You'll be okay, and Brenda will be so happy to see you." He walked around the car, lifted the hatch and gave his canine a quick and peppy rub-down.

"Brenda told me she would be finished by around two. Leaves us fifteen minutes to look around and breathe the air with some of the country's most prestigious brains in the field of medicine."

"I'm very familiar with this place. My dad spent a full week here to have one cancer-eaten side of his lung removed. Prolonged his life for about five months before the right wing caught the disease.

"That was the reason why I insisted Amos stop smoking. Sugar-infected teeth can be fixed a whole lot easier than any other part of the body infected by cancerous cells."

"You got that right," Karl knew that that remark was in reference to the sheriff's smart decision to switch from smoking to sucking popsicles.

"What?" Karl asked when he noticed Marge looking over his shoulders, failing to keep a straight face. And when he turned around he gazed into Brenda's sparkling eyes accentuated by her endearing smile that made his head spin.

And Marge had to clear her throat three times before the couple finally disengaged their embrace and Karl let the two women throw their arms around each other.

"You look a little tired, Marge, but that is understandable with what you have been through these last few days. Is Amos really alright?"

"Alright? Girl, a deputy took him this morning in the dead of night to the airport, chasing some *person of interest*," fake respect at the enunciation of the police jargon, "but I won't stand in his way anymore. I must trust him that he knows what he's doing."

Brenda wisely refrained from pursuing the matter and together the three stepped out of the hospital.

When they got back to the Jeep, Bo had to mobilize all his diminished strength to get up and stand on his feet. His inbred sense of pride would not allow him to greet Brenda lying down. And Brenda Shoemaker felt his pain. Karl unlocked the rear door for her and Bo moved to the edge where he stopped, looking at her. He stabilized his footing, breathing a little harder, his tongue hanging out slightly off-center; the rapid back-and-forth of his short tail the only visible manifestation of the canine's excitement.

Brenda embraced his neck with one arm and pressed the side of her face against his. She left it there, for a long time, and when she lifted her head, Karl noticed a couple of tears working their way down her cheek.

He pulled her to him and they kissed, it seemed, forever. "Let's go. He will be alright. Honest."

Brenda guided her husband to Broad Street, past the Cathedral and into East Bay.

"Haven't we been here before?" he asked her.

"You remember," she said and added, "you'd better," grinning from ear to ear.

The Blossom Restaurant had a delightful courtyard in the back where the women suggested having their lunch.

They decided to sit at a table next to the eight foot high red tips hedge, which gave them plenty of shade from the early afternoon sun. And after the waiter had taken their drink orders, for the ladies iced tea and for Karl a glass of imported beer, Marge had run out of patience.

"Well girl, to say we have a lot of catching up to do would be a colossal understatement. But first of all, it's so good to see you again. On top of it you look great, honey. And now let's hear all about your new career."

Brenda was all too happy to accommodate her. After the waiter had placed their beverages in front of them she took a generous gulp of her tea, and a smidgeon of self-respect joined her captivating facial features, when she enthusiastically rendered her report. "Well, Marge, if it hadn't been for this guy right here," and to reinforce what she was about to say, she gently placed her hand on top of Karl's and leaving it there she said in earnest, "I wouldn't have had the guts to even enroll after I read the curriculum.

"Karl convinced me from the first moment I had the idea, that I could do it. He was supportive throughout the entire four years. So many evenings he had to prepare the meal, and he's such a bad cook." Karl jerked his upper body away from her, cocked his head in her direction, and, faking sincere indignation, refuted her low regard for his culinary skills, "I thought I made the meanest Poulet à la Crème and my vegetable stew is flat out of sight."

Brenda had to cover her mouth with the free hand not to disturb the guests at the neighboring tables with her unladylike laughter. "Marge, sometime I'll tell you more about my husband's adventures in the kitchen. Just let me make this perfectly clear: I am eternally glad that I didn't marry him for his expertise in that field."

"Alright, guys." Marge couldn't help but release a grateful chuckle at their mock argument. It did give the innkeeper great pleasure to find her two younger friends still very much in love. For a fleeting moment she fondly remembered that she had played not an insignificant part in them finding each other.

"You have the rest of your lives to quibble over how good or bad Karl's cooking competency is. I'll just say this much: If it's anything close to Amos' I would put a NO-TRESPASSING-BEYOND-THIS-POINT sign in front of any door or opening through which he could invade the kitchen.

"But there will be no more interruptions, honey. I'm sure Karl knows everything that's behind this new endeavor of yours. It had to take courage, I can imagine, going back into the classroom after so many years. But you never were afraid to enter uncharted waters as far as I recall. So, what's next?"

"Well, as I said, we made this decision together. Believe me, having been by myself all my adult life, having someone to share that burden with, makes everything so much easier."

"Have you decided on what you want or do you need a few more minutes?" Three heads turned around, looking at the waiter as if he was intruding on their privacy. Karl smiled apologetically at the young man and said, "Yes, but we will be ready when you get back."

By now Brenda was anxious to disperse the details of her new career path to her good friend. "You're right, Marge. It wasn't easy. But not exactly because it has been so long since the first time I tried college. It was rather because the stuff I had to cram for before I was even admitted into the program. It sounded so simple. Reading and algebra at tenth grade level. I was pretty good at math in high school. So that was easy. But then it hit me: chemistry, microbiology, anatomy, physiology and finally sociology and psychology. And now ...oh, I'll have a salad, eh, romaine, and what's the soup today?" Brenda had noticed the waiter first and made sure she had an answer for him.

"A tomato based bisque, ma'am. People seem to like it," the young waiter added with pride.

"That'll be it for me then." Brenda accepted his recommendation with a smile.

Marge and Karl gave him their orders as well.

"But you could handle it, I'm sure," Marge observed with a nod of her head, confirming her confidence in Brenda's resolve.

"What, the salad? Just kiddin', I know what you mean. To be honest with you, not without his help," she shifted a little in her husband's direction when she said this. "He, some of his colleagues, and a legion of students tutored and tested me relentlessly.

"But it was necessary. Wouldn't have made it otherwise."

"She was an exemplary student. Professors and the younger classmates always spurred her on before a test. At times it was hilarious. Kids out of my class, who had nothing to do with it, curriculum-wise, came to me and asked me how she was doing."

"Anyway," Brenda felt a bit embarrassed by all the praise and quickly took over again, "four years later I have my BS degree and qualified for my exam, which I will take at home, to become a Registered Nurse, or RN, as the professional jargon goes."

"I am so proud of you, child," Marge's commendation was sincere. "And what will you do, work in a hospital or a private practice?"

"Well, Marge, I'm really not sure. There are quite a few avenues I can focus on in addition to the two you mentioned. I could also go for Nurse Practitioner, or NP. Would give me a wider range of application, uh, more responsibility, so to speak.

"But," and breathing a sigh, and it wasn't one of relief, Brenda admitted with earnest concern, "first I have to get through the exam. Let's see," she raised the right hand and ran down the list of topics she had to cram for, starting with her index finger, "there's Management of Care, Psychosocial Integrity, End of Life Care, Abuse and Neglect, Coping Mechanisms, well, there's more, but you get the drift.

"I'll just as heavily as I can rely on my coach here and hope for the best." The kiss on Karl's cheek coincided with the arrival of the food.

He gave her a quizzical look, then turned to Marge and said, "Did you hear what I just heard? Nurse Practitioner? What's next? Of course, Med School."

"Why not? Sky's the limit, right girl?" Marge's well-meant cliché to Brenda was followed by a robust wink.

For the most part the three dispatched their meals in silence. It seemed that all had something on their minds.

Karl was simply overjoyed that he had his wife back. From time to time he inconspicuously turned his head and stared at her profile. *She's so beautiful. I'm the luckiest man in the universe.* He thanked his deceased first wife Linda, as he had done so many times in the past seven years, for encouraging him in a mystical appearance that it was alright, even her wish, for him to pursue this new love, when he was still mourning her and Cookie's demise.

"Well," Marge Grimm was the first to speak. Her plate almost cleared of pesto spaghetti. "While you guys are having a mellow banana split or one of those sinful crème brûlée, I would like to be excused."

Brenda and Karl looked at each other with question marks on their faces, and Brenda was just about to protest when Marge went on.

"Amos and I have made a pact, which prohibits both of us to touch any of that deliciously sinful sweet stuff. And I'll be honest, this turned out harder for me than for him. And since there's nothing more perfect to end a fine meal with good company in an elegant restaurant than with an exquisite dessert, I don't want to be tempted."

"Are you serious?" Karl broke in with an even bigger question mark on his face.

"No," their friend answered. "Jokes aside; I haven't been to the *Catholic Bookstore* in years. Amos doesn't like the hustle and bustle of big cities. Anything larger than Georgetown is too big for him. I would be worried if we ever had to go for one reason or another to New York.

"Anyway, I've known the sisters who run the place for many years. It would give me great pleasure if I could say hello to them. It's not far from here on King Street. Also gives me a chance to take a peek into all those lovely yards in front of the old homes with those colorful flowers on the way."

Aware that the two had already figured out the real reason for her seemingly odd plan, she got up, displayed her motherly smile, and said, "You can pick me up whenever you're ready. And take your time." More smiles. "Yes, as I mentioned the bookstore is on King Street, at the corner of King and—"

"I know where the *Pauline Books and Media* is at," Brenda cut her off, shaking her head.

"Take your time, the Daughters of Saint Paul love to talk. And thanks for the lunch. It was terrific." With a brushing kiss on Brenda's cheek and a wink for Karl she weaved her way around the tables.

"That old girl certainly has lost some weight; looks like their pact is working," Brenda remarked with admiration, proud of her friend's obvious determination to steer clear of her legendary peach pie. And to Karl she added, "She's a remarkable lady, isn't she?

"No doubt."

The two shared a crème brûlée with Brenda spoon feeding her husband to the latter's supreme delight. All the while he held her free hand as if in fear she would disappear. Love and pride for this woman fought for each other's superiority inside the turbulence of his heart. It stirred up memories of their first dinner at the Pierre's in Pawley's Island when Brenda reluctantly opened up to him and told him the story of her life, a life that had been fraught with danger and sorrow.

Brenda felt her affectionate glances at him ricocheting back to her and wished for that moment never to end.

"You know, people are staring at us. But quite frankly, I don't care," Karl was unfazed. "Middle aged, over the hill, whatever they might think, I love you more than the first day I walked into the Bay Restaurant and watched you lifting the bar flap and stepping up to my table in your neat little apron, with pencil and notepad in your hands, ready for business."

"Yeah, and you didn't even let me rattle off the rest of that day's menu."

"Well, I liked crabs with a side salad and, besides, my knowledge of cuisine in general is rather limited, as you have learned in the meantime, and I just didn't think you could top that.

"But you should have seen your face when I also asked for the 12 ounce steak."

Brenda followed that up, mimicking a reprimand, "And you scoundrel let me stand there, dumbfounded, before you told me that the steak was for your dog."

They both had a good laugh remembering the amusing episode from their first encounter.

Right then, Brenda slung her arms around her husband's neck and the two engaged in a long, passionate kiss, completely oblivious of their surroundings.

"We'll explore this subject more tonight. But now I want you to bring me up to speed with the case."

Karl, looking slightly dazed, took a deep breath. "Just like this? Can I catch my breath first?"

"You can." Her response carried with it a sweet recognition of the desired effect.

"Well then, although Amos has told me this morning, or rather I should say in the middle of the night – had to catch the *Red Eye* in Myrtle Beach – that he was going to find Darren Schloss, I haven't seen all that much of him since yesterday.

"But I don't believe they could have accomplished a whole lot more. I'm sure they are still chasing after the same guys.

"Of course there's Mikey, Michelle Brown's troubled brother. The truck, from which Amos was shot at, was driven by him. He admitted to that much. You remember, the farmer's truck, which was removed from the wrecker's place."

Brenda nodded but wasn't quite satisfied. "How do you know it was *that* truck?"

"The detective, what's his name again, uh yes, Caparelli, discovered the papers belonging to Mr. Osborne, and two twenty dollar bills in his trailer. The farmer confirmed that he had left these papers in the truck together with the money.

"But there are still quite a few holes in Mr. Brown's actions and statements. For one, why did he remove the papers from the truck? Unless he saw the bills first and grabbed them together with the documents. Probably was in a hurry when he saw us leave the Emerson house."

"So," Brenda jumped in, "could he not just have been afraid the Emerson's had let something out of the bag he had reason to be worried about?"

"Well, that is one of the guys' theories too. But I think there is more to Mikey's involvement in all of this than just that. He mentioned to Amos a phone call he had received when Amos questioned him about the shooting.

"Amos, and I agree with him, believes that Darren Schloss, the liquor salesman, plays a major role in this drama. His scenario is this: Darren Schloss was dating Michelle, Mikey's sister, or at least he thought he was. Surely she must have talked to him about her brother at one time or another. The two men could have even met, although we don't have proof of that.

"When it was clear to Darren, that the woman had no serious interest in him, his narcissistic ego was fatefully hurt. Amos believes he killed her in an uncontrollable rage and began to blackmail Mikey after we had questioned him in the restaurant in Myrtle Beach. And the phone call Mikey spoke to Amos about could have been the one where he threatened to expose some of his undiscovered felonies if he didn't follow Schloss' instructions. And these should deter the sheriff from pursuing him, Schloss, any further.

"Now I don't know if Darren gave Mikey specific instructions how to go about accomplishing this or if he left it to Mikey's own ingenuity."

"Strange description, but probably a correct one," Brenda shook her head in disgust.

"Yeah it is, isn't it? But whoever of the two came up with the shooting idea succeeded in making a memorable impact on Amos and me. Too bad for him that it had the opposite effect from its intent. If Darren Schloss thinks he could prevent Amos Grimm from continuing to pursue him just because of his shenanigans he's more than just mistaken, he's brain dead.

"Two things seem to be responsible for Michael Brown to react as fast as he did. First and foremost there was the enticing promise of a generous supply of narcotics and cash, provided the job was done to the satisfaction of the caller/client.

"And the other contributing factor, thinks Amos, presented itself conveniently in the form of two vehicles: the Escort of the Georgetown County sheriff cruising north on Hwy 51 minutes after he had received the call on his cell phone, and the truck he was sitting in, enjoying his ride back to Andrews after a wild and intoxicating pot party in the shack behind Joe's Wrecker Company. In this state of mind he didn't think twice to reel the truck around, follow the Escort and fire the shot."

Right away his vigilant wife jumped in. "Where did he find the gun, in the farmer's truck?"

The slight sarcasm didn't escape the professor. He smiled, recognizing her attentiveness. After all she had been his partner in solving the Calhoun murder. "No, not in the truck, but on him. Michael had threatened several times to kill himself. And besides, for his lifestyle, hanging around with characters who know the architecture of the County Jail way better than the location of the Rice Museum, unless it stood next to a crack house, a weapon possession is almost a bare necessity."

"Oh, honey, even if you aren't stand-up comedy material, I love you nonetheless. Anyway—"

"Just let me finish and then you can ask away to your heart's delight. So, while Darren tried to get Amos off his back he drew the law's attention away from him and instead in Mikey's direction – or so he thought.

"That leaves us still with the same original two suspects; Darren Schloss as the possible killer and Michael Brown a willing accomplice."

With a quick glance at her watch Brenda's eyes widened. "I can't believe it. We've been sitting here for almost an hour. Marge thinks we have all but forgotten about her. You need to pay up. We can talk later about the case."

Karl lifted his shoulder slightly and responded, "I'm finished talking. I told you everything. We have to wait now until Amos comes back tomorrow."

He signaled the waiter for his bill and after he had settled up the couple rushed through the courtyard towards the parking lot where Bo looked up, shifting his head from one to the other.

"I know what you want, Bo, but you'll have to wait a few more minutes before I can give you a rub down and Karl will refill your water bowl."

They jumped in the Jeep and Karl took an immediate right, crossed Meeting Street and Brenda guided him to a small parking area behind the Catholic Bookstore. With one space left they breathed a sigh of relief, since even Karl had had some experience with the parking dilemma in Charleston.

Brenda kept her promise and satisfied Bo's insatiable hunger for stroking and rubbing him behind his ears, or under the chin. Years ago Brenda had discovered another place, which seemed to give the dog great pleasure, the small area above his nose, right between the eyes. Interestingly enough it was only Brenda who could touch that spot. If Karl or anybody else tried to tickle him there he either moved one paw over the nose or moved his head away.

Karl fetched the bowl and both walked around the building and opened the front door to the store.

"You already here?" Marge was sitting in a chair next to the counter with two sisters and one lay person standing around her. Judging from the looks on their faces they seemed to be thoroughly enjoying her company.

"I was just telling them a story about Father Connelly and Father Vincent Sojourner, Fr. Vince, as we called him."

Karl stood there with the bowl in his hand when one of the sisters said in a motherly tone, pointing to the chewed-up dish. "Too big for a cat, and it's not a small dog either. Am I right?"

"Uh, yes, a Rottweiler."

"There is a sink in the back. Did you park the car in the lot or up front?"

"In the back, Sister."

"Well, there is a door right behind the round table next to the sink. You can just go out there."

Karl thanked her and left.

"Well," Marge quickly regained the attention from the sisters, "several years back there was this family from Bucksport. The man did some repair work on boats over there and the woman worked in the kitchen of the Bucksport Diner. They had a number of kids, nobody really knew how many.

"Anyhow, they were in the habit of church-hopping, as in bar-hopping – a practice of which you may or may not have heard."

"We are not cloistered," replied the oldest nun with a smile and an assuring wink.

"Alright then; the two showed up in the Parish Hall every other week and asked for some financial support. Now, Father Connelly, true to his reputation, didn't turn them away, although he had never seen them at Mass.

"They also paid the churches in Pawley's Island, Garden City and even in Myrtle Beach regular visits. They had a slew of reasons why they needed help. And when they had run through the list of their *hardships* – husband out of work, wife out of work, child sick, no money for the doctor, no money for new clothes for the children, out of food stamps, wife pregnant again, and so on – then the clever duo started all over again.

"This went on for about three months until Father Connelly had a brilliant idea. "From now on," he instructed Henrietta, the secretary, "we'll only give them a check made out directly to the electric company. This way we help them a little with their light bill.

"Well, the couple didn't like this, didn't like it at all. They kept on lamenting, desperately trying to convince Henrietta why this wouldn't work for them.

"But that loyal soul of a secretary stood her ground and wrote a check for twenty five dollars to Santee Electric Cooperative. The woman snatched it out of her hand and the indignant couple stormed out of the office."

"People can be very ungrateful. But the Good Lord knows how to deal with them," one of the sisters remarked, barely hiding her anger.

"I'm not finished yet. You see, it wasn't until a month later that the church heard from them again. And it came in the form of a letter, a letter from a law firm in Aynor, I don't know the name.

"Not to drag out the story much longer, the letter contained an accusation of the worst kind; it claimed that Father Connelly had sexually molested and assaulted their sixteen-year old daughter on such and such a date.

"That same Sunday morning the youth group had gathered in front of the church waiting for the bus to take them to Surfside for an afternoon of fun on the beach. And that girl was among them. Father C. had urged the family on several occasions to bring their children to CCD. So once in a while they brought one or two of them, probably hoping that would increase their chances for the next handout.

"The letter stated that Father Connelly had approached the girl and asked her to follow him inside the Parish Hall where, in the bathroom, he committed the horrible deed.

Father had Stephen Atkins, a parishioner and attorney, send a response to the Bucksport family and have them and the daughter come to the church for a private consultation. When they came, with council in tow – who had most likely offered his services pro bono, smelling a big scandal – Stephen immediately addressed the girl and asked her if she was quite sure that the attacker was indeed Father Sean Connelly.

"And when the girl said she was positive, Atkins handed a note to their attorney. It didn't take that man longer than a minute before he crumpled the note, flung it on the floor and yelled at the three, **"Out!"** That was the second and last time these folks stormed out of the church premises."

The women just looked at Marge, wide eyed, big question marks on all faces.

"Well?" Brenda was first to speak.

"Well what?" Marge said with a smirk.

"What did the note say?"

"Oh, yes, the note. In it Father Connelly had requested Father Sojourner to say the Masses on Saturday and Sunday – the weekend when the incident was supposed to have happened – since he was going to be out of town.

"And Father Sojourner was still in transit at the time the youth group had gathered in the front of the church waiting for the bus." And a trace of naughty mischief hung on in this, her conclusion, "That circumstance made another fact irrelevant. Father Sojourner was eighty-six years old at the time."

"They must have kept that story well under wraps. I never heard a word about it. Well, it probably occurred during a period when I was not on the best of terms with the Lord," Brenda confessed.

"Well, Fr. C. is not only a holy man, he's also pretty smart. Only very few people knew about it. One of them was Amos."

Chapter Seventeen

It was Thursday morning eight-fifteen, when Karl and Brenda Shoemaker wished they could stay in bed a little longer, but "a promise is a promise," Brenda uttered with a long yawn.

Marge had already set the breakfast table in the kitchen. "Are you sure you want to do this? I can do this by myself. You just stay here, walk around town; Bo would like that too, well, a short walk, anyway."

Karl thought about that for a minute and then suggested for the women to stay behind. "I'm pretty sure you two have a lot to chat about. And Amos could fill me in on what he learned on the trip."

The females looked at each other, one trying to read the other, before both nodded in agreement. "Only if you promise to come straight back. And call as soon as he arrives." Marge knew that she couldn't control her husband if he had something else planned.

"Yes, Mother," Karl laughed, walked over to her and gave her a kiss on the cheek.

"What about me?" But Brenda didn't even wait for Karl. With gusto did she step up to him and took what she wanted.

They were still kissing when Marge put a stop to it. Shaking her head she reprimanded the two in false anger, "Enough, you guys. Sit down now and have your breakfast before it gets cold. Besides, lover boy, if you don't hurry I'll get a call from that impatient husband of mine whispering sweet niceties into my ear, like **"Where the hell are you?"**

The arrival notice listed US Air flight number 3916 as *on time.* That would give Karl another fifteen minutes. He strolled over to one of the US Air ticket counters and asked the uniformed female attendant if the plane was indeed punctual.

"This might come as a huge surprise to you, Sir, but it looks like number 3916 will be five minutes ahead of schedule."

He thanked the young woman and walked to a coke machine, slid a dollar bill and a quarter into their respective slots, shook his head, *a dollar and a quarter for a bottle of tap water,* and wandered over to the area from where he could see the incoming travelers.

And when he then saw the sheriff, briefcase in hand, resolute steps, slimmer body, his thoughts implored the understandably worried Marge, *Please let him go on a little while longer to do what he loves. And when the time comes to quit, he will tell you, I guarantee.*

"How did Brenda do with her exam?" was the first thing Amos asked after the two gave each other a few pats on the back.

Karl was stupefied and visibly moved by his friend's exemplary showing of concern for people close to him in the midst of a completely unrelated situation, a murder case of all things.

"Well, she passed it; thanks for asking. But now to the matter at hand: Did you find Schloss?"

Karl reached over to grab the sheriff's overnight bag, who released it to him with a grateful smile. "I schlepped that thing around all day."

After exiting the revolving door Amos Grimm stopped outside the airport building and took a deep breath, as if in thankful recognition of the familiar air. Then he turned to his friend and said, "Yes I did."

When they got to the Jeep Amos suggested stopping at a McDonald's on the way back for a cup of coffee.

Karl Shoemaker sensed that the sheriff was eager to brief him on what he learned on this trip without the distractions on the highway. "Fine with me, but you better call home."

"I will." Amos understood.

When Shoemaker saw a Waffle House on the side of Hwy 17 near the entrance to the former Air Force Base he asked his passenger if he also wanted a bite to eat.

"Maybe a sandwich, something light," Amos replied.

"Will this one do?"

Amos realized that Karl was not familiar with that restaurant chain, grinned, but okayed the suggestion anyway.

A couple and their two pre-school children were the only other guests in the diner. The two chose a table on the opposite side from where they were sitting. Karl went to the counter and ordered a coffee with cream and sugar for Amos and a glass of orange juice for himself.

"Tuesday afternoon I paid Mary Schloss another visit," Grimm began after he settled comfortably on the plastic bench. "Wanted to find out if she really had no idea where her husband was. Turned out he was hiding in Atlanta, at his ex wife's place. One of the children, the boy, had called and asked her if his dad was in trouble. That's how she found out his whereabouts.

"So she gave me that address, and I took off for Atlanta yesterday. I was reasonably sure he wasn't expecting me because Mary assured me that the boy was not allowed to call her and she didn't get in touch with him either."

"And when I got to the address Mary had given me, actually in the Dunwoody section, an upper class residential area of Atlanta, guess who opened the door? Our man himself. His mouth must've dropped three inches. Sure sign that he wasn't looking for me to knock at his ex's door."

Karl got up to fetch the glass with the juice and the cup of coffee sitting on the counter and placed them on their table. "Remarried?"

"Just a sec." Amos had already picked up his cell phone. "Let me just do what you told me to, before we get too far into this mess." He punched the *Inn's* number, held the gadget to his ear, and shook his head after a minute or so. "Honey, just wanted to let you know I made it back fine. Karl and I are sitting in the Waffle House to go over some of the things I found out in Atlanta." And with a grin towards Karl he added, "The fact that we chose this place to do this tells you we're not planning to remain here for long. See you." He terminated the call. "Wasn't there."

"I think they wanted to take Bo to the Bay, – if he was in the mood.

"But what I wanted to know, is his ex married?"

Amos shook his head. "The girl, a cute little thing, brought up a few times the name 'Uncle Hank'. Had the impression she was referring to the new man in her mother's life. That would also mean she hasn't remarried as of yet.

"Well, here's the gist of what I was able to extract from the elusive liquor salesman.

"After I had introduced myself to the shapely woman who peeked around the corner from one of several open-door entrances along the hallway, about to ask 'Who is it', I told her that I had come to talk to Darren about a case in South Carolina he might be able to help us with. The young lady, her hazelnut eyes looking straight at me, didn't appear startled at all, which told me that the law's interest in Darren wasn't all that unusual to her; similar to Mary's reaction in Little River.

"She was very courteous and helpful. Although I didn't see another man while I was there, she told me that her fiancé was the CEO of an up-and-coming pharmaceutical company. I think she revealed that to me, before I could ask the obvious question: 'How can you afford such a spacious home in one of Atlanta's premier suburbs?' She also told me that Darren's alimony payments were very 'irregular'. But she's obviously not hurtin'.

"I had asked Darren to step into another room with the children. He cooperated without the hint of an objection.

Anyway, back to Christi, Christi Hammond. She had changed back to her maiden name. She approved my use of the tape recorder with a wave of her hand.

"So I asked her what reason Darren had given her for coming here. Here's her simple answer." Amos retrieved the equipment, one of the old bulky ones – "Don't know how to work these modern dime-size contraptions" – from his briefcase, and pushed the *Record* button.

Christi: To see the children. Hank is out of town until Saturday, so I thought it should be alright. He doesn't care for Darren all that much. Although I must admit, I was a bit surprised, since he rarely has asked to see the children. A few phone calls here and there. Yet the children ask often about him.

Amos: Did he give you advance notice?

Christi: Well, he phoned from Conyers, GA, if that qualifies. He rang the door bell half an hour later.

Amos: Did he seem tense, nervous, or in any way different from how you remember him? When did you see him the last time?

Christi: At first he acted like the same old jerk I had to put up with for six years and three months. Still seeing chicks – *his* word, not mine –, his wife is alright with it, – which I know is not true; and then there is always his forthcoming huge promotion. You see, he can't brag about a well-paying job. He's afraid I could demand more financial support for the children. He owes us by now over five thousand dollars in back pay.

And, oh yes, how could I forget the last time he showed up here? The notice we received from him that time was the ringing of the door bell. We had company, celebrating Hank's birthday, very embarrassing. That was this past March, the eighth, to be exact.

Amos: He didn't mention a letter he had received, did he? The letter came from outside the US. Supposedly he was pretty shook up about it.

Christi: No, he didn't.

Amos: What about a woman he was seeing?

Christi: Another one? Well, no, he didn't, he's planning to stay until the weekend. What's with this woman? Anything wrong with her?
Amos: You could say that. She's dead.

Then he cut off the recorder. "Her face turned pale instantly. She just sat there and stared at the carpeted floor. I sat there, across from her, waiting. Hoping she had something else to say after this.

"And after a long pause she said: 'Well, that's certainly beyond his usual pastime. Was she, eh, murdered? I mean —"

"I stopped her from further speculations, told her that it was indeed murder, but that we had no proof of his involvement in the killing at this particular time; that he was a person of interest to us only because he knew her rather well and had a date with her the day she was found dead, all cut up, a date he had cancelled hours before.

"When she got up, Christi made one more comment. 'Right after I knew who you were it was clear to me that you hadn't come from Georgetown, SC to check into one of Darren's self-published infidelities'."

"So, are you ready to listen to the man himself?"

"You mean he was still there?"

"Oh yeah, playing with the kids in one of the countless rooms that were fanning out in two opposite directions from the entry hall, or should I say lobby?

"He was as cool as a cucumber. You sure you don't want anything to eat, a pancake, muffin, couple of sausages with—"

"Amos," Karl shook his head with a sympathetic smile, "if you feel the need to put something, well, marginally nutritional, in your empty stomach go right ahead; I won't tell."

The sheriff ordered three waffles with two hamburger patties, one egg sunny side up, butter and syrup on the side. His request was transmitted by the white-frocked middle-aged woman in such a thunderous tone of voice to the short-order cook that the poor man's spatula flew out of his hand

and torpedoed the refrigerator on the other end of the counter.

"What's the matter with you today, Bubba? Versheena smacked you around again? Oh, you hit the bottle last night." Shaking her head the woman punched the numbers into the computer.

Bubba picked up the spatula, wiped it a few times up and down his full-length apron, and went to work with trembling hands.

"That's what I like about this place," Amos clued in his friend while carving the egg, destroying the yolk in the process, "never dull in here."

Karl wished him "Guten Appetit!" but Amos wasn't quite sure he meant it.

"Now let's hear what Mr. Schloss had to say." After he had cleaned his plate, the sheriff, not even the slightest showing of guilt on his round face after the abuse he had just committed to his body, went right back to business.

"As I said, he acted as if I was trying to sell him a life insurance policy he wasn't quite sure he wanted but still willing to listen. Here we go again." Another stab on the key opened the interview with Amos making it official by announcing the purpose, date and place of the meeting.

Both men listened to Darren Schloss answering the sheriff's questions one by one without hesitation. It was only at the end when Amos, devoid of any fanfare, like a vague afterthought, brought up the letter from somewhere outside the US.

Schloss: What letter? And, uh, how did you...?

Amos: How did I what? Find out about it? Never mind that, Mr. Schloss. You were just about to confirm its existence, so, please, cut the crap and tell me what that letter was all about.

Schloss: That letter has nothing to do with what you're talking about.

Amos: Let me be the judge of that. Where exactly did it originate?

Schloss: Africa.

Amos: Where in Africa? It's a big continent with lots of countries.
Schloss: Yeah, yeah, I know. Nigeria.
Amos: Alright, making progress. What was the content of the letter and where is it?
Schloss: I told you it has nothing to do with what you're investigating. And I see no point in giving it to you.
Amos: You know I can't force you to comply with my request…at this moment. Next time we'll meet, Mr. Schloss, I'll have a search warrant in my hands. And don't try to leave the country; from now on we are watching every step you make.

The women were back, Bo in his favorite corner by the window, when Amos and Karl returned to the *Inn*.

"Guess who we saw?" Wide-eyed Brenda had been anxiously waiting for their return.

"Okay, let's see. The President of the United States."

"Very funny. No, we didn't see the President. We passed by Betty's Luncheonette and Marge suggested to stick our heads in the door. She wanted me to meet Melanie, or Missi, as she prefers to be called.

"A kind woman, a little restrained in her comments; but, as Marge mentioned, her husband makes up for that. She's from Boston, has that distinguished New-England accent. When I told her that you were from Wyoming and that's where we were living, she said her husband was from Montana.

"Wait a minute, Joe's, uh, Joseph's wife, right? I heard Marge talking about her. She's also the mother of Charlotte, the girl who single-handedly resurrected Bo from his deplorable lethargy in the neighbor's backyard."

"Oh, you met Charlotte? Isn't she the sweetest thing you ever saw? Would you believe she joined us all the way to the Recreation Center? And Bo, our arthritis-stricken graybeard, trotted beside her like a five-year old. I haven't seen him this full of excitement and energy in a long, long time."

Amos and Marge watched the two younger friends with heartfelt admiration. He was about to say something, but Marge held her hand in front of her mouth and muttered in his direction, "Just wait, she's not done yet."

"Oh yeah, I almost forgot," Brenda was right on cue, "we stopped by the Frame Shop and you know what?"

"No," Karl answered, truthfully.

"It looked as if I had never left. Molly hadn't changed a thing. The frames, the pictures, the desk, and all the stuff I had left behind, all in the same place."

Molly was a troubled girl when Karl had met her during his first stay in Georgetown, but turned out to be very instrumental in bringing Catrin Calhoun's murderer to justice. Brenda had a lot to do with her turning her life around. And before the two left for Wyoming she had decided to give her the *Frame Shop* and the efficiency apartment above.

"And you know what?"

"I still don't. But I hope you'll eventually tell me."

"She's gonna get married."

"Great."

"And you know—"

"Brenda, come on now!"

"Alright, alright. To Bucky. Remember, Bucky Hanshoe, the banker's son?"

Now for that revelation Karl was truly unprepared. And after a few moments, as if searching for the right words, he scratched the stubbles under his chin and said, "Well, I want to say congratulations, but only with a heavy load of reservations. A good part of them would be intricately connected to the mighty bank president himself."

He remembered that Mr. Robert Hanshoe Sr. had been rigorously against the friendship of his son with the murdered girl. Catrin and her family did not belong to the circle of Georgetown's blue bloods. But he also had to give him credit for presenting them with a valuable hint that led them to Brenda's whereabouts after she had been abducted.

"I'm just not sure he can handle another one of his son's entanglements with someone from outside the town's narrow community of Southern nobility. And Molly's kinfolk hadn't risen, in his haughty mind, I'm sure, one iota from the ranks of the lowest proletariat."

"Well, but according to her he must have come around even further. Checks on her from time to time in the store."

Amos lifted his index finger and mumbled, more to himself, "Better have them check on this." And to the group, "That was the word I needed to remind me of something." He searched for his cell phone in the depths of his baggy trousers and called the station. He gave Olivia instructions to have the courthouse give her the birthplace and birth date of Darren Schloss. He gave her Darren's residence and disconnected the call.

"What was that all about?" Karl asked, clueless at first.

"Don't know yet. But I think the more we find out about this guy without having to ask him or his wife, the better off we are. I don't want him to get to the point where he skips out again and we can't find him. At the moment he's still so... well, wonderfully sure of himself.

"Need a search warrant for that damn letter. Have to think of something to get around the law on that one." He looked at the three bystanders and cautioned them with a wink. "You didn't hear that."

"What about Mikey? You haven't ruled him out yet, have you? Because I think we need to work on him some more," Karl queried.

"No Karl, haven't ruled him out. Not by a long shot. But the wisdom of my wife came through, loud and clear the other day. You two are only gonna be here for a few more days. I have no right to monopolize your time the way I've been doing."

"Don't be silly, Amos." This stern retort didn't come from Karl, but from Brenda. "You wouldn't do him a favor, anyway. I have only one request. Don't leave us, Marge and myself, out of the loop. That's all we're asking, right Marge?"

The older woman nodded, somewhat reluctantly. The over-emphasized groan that erupted from the sheriff's inner layers of his belly triggered a round of amused laughter.

"Coming back to Mr. Hanshoe and his son's involvement with Molly Cordell; it really doesn't matter what he thinks about the relationship at this point."

"What do you mean," Karl asked, curious now, "oh, you mean she's —?"

"Yes, she is!"

Chapter Eighteen

"I am going to give these guys two more days. Two days, that's it."
Obviously the president of the Palmetto Steel and Wire Corporation, a no-nonsense man in his late fifties by the name of Steve Kramer, was fuming mad. He was joined by three vice presidents and two superintendents, the senior executives of his management team, in the smaller one of two conference rooms, a choice that gave evidence to the top secrecy of this meeting.

"I've asked you to come here because I think it's time to look a little closer at our investors from Africa and the reliability of their intentions. A zillion phone calls, e-mails by the dozen a day; and if I get one more of these ... what do you call them?"

"Text messages?" Buzz Stuck, VP of Human Relations, helped him out. Buzz had been with the Company longer than any of them. He wore the deep facial lines, scars from the numerous battles with the Steelworker's Union, like a seasoned veteran. He was younger than Steve, but looked ten years older. All the arbitrations, contract negotiations, hiring and firing of employees had left their marks.

Jason Strickland, twenty-seven, red-haired crew cut, incessant gum chewer, ambitious, recently promoted to head up the Sales Department, asked the first question: "What are you going to do? Break it up? We do need the injection, don't we?"

"I am well aware of that, Jason. I wouldn't even consider their offer if we weren't in such dire straits.

"It's been three weeks now, when this guy," Kramer glanced at his papers in front of him, "Okune first called me. His proposal was actually pretty clear and precise, twenty million US dollars in exchange for eighteen percent ownership in the company. From that angle, actually a pretty good offer.

"There's only one problem; we haven't seen any of that money as of today. And I think his excuses that the funds had to go through several approval stages, both in the country as well as, what he calls the '*Organization*'.

"And that's another thing I have a funny feeling about. He has been very vague about what that Organization is all about. Sort of a global conglomerate. Wouldn't we have heard about it, even if they're not publicly trading?

"So Barb," addressing an attractive brunette; her age could be anywhere between thirty-five and forty-five. Her angular stature, accentuated by a grey suit over a white blouse, no jewelry, low-heel shoes, all spelled one word: business, "don't add those twenty big ones to your next year's projection." Mixed grin on his face, stoicism on hers.

"I wouldn't dream of it and I agree with you. We need to find out more about them. The fact that they are this secretive raises a red flag for me," Barbara O'Brian, Vice President of Finances, responded with appropriate solemnity.

"You're always so cautious, Barb," Jason argued, "what do we have to lose? They won't have any votes in the decision making process until they've paid up. They would be more or less silent minority partners. And besides, I assume we'll always keep the majority of our shares. I really don't think you know how serious our situation actually is."

O'Brian's raised eyebrows revealed more than words as to what she thought of Strickland's remarks.

But that didn't stop the young executive from giving her his alarming prognosis that required immediate attention. "We are not in a position to be overly picky. I'm saying this based on the orders we have on the books for the next five to six months. We are down in most all categories and —"

"That's what I've been meaning to talk to you about, Jason," the president interrupted. "Why is that, exactly?"

A knock on the door had everybody turn their heads in that direction. "Excuse me, please. But, Mr. Kramer, call for you." And the way his secretary Louise Berkowitz shifted her eyes from one corner to the other told Steve Kramer that the call was important and that he needed to take it in his office.

He pushed his gym-trained body away from the conference table, instructed his execs to hold their thoughts until he returned, and disappeared through the massive mahogany door.

Louise Berkowitz, a seasoned professional, asked everyone if they needed anything, more coffee, "sugar-, fat-, cholesterol free donuts", knowing her movements in and out of the room would ease the awkwardness of the brief intermission.

Kramer was actually back before the secretary returned with the coffee and, just in case, a plate full of donuts nobody had asked for, but ordinarily would be depleted of the last crumb by the time the meeting was adjourned.

"That was our friend. Said the first five mill had been cleared by the government and would be in our account next week."

"Why so long?" O'Brian asked impatiently. "That could be done in a day ... or two at the most."

"I questioned him about that."

"What did he say?" Strickland this time, tapping his pen nervously on the empty notepad in front of him.

"Nothing. This guy talks to me as if he's negotiating a shady deal. I don't feel any better now than I did before that call.

"Well, we don't have the money yet, and therefore I suggest we leave no stone unturned to find a way to keep our doors open. We need to cut costs wherever possible, leaving the reduction of our work force as a last resort.

"But before we get into this I want to go back to what I asked you, Jason, earlier. Why are our sales shrinking to such an extent? Scrap prices are low, the demand for our so hard fought for specialty wires, spring, fencing, cable, even piano wire, is there. Yet we are producing more and more of *the* category we wanted to keep at a minimum, reinforcing bars.

"With the housing and construction industry in the dumps that seems to me the most illogical approach to solve this problem."

The color on Jason's face approached rapidly that one of his hair and he was more than ready not to leave these accusations unanswered.

But before the first sound came out of his mouth one of the two superintendents, both silent participants until now, beat him to it. "And the orders we *do* get for specialty wires are so small that we cannot overlook the time and money it takes to frequently change the mix of additives in the furnaces," and while Earnest Knapp, superintendent of the rolling mill, made this point, he looked for affirmation to his neighbor on his left, Dick Lambert. Dick was not only the superintendent of the melt shop; he was also a man of few words. Thus his confirmation in the form of a simple nod came to no one's surprise with the exception perhaps of a sympathetic smile on the faces of some.

"And, of course, the same applies to the rolling mill. We need higher tonnages of each size and product. We have to overrun every time we change the mill, just to keep the cost down."

"Well," Steve Kramer took over again. "That confirms what we all know. Sales have to go up, and with the right product mix. If this doesn't happen, the promised twenty million dollars will only postpone our predicament and ultimately force us to let some of our workers go. And, quite frankly, why would anyone want to invest in a company that operates on such shaky ground?

"The Africans must know how we are faring right now. That whole thing is highly enigmatic to me, anyway. But in order to keep the possibility alive, I must urge all of you not to even breathe a word about our situation, including the African offer, outside of these walls."

He looked each one of them in the eyes with an uncompromising stare before the muscles in his face relaxed.

"Now let's get something to eat."

Chapter Nineteen

The Grimm and the Shoemaker families spent the rest of the day on memory lane, consuming tidbits of Marge's legendary chow menu. They just kept munching on crisp chicken wings with a choice of three of her exceptional sauces, marinated shrimp, herring in herb-infused tartar, and all kinds of salads. Then one after another moved rather nonchalantly over to the smaller table between the refrigerator and Bo's corner by the bay window in order to top off what little room there was left in their stomachs with the most delicious pecan, peach, and blueberry pies and more mouthwatering cobblers, and, of course, vanilla ice cream on the side.

They lingered around afterwards, each in his or her favorite armchair. Gradually the conversation faded off and the room was filled with Marge's soft whistle and the more robust snore of her husband, when Brenda and Karl looked at each other and tiptoed hand in hand into the next room. Bo didn't even as much as open his eyes.

Friday morning Linus Thompson was slouched over his desk shuffling a mountain of papers. Olivia was sitting across from him, disapproval written all over her cute face. "I know how the sheriff does it."

"What do you mean, 'I know how the sheriff does it.'? First of all, kid, you should get used to calling *me* that. And secondly ... show me how he does it."

After a few seconds of testing each other they both broke into a burst of laughter.

"Sheriff Grimm always put the letters and documents back in the file from where he took them, oldest date on top. This way he felt it was easier to follow the development of a felon, or someone he was looking for. You know what I mean. 'Sort o' like a résumé,' he used to say. 'Only their career path moves mostly in an undesirable direction.'"

Linus was getting antsy. "I tell you what. You just put all of this here," sweeping a hand over the entire heap of clutter, "back in the files where they belong. I don't have the time to do all that myself right now. Have to find someone."

Having said that he pushed the chair back and swung his long legs around the desk. At the door he turned around and said, smiling gleefully, "Oldest date on top."

He called Antonio Caparelli. The detective was waiting for Michael Brown, who was still holed up in the Georgetown Detention Center.

"I'm trying to find out if he still keeps insisting on having no idea who the caller was who told him to shoot at Amos and Karl. And you know what? I'm beginning to believe him."

"That would mean so far we can only nail him for stealing the truck, and, well, what about the shooting itself? As ridiculous it is — who else could've done it — he hasn't confessed to it. And how did he get to Joe's place and back from there? He must have had help. No way could he have done that by himself."

"Well, didn't he say he hitchhiked?" Caparelli asked, sounding as if he didn't believe it himself.

"Yeah, I know he said that. And that *kindhearted* citizen took him straight to the wrecker place. I'm not buying it and I have just the person in mind who might be able to shed some more light on Mikey's travel expedition this past Friday."

Linus still carried a grudge for the ridicule he had to put up with after he had picked up one of the most unlikely prospects for questioning. And he was determined to repair his decrepit image.

He stepped into his black Ford Crown Victoria with *Sheriff's Department* stenciled along the sides and eased out of the big parking lot onto Cleland snapping on the seat belt while turning onto Prince Street.

He was still searching in his mind how to get his man to give him the answers he was looking for, hardly noticing that he had already gone over the Sylvan Rosen Bridge when the wheels of the car were unable to maintain a smooth ride.

Linus had entered into the *Bill Higgins* apartment complex, named after a beloved former mayor of Georgetown, although the sight of the low-income housing expanse suggested rather the opposite.

The pothole-riddled parking lot allowed owners and visitors to drive their vehicles as close to the house as they wanted to. There were no fences or curbs to prevent someone from slamming the brakes a couple of inches too late. Proof that this happened to a number of those row house-style homes became apparent to the interim sheriff after he halted the Crown Vic and the dust had settled.

Thompson was looking for 21B, but couldn't find it. Mumbling to himself, *I ain't gonna walk from house to house to find it,* when he recognized the faded remnants of the number 21 and, what looked like an A. He returned to the previous house and knocked on the metal door, whose corners were in an advanced state of decay. And at least one hole made a good argument that it was conceived by a 22 caliber bullet.

There was no reaction and Linus tried it again, this time harder, hoping he wasn't tempted to perform his karate kick, which could get him in trouble as it had done quite a few times before.

He paced a couple of times back and forth in front of the house when he heard the uneven footsteps, telling him that not only was somebody in the house but that it most likely was also the man he was looking for.

Clarence Woodburn had a bum leg. Claimed he got shot during the Vietnam War. But there existed at least half a dozen more reasons, most of them a lot less heroic, for the slight limp.

"You again. What d'you want now?" Clarence showed no exuberance to see the lawman who had questioned him about the murder of that young woman in Garden City.

"Well, aren't you letting me in? Would be fine with me. I can take you again to the office; we can have our chat there."

Woodburn opened the door a bit wider and let Linus step inside. "Yeah, and I told you last time that I had nothing to do with that murder."

Linus went ahead of Clarence and looked around the first one of the two-room dwelling and wasn't thrilled with what he saw. "You have a clean towel somewhere? I'm not going to sit on *that*." And he pointed at a sofa and the only chair, both covered with dirty clothes, tools, huge piles of newspapers, mostly inserts with advertisings.

"I ain't askin' you to." Clarence Woodburn shot back in defiance. But after a quick glance at the couch and the chair he decided clearing the latter to be less work. His limp and groans seemed way overdone to Linus, but he refrained from telling the man to stop the act.

Notwithstanding the seriousness of his visit the lawman did feel kind o' sorry for the man.

He had known Clarence all his life. Maybe five years younger than himself, Clarence Woodburn was raised by his grandmother. After his unmarried birthmother was unable to keep him he was passed from one foster home to another until he was about eight years old. That's when his grandfather died. He never wanted to have anything to do with him. So after he was gone his grandmother took him in.

After the man had dumped the laundry on the floor, Thompson perched on the wobbling piece of furniture and proceeded to interrogate the pathetic man who miraculously had found some room on the sofa.

"Listen, Clarence, you know why I'm here. When I questioned you the other day you were either unable or unwilling to tell me where exactly you had been on that Wednesday when the killing occurred."

Woodburn threw his hands in the air a few times; one eye began to twitch rapidly, constantly shifting his position from the right backside to the left.

He's nervous. Need to calm him down. Make him feel safe. Thoughts that he was on the right track seeped through Thompson's mind. He reached into the inside pocket of his uniform jacket, retrieved a pack of Marlboro cigarettes, pulled one out for himself and threw the pack with the two remaining fags at the man on the couch who feverishly snapped them out of the air.

"What are you so nervous about?" Linus asked casually, trying to maintain professional conduct. "If you haven't done anything illegal, you have nothing to worry about."

"Look," Clarence took a drag from the cigarette that could have burned a hole in his socks if he were wearing any, "I only heard about it from somebody. Didn't even know who the woman was.

"I know I done stupid things."

"You can say that again," Linus considered it his duty to confirm this.

"Yeah well, but I haven't killed nobody."

"Okay, then why can't you tell me where you were two Wednesdays ago. You surely couldn't have forgotten what you did where a week and a half ago." *Although, with him, that can't be totally ruled out.*

Woodburn's demeanor deteriorated further. He was unable to sit still, the eye was twitching non-stop now. And unable to expose himself any longer to the lawman's unrelenting stare he pushed his brittle torso out of the littered couch, shook his damaged leg and began to pace up and down the crammed room. And when he stopped in the middle of the room he said, gasping for breath, "Alright, alright. I was short of cash. Hadn't had anything to eat all day. So I picked up all the advertising pages they put inside the paper from Tom Hibbon's trash can. He gets the Gazette regular. I cut out the coupons and took'em to Walmart. Got me a few bananas and a bag of peanuts. But the woman at the cash register didn't accept some of the coupons on account that they were from Food Lion. So I returned the bananas and came home."

It took Linus a substantial amount of strength to keep firm. Clarence Woodburn, regardless of what mischief he had been accused and found guilty of, was just a pathetic creature. "About what time was that?"

"Way after lunch, two, three o'clock."

"Do you know the woman who refused to accept the coupons?"

Clarence was ready for that answer. "Oh yeah, sure do. Loretta King. Lives here, in the compound, 46 A."

The detective shook his head. *This man is unreal,* he thought to himself. *I need to get out of here, before they have to switch my uniform with a straight jacket.* "What about the following day, on Thursday?"

Still standing, but visibly calmer, Woodburn answered, almost self-assured, "Working."

"Working what, where?"

"Walmart. Loretta helped me to get a job offloading fertilizer, stuff for the garden."

At this moment Linus wasn't sure what was more amazing, the story itself or the bare casualness with which it was presented. *No one could make this up. Let me get this over with. It's getting downright creepy.* "And what do you know about the stolen truck?"

"What stolen truck?"

"Now don't play games with me, Clarence. I know that you and Michael Brown are buddies. I also know that you and Mikey have been hanging out occasionally in the shack behind Joe Grubbs' place with a bunch of other guys. I'm not asking you what y'all been doing there. That's not what I'm here for. I just want to know if you were there that Friday night."

Woodburn's frown indicated that he didn't like the direction in which these new questions were going. He picked up the pacing again. "Uh, maybe."

"Maybe, huh? How does this sound? You, Mikey and the other vandals were having a good time; all kinds of dope had already been passed around when you heard Joe's wrecker coming through the gate, with another pick-up in tow. How am I doing so far?"

Clarence just stood there, saying nothing.

Linus went on. "The whole gang watched how a man worked on that truck, fixed it and left. The truck was then unattended, when Mikey came up with the idea to use it for a ride.

"And here's where I need your help. Did Mikey tell you what precisely he intended to use that truck for? And may I tell you also that lying to an officer of the law is a federal offence which could put you in a Federal Penitentiary for a considerable portion of your current life expectancy. Just in case you are planning something this stupid."

"I know nothing about why he wanted the truck." Woodburn had resumed his position on the couch, and the twitching in the left eye was back.

"You see, Clarence, now I know that you were there without telling me. So I am warning you again. There's a huge difference between the Georgetown jail and a Federal Correctional Center.

"One more time, what did Mikey say he needed the truck for?"

"Said he could make some cash and dope." By now Clarence Woodburn looked like a beaten man, hunched over, supporting his head under the chin with both hands, elbows bent ninety degrees, planted on his thighs.

And Linus Thompson smelled victory. He felt confident that his man would also answer his next question. "What did he have to do in order to earn the cash and the drugs?"

But there was no answer coming from Clarence. Yet it seemed to Linus that it had less to do with him still being unwilling to cooperate but rather his inability to utter the words. And when he asked him, if it had anything to do with the shooting at the sheriff, he nodded twice. But then he whispered something under his breath that stunned the detective:

"They'll probably kill me."

Linus wanted to follow up on that but knew that he would not get any more out of Clarence Woodburn.

Then he called Caparelli.

Antonio Caparelli was sitting in the interrogation room of the Georgetown County Detention Center on Hwy 51 waiting for the officer to drop off Calvin Michael Brown. He had pulled another wooden chair closer so that his legs could comfortably rest on it. The call on his cell from Linus provided him with valuable information.

When Mikey was brought in the accompanying officer appeared to be more than just slightly annoyed. "Here's your boy. Thinks he has celebrity status."

Half pushed by the prison guard Mikey tumbled on the nearest chair from where he sized up the man on the opposite side of the rectangular table, raw defiance on his hollow-cheeked face.

Caparelli abandoned his relaxed position and faced the troubled young man. "Hi Mikey, good to see you again. Are they treating you satisfactorily? If not, I can check with the Hampton on the Bay if they have a vacant suite for you."

But the sarcasm quickly changed to the business on hand as it was reflected in his tone of voice and the tightening skin at the edges of his mouth. "Look, we know you stole the farmer's truck and drove it to Andrews. You admitted that much yourself.

"And at some point during that time frame you received a phone call, or placed it yourself. Now listen to my rendition of the events that followed including your shooting at the sheriff's car."

"Who told you that I shot at the sheriff?" I didn't—"

The detective cut him off instantly. "Unfortunately for you, asking questions is my prerogative, and **only** mine, *capisce*?

"The person on the other end offered you a deal. And the deal was for you to give the sheriff a scare. And when you heard that you would be reimbursed with cash and narcotics, which I found all or part of when I visited you last Monday, you didn't ask to what extent you were to 'scare' the sheriff, or even ask who the caller was. So that truck came like a gift from heaven and the timing couldn't be better, since you had seen the sheriff's vehicle in front of the Emerson house a while ago. Correct me where I am wrong, so that we can go on and explore the next phase of the drama."

With these mostly unproven accusations the detective was trying to get Brown come up with his own version of the event.

But Mikey's rebellious attempt to just protest against the accusation without any explanation was again stopped cold by the detective. "Since you insist on wasting my time I'm just going to assure you, we know that you did it. Couldn't keep your heroic accomplishments to yourself, could you? Had to brag about it.

"When was the last time you saw Darren Schloss?"

Now Brown looked at Caparelli with seemingly upright surprise. Then he said, "Don't know; two, three weeks ago."

"Well now, you're really pissing me off. Maybe there was no phone call at all, at least none that had anything to do with the case.

"Let's take a look at *this* scenario. You were in desperate need of a fix. Michelle was the only person left who might help you out, again. You got on your bike and hauled your sorry ass to Garden City. And when your sister refused to give you any more money, you lost it."

At that point a momentary fury was quickly replaced by the sober realization of his predicament. "You're crazy, but I am not saying any more without a lawyer."

Detective Antonio Caparelli got up, opened the door and called for the guard, "I'm done with this piece of shit. I know enough." And when the officer came, the prisoner and the detective locked their eyes on each other. Only one pair was smiling.

That same Friday morning at eight-fifteen Amos Grimm was sipping on his coffee, half decaf halve regular, reduced-fat milk. He and Marge were the only ones up. Brenda and Karl had not yet emerged.

The innkeeper had positioned herself in front of the cook top, watching the development of a heap of sun-golden scrambled eggs, joined by a few of her husband's favorite fried potatoes and bacon. And while she was gently stirring the fare she smiled at Amos. "Well, honey, I think your honorable attempt to cut back on caffeine and too much fat in milk will be shot after you are finished with this here," pointing the oil-dripping spatula at the sizzling frying pan.

Lifting up his mug Amos replied, acting seriously, "I'll just have another one of these to make up for it."

They both laughed at Amos' astute perception of nutritional science. "Look, I figured you had a rough week and—"

"Oh, sweetheart, it wasn't that bad. I had no trouble on either airport, had a car in Atlanta and Karl picked me up in Myrtle Beach—"

"That's not what I meant." Marge swallowed hard before she continued. "I meant I was a bit rough on you the other day. Spoke to Father Connelly about it. I understand what you're trying to accomplish. Just know that I am only concerned about your safety. That shooting didn't help reduce that concern, much less eliminate it."

"I know all that, honey. Let's get this case over with first and talk seriously about my retirement again afterwards. Would that be okay with you? Cause I know I wasn't quite honest with you about it."

The telephone rang before Marge's intended reply made it out of her mouth.

Amos pushed himself out of the chair and looked around. "I hate these wireless phones. Can never find the stupid thing."

But Marge had already found it and was sending her friendly *hello* into the speaker part after she didn't recognize the number on the narrow screen. "Oh hi, uh, Mary...yes, he's right here." Mouthing the name Mary Schloss to Amos she handed him the phone.

The call took about two minutes. "Schloss is coming back. She's a bit scared. His ex said he's behaving kind o' strange. I think I'll drive to Little River and on the way back I'll probably stop at Gwendolyn's; see if she has remembered a few more things about that triangle."

Marge looked at him, confused. "Who is Gwendolyn and what is this triangle?"

"She is Michelle Brown's and her brother's aunt. The two siblings and Darren Schloss constitute the triangle. And I'm sure in that triangle lies the answer to our puzzle."

The phone rang again, this time it was the one in his pocket. "Linus, anything new?"

"Well, sheriff, I just came from talking to Clarence Woodburn. He spilled the beans on our friend Mikey, who is being grilled right now by Caparelli." The satisfaction in Thompson's voice was unmistakable.

"Alright. Now call Tony and tell him to meet us in the office as soon as he's done with this Brown guy. Good work, Linus."

When the sheriff arrived at the station, Thompson and Caparelli were already there. The sheriff refused the coffee Linus was anxious to pour for him.

Both men rendered their report with professional ease. When they were finished Amos submitted this synopsis: "So, thanks to Woodburn we have Mikey on the hot seat. Wants to talk to a lawyer, huh? For the shooting alone he'll wind up behind bars for a long time. As you pointed out, Tony, he could've done it all by himself, including the murder of his sister. His capacious appetite for the wrong stuff gives us a pretty solid motive.

"He's not going anywhere. And I still want to find out if there actually is a caller who made that phone call from the empty hospital room and made him the offer he couldn't refuse." The sheriff got out of the chair and made a few steps toward the door when he turned around and faced the two men. "Just thought of something; although we have pretty much narrowed it down to those two guys, we still shouldn't leave anything to chance.

"Therefore I want you two to revisit also those folks who have given us helpful information in the beginning. Find out, if they can add to what they told us before. I'm thinking of the Emerson's in Andrews, Greta, Michelle's neighbor, even the waitress at Mama's Kitchen in Myrtle Beach – wait, I wrote her name down, yeah, here it is: Jamie Hendrix.

"And you know what, I was about to go by Michelle's aunt, Gwendolyn Brown. You might as well see her too, saves me a trip. Olivia has all the addresses. And I'm going to make sure we don't lose track of the elusive Darren Schloss. We want to find out if it was him, who placed that hospital call."

The two detectives looked at each other. Both had questions but kept them to themselves. Finally Linus spoke. "Let's get the addresses from Olivia."

The door to the Schloss house opened before the sheriff had even knocked. Mary Schloss literally pulled him inside as if to make sure nobody saw him.

"What's wrong, Mary? You look like you had been fighting off a grizzly bear," Amos questioned with elevated concern.

Mary Schloss gradually regained her composure, but had to heave a deep sigh before she could say anything.

Amos led her into the living room by giving her back a gentle push. "Now, Mary, before you say anything, I want to make sure if you're alone in the house."

She nodded, gripping her handkerchief a little harder.

"Alright then," the sheriff let her take a few more breathers before he encouraged her to speak. "Whatever it is that upset you; he is not going to hurt you; I vouch for your safety as long as I'm here and we decide what needs to be done afterwards."

Eventually she was ready to talk. "I am not in danger, at lest not right now, Sheriff. It's Darren. His ex wife called me last night; she's actually a very nice person.

"She wanted to let me know that Darren had gone from there. But she was unsure if he was coming back here. 'He was in a strange mood. I never saw him like that; kind o' detached; walked around like he was in a trance,' that's what she said. First she thought he was on something, you know, but before she could rule it out, he was gone.

"And then she told me why you are *really* looking for him."

The sheriff raised his eyebrows, but didn't say anything.

"If there is any truth to this, I mean, if he was involved in a murder, I am not sure if I should stay in this house." Then she forced herself to ask the unthinkable question. "Was it the woman from Garden City that was killed so brutally last week?"

"Yes, that's the case we are investigating. But by no means are we accusing your husband of that crime. Until we have solid proof, which we do not have as of yet, he's merely a person of interest." The sheriff's intention to calm her down a bit by giving her this glimmer of hope, failed. It seemed as if every ounce of blood had drained from her face.

"What we do know, however, is that Darren had been seeing this woman, Michelle Brown, for a while.

"But other than his whereabouts, there is only one more question I have for you. Has Darren ever mentioned a letter to you? A letter supposedly from Africa, actually Nigeria? One source has told us that he reacted to this letter visibly disturbed."

"He did not." And when Mary Schloss said this her eyes did not meet the sheriff's, but appeared to be fixated on a point in the far and hazy distance.

"We are going to have a patrol car stationed in front of your house tomorrow," Grimm assured her, not knowing if she was even listening.

He gently laid his hand on her right shoulder and left the house without a further word.

Karl and Brenda had managed to persuade Bo to accompany them to the Bay. After their *Snackathon* the previous day they had a late and, as always, delicious breakfast with Marge. Karl felt bad about having Amos leave without him and said so to the innkeeper.

"Amos wouldn't want it any other way. And so did I. You're only going to be here for two more days and should enjoy this time together. Have another sausage. You two skinny ones can absorb them. With Amos and me it's a different story."

Now they were relaxing at the tiny beach behind the recreation center, soaking in the midday sun, which did her best to dazzle the two with her warmest rays she was able to dispense this late in the year.

A few heavy sighs in between a steady breathing told them that Bo had recuperated from the rather long walk. With only the eyes shielded from the sun the rest of his weary body dared the daystar.

The couple was still amazed at the improvement of the canine's agility since Charlotte had achieved the almost impossible, when she was able to coax him away from his self-imposed exile under the holly bush in Mr. Meehan's yard. "It still baffles me how she related to Bo. Such a sweet girl."

But then Brenda returned to the presence and sighed, "I wished I could stay in this place forever."

"Yeah, me too," Karl agreed. "If Paradise was anything close to this it would be a lot harder for me to forgive Adam and Eve."

Brenda thought about Karl's remarks and wanted to ask him where this came from, but with a mischievous sparkle in her soft green eyes, whispered, "Yeah, this spot is simply out of this world. But that was not the place I had in mind. I was more thinking of my comfortable position."

Karl just shook his head and smiled. And eventually the woman who had rescued him from a life of regret, loneliness, and a complete lack of purpose lifted the back of her head off his lap and slung her arms around his neck.

They decided to get a sandwich at the *Bay Restaurant*, but approached the task reluctantly. With Bo it was more a passive rebellion. Karl watched his dog's flawless sign-language maneuver with great joy: first the removal of the paw, followed by a two-inch head lift and the eye contact with his master, before every part falls back into its previous position.

Translated into plain English all of this meant:

"What? No! Leave me alone."

And that ritual told Karl that his dog's refusal had nothing to do with age-related muscle pains.

"Alright then, we'll be off, Bo." And to Brenda he said, "Let's find out how long it takes him to give up and follow us."

Before they had reached the road behind the ball park the predominantly grey features of the creature appeared in the opening about a hundred yards behind them. They waited for him and together they strolled along Main Street, passed the Maritime Museum, which now housed also the Chamber of Commerce, the impressive building of the *Georgetown Gazette*, the Rice Museum with its landmark tower, before they reached the *Bay Restaurant*.

And when they got there, they didn't recognize it at first. A huge tent had been erected in the memorial park in front of the restaurant. A few boats were already parked along both sides of Main.

"Look over there." Brenda pointed to the right, where another long tent occupied a stretch of the mid section where Broad Street dead ends into Main. "That's where they are going to build the little skiffs for the races. You will see it all tomorrow."

They left Bo at the same lamp post that had served them for that purpose the first time Karl and his dog came to Georgetown.

Amy was talking to one of the waitresses. Her face lit up when her eyes caught the newcomers. The two women kept their embrace for what could almost qualify as a small eternity. It had been almost four years since Brenda had seen her former boss the last time. Brenda still felt deeply grateful for them to have given her a job when her life was in a tail spin.

"Bobby is in his office with the rest of the organizers for the show tomorrow. They're all a bit edgy at this point of the game. Let me get him. Are you going to eat?"

"That was the plan," Karl answered.

"Okay then, let me seat you."

A few minutes later Bobby Moore appeared in the aperture, looking for them. He smoothed his bushy moustache with his thumb and index finger and then stepped forward to meet his guests by the window. "Well," he said, after greeting them by pushing their partially raised bodies back onto the chairs, "don't get up."

Bobby Moore was not known for showing great emotions. What he was known for, however, was phrased by Henry Jones, the owner of the largest real estate company in Georgetown County: 'If you make a deal with Bobby Moore you don't even need to shake hands on it.'

"Well, it's really good to see both of you. I know we're all looking forward to the show tomorrow, and it's great that the event is growing, has been, every year. This one is going to be the twenty-first show. But the work is growing too. And on top of all that I still have to deal with this Sutton jerk; idiot doesn't give up. I really wished I could spend some time with you."

"That would be nice, but we'll be watching tomorrow. I'm sure we'll run into each other a lot."

"Well, I better get back; still fighting the City over a concession to allow visitors to consume adult beverages outside the buildings. By the way, you're both my guests in the sponsor tent tomorrow, and, of course, dinner tonight is on the house."

The Enforcer contemplated again and again upon the meeting in Atlanta. Babatunde had informed him that the project was about to be wrapped up. They had gone as far as they could without jeopardizing their cover. But not unlike most of his previous assignments *his* job wasn't finished yet.

This time he had to be painfully meticulous, more so than ever before. The person who had to be eliminated could only be reached or approached without his disguise. He had disposed of all his prop-ups and canceled the lease of the room he had used to prepare for the execution of the woman in Garden City.

He felt that his call from the hospital the other day had, for the moment, kept the sheriff's attention focused on that crazy drug addict.

Yet he knew it would be another restless night. And recently he had increasingly been visited by the first voice, urging him to abandon his criminal activities while there was still time. But he didn't trust the Organization and Babatunde to leave him alone if he told them that he wanted to get out. Blackmail was one of the strongest deterrents to keep the members in line.

And then it was there, surrounded by complete silence. Gradually his mind drifted into the familiar dream- like state. What did it really mean, anyway, reason? One of the answers to that question would be justification. And he felt absolutely justified to avenge the slaying of his father and the early demise of his mother. There were no innocent people. Anybody who got in the way of the Organization was against him, and therefore deserved to die.

I never told you that I was your voice of reason, although that's one part of me. I listened to your thoughts just now with great concern.

You shattered my hope, which is another part of me. But you are not even close to understanding that concept. I said it before, you need to ask God for forgiveness and run away from this cobweb of sin. But the One who sent me ordered me not to give up on you before your last breath on earth. So listen, this could be your last chance. Another part of me is love, unconditional love.

Ask the one who is no doubt coming after me what he knows about love. Remember, your time is running out. I surely wished I had more time to win you over. Sorry and may God have mercy on your soul.

And it came as no surprise to the Enforcer when the ear splitting screech announced the arrival of the other voice. The foul odor penetrating the car was even more repulsive than previously. But again, neither the inhuman sound nor the smell seemed to turn him off.

I didn't interrupt this time, because I wanted you to hear every word that liar threw at you.

There isn't very much to be added to what I told you a few days ago. But the choice is still yours. You can bow out now. In that case, however, I cannot guarantee your safety. You have signed up for this. And after it's all over you will recognize that operation XP 012 was a worthwhile endeavor. Poorer countries will benefit from this.

"How?" the Enforcer asked, surprised at himself for daring to interrupt the voice.

*I just told you, **after** the mission is over you will know. What's important for you to remember is that the end does justify the means.*

Remember, all bets are off, if you quit now.

Chapter Twenty

When the sun appeared Saturday morning over the tree line and ascended into another cloudless sky, the day promised to become just shy of spectacular. And by eleven o'clock it turned out to have kept its promise.

Karl, Brenda and Bo had left the Inn and were on their way to join the thousands of boat enthusiasts for a day of fun. The wooden boat show had over the years advanced to one of the most eagerly anticipated outdoor events on the south-eastern seaboard. What used to be a gathering of folks from Georgetown and Horry Counties had mushroomed into an affair that attracted visitors from as far away as Florida in one direction and Virginia in the other.

When Karl turned the Jeep from Church Street into Screven Brenda said, "Amos said the reserved parking for law enforcement was in the parking lot across from the old courthouse. That was really nice of him to do that for us."

Karl agreed and pointed to all the cars that were lined up on both sides of the street even before they had crossed Duke. "Where *would* we have left the car otherwise?"

"As of noon nowhere in the historical district." His Georgetown-born and raised wife obviously knew what she was talking about.

They found their spot right next to the sheriff's. The makeshift sign was marked *Sheriff's Department.*

"Now let's see if we can find us a boat that you will buy me one of these days," Brenda's smirk didn't deter Karl from playing along. "Yes, that's great. Maybe one of those builders will sell us his rowing skiff." The handbag hit him square on his left ear.

In mock surprise he declared, "Didn't know you had it in you."

The occupant in the back was tempted to shake his head, but refrained from doing so. Bo was not about to lower himself to the level of these two crazed humans. But he felt kind of a relief that they didn't want him to come along. With a bungee cord attached to the hatch and the trailer hitch as well as all the windows rolled down, Bo should be comfortable. And from the looks of it he already was.

Boats of all sizes and shapes were lined up on both sides of Main Street as far as the eye could see. The Shoemakers ambled along, stopped here and there to inspect a boat a little closer or listened to a proud owner give them a résumé of their craft.

The two admired the glassy-smooth mahogany rail of the Gloucester Light Dory, or the elegant symmetry on the modified Stephenson Weekender.

"It says here 'self built'. And were you that person?" Karl, the landlubber, was glad that he could start a conversation without giving away his total ignorance of boats made completely of timber.

"Sure am, yes sir. Took me three years."

And the cheerful gentleman sitting on a tripod chair next to a 20 foot boat, described as a *Simmons Sea Skiff*, skipped any kind of introduction when he noticed the couple stopping in front of his craft. "Got married on this one." At this point the weather-beaten face of this proud captain lit up even more. "Met this beautiful woman in Myrtle Beach six years back. When she saw the boat she didn't want to leave. And when I told her she had to take me too in the bargain, she agreed."

Karl and Brenda laughed politely and moved on. "Well," Karl was still grinning. "He was obviously more interested in sharing his private life with us than giving us the history of his skiff. He seemed to be warming up to handing us more details about his conquest."

"Well, he may have had his share of expert visitors requiring real answers from him, I mean technical answers pertaining to his boat."

They leisurely went on, passed the *Bay Restaurant* with the sponsors' tent to their left, and were about to leave the hotdog stand behind when Karl looked at Brenda and ...

"Let's have one, with everything," his wife looked back at him and smiled.

"ESP again?" Karl drew her closer to him.

They took the hot dogs and resumed their stroll along the sidewalk. There was a stand where children tried their skills in building a boat and tested its seaworthiness in a tank next to the stand.

Karl read the description of the next boat they stopped: *"Fourteen foot semi-Dory with center board moved six inches forward."*

"Look at this one: *Camp Cruiser with sail.* And here it says: *cumulative errors.* There must be a reason for such a confession. But let's not try to find out. We have lots more to see. I want to watch the boat builders."

And after a *Clancy – sail ten foot,* a *fifteen foot Runabout,* Karl read, almost with relief, *"Chris Craft twenty six feet.* Finally, a name I recognize."

Next were canoes and kayaks. "I heard they are new additions to the exhibit this year. Why shouldn't they? They are made of wood, aren't they?" Brenda remarked in defense of the more primitive, nonetheless masterfully crafted representatives in the show.

Clusters of people surrounded the canvas roof under which the row-skiff building race was underway. Karl and Brenda went inside where onlookers could watch the progress of the construction. Karl picked up a paper from the wood-chips covered floor. It was a special supplement to the Georgetown Gazette titled:

Twenty-First Annual
Wooden Boat Show

"Wow, there's more to the competition than racing on the river. You didn't tell me that."

"I only know about the race, that's all. What else is there? Read it."

Karl skimmed the article:

Wooden boat challenge
The wooden boat challenge
will begin at noon under the big tent
on Broad Street.
Two-man teams will race to
build a rowing skiff within a
four-hour time limit.
At 5p.m., the competitors will
test their completed skiffs for
seaworthiness in a rowing relay
across the Sampit River
The teams will be judged on
speed of construction, quality of
work and rowing ability.
Cash prizes ...

"To build a whole boat in four hours?" Karl shook his head in disbelief.

"Yeah," Brenda was eager to prove her superior knowledge about the process. "You see all these bottles lying around? If the boards aren't put together just right, neither more epoxy, caulking nor nails can improve the little doodad's chances to stay afloat."

"So, you know something about this?"

"No, I've only seen quite a few brave contestants freestyling it for the last ten yards to the dock, forcing to donate their disintegrating dinghy to the good old Sampit River."

"Alright," Karl chuckled at his wife's spontaneous sense of humor, but also knew that when this Southern girl was on a roll it was almost impossible to stop her. "On this charming note we might as well take Bobby up on his invitation and pay him a visit in the sponsors' tent. We'll have a few hours until the race across the *Channel*."

The inside of the sponsors' tent was invisible to the meandering public which gave them the apprehensive feeling of crashing a private party.

But this didn't last long. Bobby Moore, who stood right next to the entrance, stepped up to them and asked for their drink preferences. "I know that Brenda will recognize quite a few of her former patrons and friends. And so will you, Karl. I told the Stammtisch crowd that you were coming. But I don't think you know this gentleman," saying this he pulled at the upper arm of the middle-aged man next to him. "Steve, meet Karl Shoemaker; the man I talked to you about."

"Oh yes, I heard so much about you I feel I know you. I'm Steve. Good to meet you." Steve Kramer, the president of the Palmetto Steel & Wire Corporation, turned to face Karl and the two shook hands. "Likewise, and I am Karl."

Then Bobby introduced Brenda to Steve. "If she had left us for any other man I would personally have brought her back. There are even today, after – how many years has it been since he kidnapped and dragged you across the entire country?"

"Oh, Bobby, cut it out; he did neither. But it has been seven years. And I still love him not an ounce less."

"What I was about to say, Steve, even after so many years, visitors from as far as Canada ask about her."

"She must be a very special lady."

"Enough, you guys; wait, over there, Bobby, is that Louise, Louise Berkowitz?"

"It sure is." To her surprise it was Kramer who answered her question. "She is my secretary."

"Oh yeah? Haven't seen her in ages. Come on honey, let's go see her. Really nice to meet you, Steve."

Louise and Brenda had been close friends in high school, but hadn't seen much of each other after that. And after Brenda had introduced Karl to Louise he brushed her cheek with a fleeting kiss and said appropriately, "You guys must have a lot of catching up to do. I am just going to say hi to the mayor. First time I see him with a full set of hair." All three had a good laugh at that remark, since the haircut-incident many years ago had been broadly publicized.

The mayor seemed to be enjoying himself, judging from the boisterous laughter that was shaking his upper torso. The reason for his enjoyment seemed to be provided by the gentleman to his right, who introduced himself as Ernie, Ernest Knapp.

"Ernie is one of the big shots over at the steel mill," Jim Livingston slung his arm over Karl's shoulder and introduced him to Ernie. "This is the man who always shows up when someone gets killed in our neighborhood." And to both men he said, halfway seriously, "But let's give that unfortunate incident a rest tonight. We'll have to deal with it soon enough.

"Ernie was just telling me a few stories from way back, when the steel mill had just been built. They didn't have enough room in the main building for all the employees they had to hire for training and the subsequent start-up.

"So they put'em in trailers and placed them all alongside Frazier Street. And one day GTE had set up a telephone booth right across the street and in front of Ernie's trailer. You remember a few more of those strange calls, Ernie?"

"Maybe; we were such a crazy bunch then. I had just gotten my degree from Clemson and hadn't quite made the transition from a good-for-nothing student to the solemnity and responsibility of real work.

"Anyway, one day two guys in a pitch black late model Corvette, late as in the late fifties, parked in between Randy Southerland's Esso station and the telephone booth, which by that time was affectionately nicknamed Bertha by the informed.

"Luke Bingham was our man on the phone. He could imitate all kinds of voices, like the one of Jonathan Winters', when the comedian portrayed the oversexed grandmother; you remember... *'all over my body'*?

"So the two guys, one as tall as Joe Pesci, the other a bit shorter, their slick hair combed back, leather jackets the same color as the car, strutted past the booth in route to the *Swamp Fox Restaurant,* which was renowned for its legendary bread-pudding dessert. The demand for that delicacy was in fact so strong, that its availability and freshness had to be secured with the help of an eighteen-wheeler from the Pilot Trucking Company, which delivered two pallets of the stuff every quarter, come rain or shine.

"Although the outfits and the out-of-state license plate didn't particularly make those two guys more endearing to us, the prank was, as always, aimed at our good buddy Leonard Sharpstein, co-owner of the *Swamp Fox Restaurant.*

"Now, the real stimulus why our gang took such a shameless pleasure in Len's meteoric rise of his own blood pressure was his undeniable, gospel-true stinginess and self-destructing irritation following any disruption of his carefully honed business philosophy that centered around three areas of importance: *profit, accelerated profit, maximum profit* — and not necessarily in that order."

A few more people waved at them or nodded their heads in their direction; most, of course, were addressed to the mayor, who liked the attention for more than political reasons. To Karl's surprise, he too recognized quite a few of his acquaintances, old and new ones. Other than almost the entire Stammtisch crowd he spotted Bucky Hanschoe and his dad, the stern banker, the ever busy Joseph Hughes, who helped the caterers carrying drinks to thirsty guests, and of course Lois Catbury was yapping in all directions, at the same time, it seemed.

And there was a woman he was surely not expecting to see; Betty-Lee whatever her new name was now. Based on the younger man at her side she had obviously escaped that dark period in her life without as much as a blemish on her perfectly made-up face.

Brenda was still reminiscing with Louise and Karl turned his attention back to the telephone story. And Ernest Knapp was ready to share it.

"Well, in exactly that moment the shrill sound of the telephone in the booth stopped the two Pesci brothers in their tracts. On a scale of one to ten our success rate had been a nine and a half. As a matter of fact, we were so sure that they wouldn't resist the temptation, that some of the guys in the office added the words to the silent movie on the other side of the street.

"What the hell is that? You see anybody?"

"No, you?"

Both men are looking at each other.

"Let's see who that moron is who calls a public phone number. Didn't even know you could do that." He steps back and picks up the phone. *"Hello!"*

Now Luke Bingham enters the scene. "Well, who the hell do you think you are? Just because you're from New York and drive a Corvette don't give you the right to park that piece of shit in my parking lot."

The guy on the phone looks at his friend, then at the parking lot, which would be completely empty, if it weren't for the Corvette. "What the f ... are you S.O.B. talkin' about? We were just gonna have—"

"Not in my place, you arrogant dirt bags. Get back in that contraption of yours and haul your asses out of here. Pronto!"

The man slams the phone against the wall. There is no reenactment necessary anymore. The two little fellows have turned into raging bulls, yelling obscenities at no one in particular, throwing their arms in the air and pointing the infamous fingers at the restaurant.

"I bet you they're not going to the car," offered by one of the office guys, turned out to be a safe bet. The two Pesci brothers stormed straight into Leonard Sharpstein's Holy Grail.

"A few days later we learned from patrons and kitchen staff what happened. Apparently one of the New Yorkers punched the welcoming smile off of Len's face and the other one retrieved the first full bucket from the kitchen and dumped content and bucket over his head.

"Leonard Sharpstein didn't talk to us for three weeks. However we felt better when the waitresses told us that they were under strict orders not to give us any dessert, which was included in the price of the meal, for six months to make up for the loss of a bucket full of the finest bread pudding in all of Georgetown County, ... which the waitresses equally strictly disobeyed.

"One of Ernie's telephone jokes?" Bobby Moore had been swiftly moving from one group to another, talking or listening, thanking people for their support. "Did he also tell you the one with the school children?"

Karl shook his head, not quite sure if he was ready for another of these Southern-flavored tales.

"From time to time the steel mill conducts group tours of the plant. This one was for a class of fifth graders, who were as interested in the steel-making process as I'm in the art of basket weaving. It was also one of the hottest days of the summer. When they came out this Bingham kid – fittingly he's now a vice president in the Burroughs and Chapin Company in Myrtle Beach, in charge of the Amusement Park – dialed the phone booth number and it didn't take more than two rings before the first boy answered it while the teacher was still ushering the rest of the class across the street.

"'Hey, you guys must be thirsty like the dickens. I am the owner of the restaurant you're lookin' at. Why don't y'all come over for a free coke.'

"Luke hadn't quite finished when the kid stormed out of the booth and without stopping waved at the cluster of dumbfounded classmates yelling the two earthshaking words, '**free coke**'.

"Three or four kids made it out of the restaurant with the broadest smiles on their faces, cherishing their golden prize, when the embodiment of the devil appeared in the door and demanded his pay with the reinforcement of a few choice words that made the clueless Mrs. Fenton cringe."

While he was telling that story he nudged Karl forward until they were out of earshot from the mayor and Ernest Knapp. "I hoped you didn't mind me dragging you away from those two. Want you to meet some more of our most generous supporters. And for the next thirty minutes Karl Shoemaker shook more hands than he probably had the entire year prior to this day.

"Well, I'll be ..., take a look at the fellow over by the bar, right next to one of the coolers, white hair, respectable beer belly, yellow short-sleeve shirt. See him?"

"I do. Seems to be having a good time."

"He always has a good time. He's a character alright; name is Closecall Overstock. His real name is Alfred, but everybody calls him Closecall; stems from a time when Georgetown had the dubious reputation of being the only municipality in South Carolina and beyond that allowed a dozen or so ladies of the night to practice their craft in a house called *Sunset Lodge.*

"And when his wife Mathilda received an anonymous phone call that her husband's car had been seen there she decided to pay him a visit.

"Seeing his wife driving up Closecall has to act fast, real fast. He tells the *staff* to stall her and calls a couple of friends at EMS.

"All the wife sees is a stretcher with a body on it covered with a blanket from head to toe. When Mathilda comes home, she confronts him. 'Don't even attempt denying it. I saw your car at the brothel and—'

"'You **did?**' He picks up the phone and dials seven numbers. 'Is the chief there? Oh, well, let me talk to Linus... Yes, Alfred Overstock here. Just wanted to let you know you may call off the search for my car. We found it. Yes, and thank you very much.'

"From that day on Alfred became Closecall."

Laughing hard, Karl thought he heard that story before. "After this I need another beer. My mouth is dry and I have hardly even said a word. Do you guys ever get serious around here?"

Bobby just stood there, looking intently in one single direction. "Yes, at least *I* am, in fact, right now. Look who has honored us with his presence."

Karl followed the restaurant owner's line of vision and couldn't believe what, or rather who he saw. Jacque Sutton stood near the entrance, engaged in what seemed like a heated discussion.

"You have to give it to him," Bobby conceded, still furious. "He's no dummy. Knew exactly we didn't have time to return his donation before the show. We received his check for 200 bucks yesterday. So he has all rights to be here. But I don't like it, don't like it one lousy bit."

"Just try to ignore him, Bobby, uh, Robert Forrest," Karl suggested with a smile in an effort to defuse any bad intentions his good friend might harbor, and earned a small grin in return.

"Who is the man with the red crew cut he is lecturing?"

"Oh, that is the new exec they hired at the steel mill; runs the sales department; supposed to be really sharp."

Bobby looked at his watch and with a surprised expression on his face uttered under his breath, "Wow, where's the time gone? The race is gonna start in ten minutes. They must have already picked the winner for the first part. I've got to go, Karl. See you outside." He took a few steps, then turned around, gave Karl a thumbs up, and didn't give Sutton as much as a look.

Time to break my wife away from her longtime friend. Don't want to miss that race.

And while Karl was snaking through the crowd – the canvas pavilion had filled up considerably, and with it had the intensity of the noise – he almost brushed against an older guy, who showed already some signs of inebriation.

He apologized to the man. His bloodshot eyes were riveted on a slender brunette who was trying to maintain her catwalk-style steps towards the wine bar.

And by the singsong slur in the tone of the man's voice he believed to recognize one of the regulars in the bar of the restaurant. "She still has the moves."

There was no guessing necessary, however, to identify the author of the ostentatious announcement that followed:

"Otis, shut your trap. The only moves you should worry about are the ones of your bowels."

Sorry Lois, not now. He made himself a bit smaller, turned his head away from where that sagacious counsel originated and was more than modestly pleased when he had reached the safe haven in the form of Brenda and Louise.

The women seemed to be wrapping up their mutual trip on memory lane. "And I ought to go over and chat a bit with my boss. He looks somewhat lost. I have your e-mail address now. Let's promise to stay in touch," and to Karl the secretary said warmly, "It was truly nice meeting you Karl."

Brenda and Karl joined the huge crowd gathered along the boardwalk, all ready for the highlight of the day, the boat race across the Sampit River. The first two contestants had already taken their skiffs to the starting line.

Right at that moment Karl's phone rang. "Having a good time?" It was Amos.

"Aren't you coming?" Karl had been expecting him hours ago.

"Well, two things happened. I got another call this morning from Mary Schloss. She was really shook up this time. Her husband had been in touch with her. Told her he was coming home to pack some clothes. He also asked her to get some of his personal papers together. He had to stay away from South Carolina for a while. That it wouldn't be for long and for her not to worry. He had done nothing wrong."

"That must have been immensely comforting to her," Karl infused cynically.

"Yeah, I bet. She's scared stiff of him. Afraid what he will do to her if she doesn't follow his instructions.

"And listen to this. While she was looking for his personal files, she found his birth certificate. Guess where Mr. Schloss was born?"

"I'm waiting."

"I think she said Liberia. But it could be that other country; sounds similar."

"Nigeria?"

"Yeah, I believe so. They're both in Africa, aren't they?"

"They are," Karl wondered where the sheriff was going with this. But he didn't have to wait long for an answer.

"You remember Caparelli's description of the way Michelle's body looked, 'covered with zigzagged slash wounds.' Don't sound like the killer used a kind of tool we here are familiar with. Toni once mentioned to me her torso gave him the impression as if she had been the victim of a tribal slaying in the jungle of Africa."

"Doesn't that sound a little far reaching to you?" Karl was less than convinced.

"Yeah, but what about the books about Africa you found in Michelle's apartment? You yourself found them out of place among all the legal and medical reference books."

"Hmm!"

"Then there is the ominous letter he's allegedly so concerned about, which according to Gwendolyn came from Africa. Too many coincidences, if you ask me."

"And what is the second thing?" Karl asked.

"What thing?"

"You said two things happened."

"Oh yeah, I got the search warrant. I'm gonna ride over to Little River. Don't want to miss our boy."

Karl had to admit, Amos had done his homework. *Well, that's why he is the pro.* "I'm going with you. Can you pick me up here somewhere? Then Brenda can stay here and watch—"

"No way, you two stay right there and enjoy that spectacle together. I am taking Tony with me. All we do is put the cuffs on the guy and bring him here. I'll be in touch when we get back. By the way, Linus is also on Main Street, just in case somebody should step out of line."

"Do we have to leave?" Brenda made sure her spouse didn't miss the inclusion of herself.

And Karl didn't. "No, *we* don't have to leave."

She had to tiptoe in order to plant a loving kiss on his lips.

With their arms around each other's hips the couple moved a little closer to the edge of the river hoping to get a better view of the rowers. "I need to be excused for a minute. The wine, you know."

Karl smiled, walking with her and said, "Might as well go too, the beer, you know."

Laughing at their childish behavior they stepped through the entrance of the restaurant.

Karl was by himself in the men's room, so he thought, until he overheard a heated discussion between two men behind the door separating the urinals from the toilet. The discussion escalated to a vicious argument in a hurry. Karl didn't recognize one voice, a very boisterous one at that, and every time the second man spoke the toilet was flushed. *This is weird, I better get out of here before the fists are flying and one of them crashes through the partition.*

He mentioned the incident to Brenda after she returned. "One of the two didn't want to be heard, while the other obviously didn't care."

"Why do you say that?" Brenda didn't follow right away.

"Because every time the loudmouth stopped and it appeared that the second combatant was about to retaliate, the toilet was flushed and drowned out most of what he said."

"Interesting, let's hope they work it out without hurting each other.

But now we're going to enjoy the race. Look here, the first two are already on their way."

They were pretty even, weaving erratically from one side to the other, both took a wide turn and rowed as hard as their remaining strength allowed.

Then one rower took a small lead, just about twenty yards before the finish line. One could see the victory smile on his face through the strain. A large group of people cheered him on. That's when he lost one oar.

Complete silence ... for about ten seconds. Then another group spurred on the second skiff which was now catching up in a hurry.

And with about ten yards to go it was a dead heat. Karl and Brenda craned their necks to see who would emerge as the winner. But all they saw was a sideboard all by itself floating aimlessly in the water.

Someone shouted, "He's losing another one."

"Don't they have to bring the whole skiff in? Oh, now he's takin' on water," a second observer's voice was about to crack.

"Yeah, but skiff number two didn't finish with a whole boat either. He lost an oar. Aren't they part of the boat?" This comment by a woman in her forties made the speculations of the outcome more intriguing.

Karl and Brenda had a fantastic time, laughing themselves silly. "Let's hear what the "official" ruling will be." Karl pointed to a young man with a megaphone in his hand.

And when it was ruled a tie Karl applauded the verdict: "Worthy of Solomon!"

"Where did that come from? Just hold your answer. I think I left my light sweater in the pavilion. I'm feeling the chill a bit. Be right back."

"Young lady, if you think I'll let you roam around by yourself again, you're out of your mind."

"Are you jealous?" Brenda slipped into her playful disposition.

"Constantly."

Most of the sponsors and invited guests were still inside. Brenda fetched her sweater and was about to go back outside. But Karl quickly stepped in front of her, gently cradled her head with his hands, and kissed her passionately.

"Look, you and I are going to take a time-out. I'm sure this guy over there at the bar will be happy to pour us a glass of wine. What do you think?"

"I think that's a wonderful idea."

The bartender poured them both a glass of Piesporter Riesling Spätlese.

Three quarter of an hour and two more glasses of wine later Brenda said with honest regret in her voice, "I wanted so bad for you to see the little boat race, but," and her face brightened up momentarily, "I shall relish this endearing time more than you will ever know.

"Incidentally, did it occur to you that our intimate tête-à-tête took place in the company of, what, eighty people?"

"So?" laughing at his unusually brave display in those matters. "But, alright, back to the race."

They were passing through the entrance when Linus Thompson stood in front of them, out of breath, his face chalk-white.

"What is it, Linus?"

"Need to talk to you." His sidelong glance at Brenda told Karl the interim sheriff intended to talk to him alone.

"It's alright, go ahead."

"There's a male body in that little storeroom where the restaurant keeps their trash. I called the sheriff."

"What did he tell you?"

"Not to let anybody other than EMS and the coroner close to the place. We've taped off the area."

"Is he dead?"

"Yes."

"Who found the body?"

"One of the dishwashers, when he took out the garbage. He's in a squad car. He only told one of our officers. Public doesn't know the man is dead."

"Okay, keep it that way. And communicate with the sheriff."

Linus stretched his neck sideways and cupped a hand around his left ear. "The ambulance, need to go."

Karl took the first deep breath and a quick glance around the interior of the tent. Into Brenda's ear he uttered, "You see Sutton?"

"No."

"Let's go!"

The two sprinted down Main, into Screven, where the news had not yet spread to.

Bo's snout was leaning out of the open space in the rear, but the two jumped into their seats and Karl maneuvered the Jeep out of the parking lot.

"Passed Hobcaw Barony," Brenda wheezed, trying to catch her breath. "Go straight to Church. Then hang a right. Wait, not here," she was shouting now, "that's Highmarket. Now go to James, then left back to Church.

"Karl, what are you doing? I said James, not Cannon. What's wrong with you? I thought you could hold it better together. Now take—"

"Someone else was missing."

"What are you talking about, Karl, listen to me."

But Karl didn't. About hundred yards further he brought the vehicle to a screeching halt, on the sidewalk.

He thrust himself out of the car and bolted for the door, which gave way without a lot of resistance.

The front room revealed no clue, and neither did the second. Karl's brain was in overdrive now. *What if I'm wrong and let the real murderer escape?* He turned around to catch at least a glimpse of encouragement from his wife.

But, if anything, Brenda felt sorry for him.

He left that place and stepped back onto the narrow hallway. At the end, against the back wall, some boxes were stacked all the way to the ceiling. Although it was almost totally dark in the hallway, Karl thought he could make out the outline of another opening.

When he got there, that door was closed. Or was it? There was no keyhole and the doorknob turned easily. "Something behind that door is blocking it," he whispered to Brenda behind him.

"Or somebody," her frightful remark hung in the murky air like a flock of bats in a cave, ready to burst into their nocturnal hunting ground.

Ever so slow, inch by inch, was Karl able to push the door open, enough to squeeze through. "You stay here."

And then he saw it. The woman had already lost most of her blood. Trickles of it joined the huge pool around her. When Karl took a closer look from where the drops of blood came from, he noticed that both carotid arteries on either side of her neck were severed.

Brenda, still on the other side in the hallway, was trembling and a cold sweat was taking over her body. Afraid of a panic attack she hunkered down and began to weep.

"I'll be out shortly, baby. Hang tight. I love you."

"I love you too, hurry."

Karl noticed a sliver of daylight brightening a tiny area of the room. Carefully he felt his way to that spot. It turned out to be a window with the blinds drawn. He rolled them up and could see the rest of the room.

And in the far corner he discovered another lifeless pile. The man wasn't even clinging to his life any more. The shifting eyes, the erratic, almost indiscernible pulse beat gave Karl Shoemaker solid reason for the conviction that Joseph Hughes wasn't going to be among the living much longer, less than a hundred of those fading heartbeats. Then he saw the empty bottle on the floor, looked at the description and murmured, devoid of any sympathy, "Make that half of that."

The words that barely oozed out of the dying man's mouth made no sense to Karl. "Sorry man, that's not going to improve your legacy," was Shoemaker's reply.

Brenda hadn't moved one inch from where he left her. She was still shaking uncontrollably.

"Alright, sweetheart, there's nothing else we can do here." He helped her up and held her tight until she had steadied herself.

"Now we have to find the girl; I am so scared ... look at that!" There was Bo looking at them around the corner from one of the rooms they had searched earlier. He barked twice and then disappeared, back into the room. When the two got there they witnessed the most amazing thing. Bo was on his hind legs, howling incessantly, and scratching at a door that they had overlooked earlier. The canine was trying to turn the knob, but the strain on the back legs was too much for him to stay in that position long enough to accomplish the task.

Karl and Brenda were at his side momentarily and finished the job he had started.

Charlotte cowered inside of what looked like a laundry closet. Right away Bo was all over her, licking her endlessly until the girl, frightened beyond comprehension, slowly began to respond to his caresses.

Chapter Twenty-One

On Sunday afternoon Amos Grimm had invited Steve Kramer, the president of PSW and Robbie Clemens from the Georgetown Gazette to his office at the Sheriff's Department. He had summoned interim sheriff Linus Thompson and detective Antonio Caparelli. Karl Shoemaker had come with the sheriff.

"You may wonder why I asked Steve Kramer to join us this morning. But the murder of the head of his sales department yesterday, as heinous as that one was by itself, has also shed a different light on our investigation into the homicide of Michelle Brown. And I'll let Steve explain to us shortly why he thinks these two are linked.

"I had offered Robbie to have the first crack at the story. And I did this for two reasons. First I gave him my word and second because he kept his. And I thank you Robbie for being patient. You'll see it was the smart thing to do. The paper will thank you."

This well-intentioned praise coming from one of the most respected leaders in the region made the young newspaper man blush more than he probably felt comfortable with.

"Now, before I ask Steve to tell us how his company fits into all this, I want you two, Linus and Toni, to give us your take on Clarence Woodburn and Michael Brown."

"Well," Thompson looked at his notes, but immediately shoved them aside. "Clarence Woodburn is arguably the most dejected person in Georgetown. Even his various stabs at crime turned out to be a string of tragic comedies. But Sheriff, I don't think he had any part in this murder affair, not even in a supporting role. And let's not forget, he helped us to establish the link between Brown's stealing the truck and the shooting.

"I wanted to ask you something while we're talking about Clarence. We need to get him off the streets. He has too much time between his sporadic labor jobs. His nutty break-ins always happened when he was out of work.

"Bubba Fulps, the janitor over at the jail, is about to retire. He can hardly lift the broom anymore. I felt sorry for him the other day. Maybe we could give that job to Clarence. He would have some regularity in his life and the close proximity to the jail cells might discourage him from launching any more of those lunatic misdemeanors."

"That's a fine idea, Linus. We'll have to run it by County Council, but I don't foresee a problem.

"But I don't believe that Michael Brown will get off that easily, right, Toni?"

"Absolutely not, Sheriff." Caparelli had been anxiously awaiting his turn. "He will spend time in jail, and possibly a lot of time. Possession of illegal substances, theft, and attempted murder would require a lawyer the likes of F. Lee Bailey to get him off the hook."

"Yeah, but that will no longer be our responsibility. And thank God for that, if you ask me.

"And when all this happened here in Georgetown I was on the way to Little River, to wait for the arrival of our, at least at that time, primary murder suspect, Darren Schloss. I had received a hint from his wife that he might be coming home, just to pack some clothes and take off again.

"And the timing was perfect. He could have killed Mr. Strickland in Georgetown and be back in Little River not much after I got there. That's the reason I kept going when Linus called me. I parked the Explorer around the corner where it could not be seen from his house.

"Mary's discovery that Darren was born in Africa made that notorious letter all that much more important. And when he showed up about twenty minutes after me I asked him from where he just came. His response that that wasn't any of my business didn't surprise me. Modesty just isn't part of this man's DNA.

"Then I showed him my search warrant and for the first time noticed a change in his demeanor. But that change was not in the direction I hoped. With the level of his conceit a notch higher he pulled out an envelope and handed it to me. I don't even want you to guess the content of the letter, because in contrast to the grisly murders it sounds almost comical.

"A woman in Lagos, Nigeria, had tracked him down and claimed that he fathered her child during his stay there while serving a year in the Peace Corps. The letter was written on official stationery from the Ministry of the Interior in Abuja.

"And while I was reading that he said, 'And to answer your question, I just came from my lawyer to find out how or if I should react'.

"We were able to confirm this. Does this remove him as a suspect in the murder of Michelle Brown? Not by itself. But in light of what happened yesterday there is little doubt who the killer was. The same zigzagged wounds inflicted on Michelle and described by Tony as the most gruesome he had ever seen were found on the torso of Mr. Strickland. And the weapon, a cut-off machete, located on the premise of Mr. Hughes, his prints all over it, can now officially be declared as the murder weapon. All that was confirmed by the lab.

"Unfortunately there is nothing in our law books that punishes someone for being a jerk. And that's what Darren Schloss is, a certified jerk.

"Well, let's move on here. Don't want to keep Steve waiting much longer.

"Now, Steve, you may very well be the one delivering the smokin' gun in this horror movie that could have come straight out of a Steven King book."

The president of the steel mill gave them a quick account of their financial situation, and the offer from this

Nigerian outfit to buy shares from the company, which never materialized.

"As I told the sheriff this morning, after Jason's body was found yesterday, I smelled a rat and we did some investigating ourselves. He was the only one among our top managers who wanted us to hang on to the African proposition, even after I had suggested giving the guy a two-day ultimatum. And I told that to the man, who called himself Samuel Okune, in no uncertain terms that same day, Thursday.

"We all know of these scam artists from that corner of the world who lure old grandmothers into giving them their social security information and what else to deposit huge amounts of money into their bank accounts.

"So in order to rule out any kind of foul play, we had a law firm in Surfside Beach check them out."

At that point the sheriff raised his arm a couple of inches off the table. "Excuse me, Steve, for interrupting, but you just brought up the point where I have to jump in.

"And for that law firm, *Harper and Cornelius,* our first victim, Michelle Brown, did some paralegal work in her apartment."

Turning to Karl he added, "Remember the literature you found in her apartment, you thought a bit out of place?"

"Well I'll be damned," was all that came out of Shoemaker's mouth.

Kramer went on. "But when we hacked into Strickland's computer we couldn't believe our eyes. Entire systems specifically developed for the production of steel in electric arc furnaces, the newest designs in the field of direct reduction methods, even charts outlining the mechanics of operation processes like production planning or quality control. I don't want to bore you with shop lingo, but believe me; he has, or rather was about to, give the store away, technically and financially.

"He obviously felt so secure; he even left a personal income statement in his desk drawer. And that income was not shabby. We at the mill understand now why our sales figures were so low in a reasonably stable market. He had raised a real cash cow which he intended to milk for as long as possible.

"Jason Strickland had become a greedy collaborator in an international industrial espionage heist, whose ramifications could've been far-reaching.

"And it was greed that finally caught up with him. His insistence to keep the deal going brought him face to face with his killer."

The sheriff thanked Mr. Kramer for his quick and effective response to the tragedy. "And if you ever get tired of the steel industry, I'm sure you could have a great career in law enforcement. We were truly tapping in the dark until yesterday.

"I am also very proud of my two colleagues Linus and Toni for their diligent and methodical police work. When I heard that the festivities went on after the body was discovered I was impressed.

"So I am announcing my retirement ... for the second time. And this time I mean it. Linus, I suggest you take Toni here as your assistant. With both of you at the helm the department will be in good shape.

"And last, but definitely not least, do I want to thank my friend Karl again. His keen recognition of the situation is about to become legendary in Georgetown."

It was on extremely rare occasions that emotions got the better of the seasoned lawman. This was one of them.

On the way home Amos was shaking his head, and turned to his passenger. "I still don't get it. People liked him. You wonder what goes on in someone's mind that is capable of committing a crime with such evil intent. And why did he not use the same weapon when he killed his wife? You think he would have killed the girl too, but didn't find her?"

Karl Shoemaker shook his head. Could there even *be* an answer to these questions?

Yes, there was somebody who knew the answers. But Luca Babatunde, aka Samuel Okune, was at that very moment flying over the Atlantic Ocean, enjoying a glass of Christian Moreau Chablis Les Clos in the first class section of West African Airways.

Brenda had spent most of the night at the Georgetown Memorial Hospital. Charlotte had been brought to the trauma unit for observation. They had given her some sleep-inducing medication that it was no surprise to Brenda that she was not awake at ten o'clock.

She had taken the Jeep to get a shower at the Inn and freshen up. It all had happened so fast. Three savage killings and a suicide in a little over a week. While her brain refused to assimilate information of such barbarous nature at the present time, she shifted every ounce of her concentration and strength to the care of the little girl.

Late yesterday evening the physician in charge of the trauma unit told her that she was amazingly coherent for having witnessed something that horrendous; even if she didn't see everything. "In rare cases," the doctor said, "if children are showered with love and compassion immediately after or better yet, during the ordeal, they don't go through all the traumatic set backs that usually afflict young victims or witnesses of violent acts. It seems Charlotte was very lucky to have had you and your husband to have come to her rescue."

Thank you Doctor, but if Charlotte will be alright, it has nothing to do with either Karl or me, but everything with a four-legged, grey-bearded, hundred and twenty-pound canine.

Due to the tumultuous weekend Karl and Brenda agreed to postpone their departure until they knew that Charlotte was going to be alright and a good relative found to raise her.

Brenda and Marge were the first visitors at Social Services Monday morning. The innkeeper looked around and her eyes lit up when she recognized a familiar face. They both strode up to that window.

"Now I declare. What in the world brings you here, Marge? You and I are too old to still have runaways at home." A woman with a friendly round face, got up right away, opened the door next to her and greeted Marge in the lobby with a warm embrace. And when she tried to introduce Brenda, the seasoned social worker took one look at her and exclaimed enthusiastically, "Well, if this isn't Larry Davenport's little girl, I ain't Eula-Mabel Watkins. Come here, girl." And Brenda, too, received a big hug from this hospitable Southern lady.

Mrs. Watkins led them into a separate room, where bright furniture, a not too large round table with about eight chairs, cushioned in a soft green color, and paintings on the wall with scenes of sun-lit local beaches, gave whoever came here to seek help an uplifting boost.

The three lamented over the lives lost during Saturday's massacre before Marge and Brenda brought up Charlotte. "We need to find out if and where there are close relatives," Marge stated, urgency in her tone of voice. "I just hope there will be some good kinfolk, on her *mother's* side, to take her before you let her embark on the foster-parents' circuit."

That thought sent shivers down Brenda's back and she gave her friend a frightful glance.

"Well, there are some wonderful families who are looking for children to adopt, some even more suitable to raise children than a few birth parents I know.

"The question of existing relatives would have come to our department eventually. However I can tell from your appeal that 'eventually' won't do in this situation. And I agree with you. We have to find a stable environment for that poor little thing as soon as this is possible.

"I'm sure that the police have all of the family's documents at the moment." Winking at Marge she added, "I know somebody who has connections to the sheriff. He could speed up the bureaucracy. In the meantime I'll have one of the girls in our office go to the courthouse and copy the records of the, what was that name again?"

"Hughes, Joseph, but I wouldn't hold my breath on that," Brenda cautioned.

At ten-thirty Brenda was back in the hospital and hurried straight into Charlotte's room. One of the doctors on duty was chatting with her. Brenda was overjoyed to hear the little girl's voice.

The physician asked Brenda if he could have a few words with her before she talked to the girl. And with Charlotte's hazel eyes riveted to hers Brenda mouthed the words *I will be right back – promise.*

"Mrs. Shoemaker, I am not very familiar with the procedures in this case, since it is my understanding that you are no relative of hers. So I have to ask you to take this up with administration.

"My colleagues and I observed her for any repercussions, psychological as well as physical, and have no objection to releasing her today. Of course, there's bound to be some emotional backlash later on. That will have to be expected and dealt with when it occurs. But for right now she needs a lot of TLC."

When Brenda returned to the room and gently ran her hand across the child's brow and temples Charlotte asked her a question that brought Brenda almost to her knees: "Is my mummy in heaven now?"

If nobody told her, how could she know, unless she saw something.

Fighting and holding back the tears she answered, not able to completely hiding the tremble in her voice, "Oh, sweetheart, I am absolutely sure of this. But now I have to sign a few papers to get you out of here.

"Would you like to come with me to the Inn and Ms. Marge ... and Bo?"

"Yes," there was a frail, but irrefutable glow in her innocent eyes.

"Just sign here," the lady who took care of Charlotte's discharge had already erased the word closest relative with closest friend. She noticed Brenda's surprised look and said with an informed smile, "The sheriff took care of the rest."

Brenda silently thanked Amos, picked up the bag with some clothes for Charlotte, which she had bought earlier, and darted back to the elevators.

Later that afternoon Amos was reading Robbie Clemons' first-page article in the Gazette entitled: THREE DEATHS AND ONE SUICIDE BELIEVED TO BE THE RESULT OF AN INTERNATIONAL INDUSTRIAL ESPIONAGE ATTEMPT

After he read it he tossed it back on the table and said, "His daddy will be mighty proud of him.

"Contrary to the murder of Michelle Brown Hughes threw all caution in the wind this time. Apart from the fact that there is absolutely no doubt that he's responsible for the killings, including his own, he didn't even make a serious attempt to hide the murder weapon in the Strickland slaying. He probably knew this was the end."

"That," Karl added, "or time, rather the lack of it, didn't allow him to be as tedious as he was in Garden City. And as far as trying to make sense about the horrendous attack on his wife, your guess is as good as mine. But I suggest we abstain from any speculation here and trust she has already passed through the gates of heaven."

"Amen to that," Marge applauded that wish before she had to answer the phone.

Although the mood among the friends at the Inn was still somewhat subdued, the outlook wasn't that bad, actually not bad at all.

Charlotte and Bo were inseparable in the room adjacent to the lobby.

Amos' decision that he really would retire now brought tears into Marge's eyes. And this time she actually believed him. Times had changed, crimes had become more brutal. The wear and tear on his body was visible and both knew it.

And when Marge got off the phone she informed them that Eula-Mabel Watkins had been unable to find a relative to take care of Charlotte. "At least not a suitable one. There is an aunt of Melanie's ... she resides in a nursing home. It seems that Charlotte's mother was a late-comer to a family who had already three children, all boys, between fifteen and twenty years her senior; two of her siblings are deceased, and the third one lives in Australia. Yeah, and Melanie's parents died of natural causes in their nineties.

"Charlotte's birth father, a man by the name of Ben Carson, Melanie kept that name for both of them, died of pancreatic cancer shortly after Charlotte was born.

"And she couldn't find anything about Joseph Hughes, much less a relative. Strange, if you ask me.

"All of this is devastating news for Charlotte. But what else can we do?" She had directed that question at Brenda who looked as if she was thanking the Lord for that *devastating news.*

"How can you be so—" she twisted her head in search of Karl, who was clumsily hiding behind the sports section of the newspaper.

"Oh God Almighty! Amos, those two here are about to spring another big one on us. Look at them. She almost fell on her knees when I said that there were no suitable relatives who could take the poor little girl. Karl, you can come out from behind the paper."

The revelation of the younger couple's intent to take Charlotte with them to Wyoming brought rivulets of tears to the eyes of the women, and prompted the retired sheriff to open a bottle of Alfred Basely Brut Champagne, the only one in the house, held in reserve for very special occasions.

It goes without saying that the grown-ups were thoroughly enjoying their last evening together with both couples toasting to the success of each other's new beginnings.

But Brenda knew she had to do one more thing. *What if she doesn't want to come with us, or if this would be too much of an adjustment after losing her parents in such a barbaric fashion?*

Bo had taken residence next to the kneeling girl who was stroking him gently behind the ears and talking to him; the peace that engulfed the child and the creature draped Brenda's heart with such a warm embrace that made her pause for a few of the most endearing moments of her life.

But the canine heard her first. From his supine position he gave his dignified head a sharp jerk, and with one eye gazing at her Brenda heard his silent reprimand: *Can't you see she's busy?*

Thus having been reunited with the reality of life Brenda joined Charlotte and Bo. Cross-legged, she faced Charlotte and contemplated about the right words to use, words that would not add to the confusion that must be troubling the child's unblemished mind and chaste faith.

And in the midst of her considerations the right words came to her, only they didn't come from *her*, but out of the mouth from this precious little girl herself. And the words were simple, unadulterated, and from the heart: "Can I stay with you?"

"Did Hughes, or whatever his real name was, die from the stuff I saw lying on the floor?" Karl asked the question more to bridge the time waiting to see Brenda's face since he knew the reason why she went into the next room.

"Cyanide? Yes. They found it in his blood. He took cyanide, the cowardly bastard. Butchered the others like swine, let them suffer under unimaginable pain until their last drop of blood had dripped out of their dying bodies, while he drank a bottle of poison and awaited death in reasonable comfort until the effect of the stuff set in; and then it was a matter of seconds before he took the shortcut to hell.

"We'll never know why he also killed his wife. And what about this precious little girl? Thank the Lord for providing a safe hiding place for her.

"But you never told me, why you picked this monster so suddenly? You were first after Sutton, which would have been my choice too in that situation, and then you changed your mind in mid-course. Where did the intuition come from?"

No sooner than the mischievous grin appeared on Karl's face it was gone. "I didn't really exclude Sutton, but used instead a highly scientific formula."

"Oh?"

"Yes. While we were speeding in the direction of Church Street, a rather insignificant episode flashed by my mind. You remember the day I picked you up from the airport in Myrtle Beach?"

Amos nodded.

"Marge and Brenda had been to see Melanie Hughes, or Carson, at her store. And Brenda said that after she told her that I was from Wyoming she mentioned that her husband was from Montana."

"So?"

"Well, the vernacular in Montana isn't a whole lot different from the one in Wyoming. But from the three times I had the misfortune to listen to him, Joseph Hughes' accent wasn't even close. He was another guy I didn't see in the tent when Brenda and I looked for Sutton, and his store was practically on the way to Sutton. Three solid clues. What else do you need?"

Now Amos Grimm smiled; but it wasn't a mocking smile, rather one of admiration. "Your solving the case, and that's what you did, again I might add, may not have been based on a highly scientific formula, but on an extremely astute talent for detail. Thanks, my friend.

"Uh, before I forget, was he still alive when you got to him?"

"Just barely, for a few more seconds."

"Was he able to say anything, a few words? Might be important."

"No, not really, well ..." Karl had all but forgotten that the man did sputter a few unintelligible words. "Come to think of it, I remember he did stammer a few words, incoherent as they were. Don't believe they'll do you any good."

"Well, what were they?"

"I heard something like 'I ... followed uh, the wrong ... voice.' Or something like that."

"Oh well, you're right. Didn't expect anything revealing coming from a professional psychopath."

Epilogue

On December 23 the Shoemakers received the adoption papers, making them the proud and lawful parents of Charlotte Elizabeth Shoemaker, age nine.

On December 31 they said their good-byes to Bo. He was comfortably lying on the bed of the girl, whose gentle presence had enabled him to gracefully accept the inevitable.

Although he knew the day was coming, Karl took it hard. And when he looked for the last time into the tired eyes he saw behind their waning strength a champion, strong, fast and proud; from the stubborn three-month old puppy who refused to leave the burning house in which his first wife and seven-year old daughter perished, the countless times when the adult canine kept him out of harm's way, to the last heroic act, an act that allowed their new daughter to bypass the customary traumatic-shock syndrome that could have created substantial damage to her psychological development.

But more than anything he saw a companion and a friend of thirteen years.

"Go to your heaven, my dear friend. The memory of you will have a special place in my heart — forever."

There were three more heartbeats and Bo had arrived.

Society Hill Library
114 Carrigan Street
Society Hill, SC 29593

WITHDRAWN